PRAISE F
Sound Choices

"Bravo! Sound Choices *brings the ear, the heart, and the body into harmony. An important book, its practical and visionary uses of sound will help many generations stay in tune."*

— Don Campbell, author of *The Mozart Effect*

"Sound Choices is a treasure, revealing the power of music to heal, to inspire, and to help us act skillfully in a stressful world. This practical and delightfully readable book is full of wisdom for designing auditory environments that facilitate learning, creativity, communication, and health. Written by two master musicians with years of experience in classroom, hospital, and performance settings, it is a much-needed addition to the literature on transformation and healing."

— Joan Borysenko, Ph.D., author of *Minding the Body, Mending the Mind*

"Music can be a potent force for healing—far too powerful to be considered mere entertainment. Mazer and Smith are music professionals and pioneers in bringing music into our hospitals and healing institutions. Their music is magical, and so is their book. Highly recommended."

— Larry Dossey, M.D., author of *Prayer Is Good Medicine*

"For many years I have listened to the sound environments created by Susan Mazer and Dallas Smith. This book, which is destined to become a classic in the field of sound and environmental design, is a testimony to their outstanding vision and pioneering work in the developing arena of music and environmental design. It is a powerful statement about the healing power of music."

— Leland R. Kaiser, Ph.D., health-care futurist;
president, Kaiser and Associates

"Sound Choices *reveals the power and majesty of music in the healing process. Music is being used as a natural complement to drugs and surgery in health care. To understand how music can refresh your soul and spirit and aid in your healing, read this book.*"

— Barbara Dossey, R.N., M.S. F.A.A.N., author of
Florence Nightingale: Mystic, Visionary, Healer

Oct. 13, 2000

For Bill —
   With appreciation for your
work with yoga and healing healthcare
         Best wishes,
         Dallas Smith

Sound Choices

Other Hay House Titles
of Related Interest

The Healing House
*How Living in the Right House Can Heal You Spiritually,
Emotionally, and Physically*
by Barbara Bannon Harwood

Your Personality, Your Health
*Connecting Personality with the Human Energy System,
Chakras, and Wellness*
by Carol Ritberger, Ph.D.

The Western Guide to Feng Shui—Room by Room
by Terah Kathryn Collins

You Can Heal Your Life,
by Louise L. Hay

(All of the above titles are available at your local bookstore, or may be
ordered by calling Hay House at 800-654-5126.)

Please visit the Hay House Website at:
www.hayhouse.com

Sound Choices

Using Music to
Design the Environments
in Which You Live, Work, and Heal

SUSAN MAZER
and
DALLAS SMITH

Hay House, Inc.
Carlsbad, California • Sydney, Australia

Published and distributed in the United States by:
Hay House, Inc., P.O. Box 5100, Carlsbad, CA 92018-5100
(800) 654-5126 • (800) 650-5115 (fax)

Editorial: Jill Kramer   *Design:* Jenny Richards

Library of Congress Cataloging-in-Publication Data

Mazer, Susan.
        Sound choices : using music to design the environments in which you
live, work, and heal / written by Susan Mazer, Dallas Smith.
            p.   cm.
        Includes discography, bibliographical references, and index.
        ISBN 1-56170-569-1 (tradepaper)
        1. Music, Influence of.   2. Environmental music—Analysis,
appreciation.   3. Architecture—Environmental aspects.   I. Smith,
Dallas.   II. Title.
ML3920.M3   1999
781'.11–dc21   99-31742
                                                                    CIP

ISBN 1-56170-569-1

02 01 00 99   4 3 2 1
First Printing, November 1999

Printed in the United States of America

"Music is painted on a canvas of time.
Music is created by all of us when we fluctuate our voices
to well represent our intention.
Music is a child speaking in syllables that are songlike,
but not yet discernible in language.
Music moves us beyond our thoughts and feelings
to a place of authenticity.
Music expresses feelings that words can only approximate.
Music is so necessary to our quality of living that
we will create it rather than live without it.
Then, there are the music makers."

— Susan Mazer

"We dedicate this book to the musicians whose
music transforms space and time
to heal and regenerate the mind, body, and spirit."

Contents

APPENDIX

Acknowledgments

We would like to acknowledge and thank the following individuals for supporting our work and offering continued inspiration and encouragement in the writing of this book.

First, let us thank our parents and families: Judge Oscar and Latane Smith; Albert and Dotty Mazer; Beatrice Mazer (my mother, whose legacy, dedication as a teacher, and spirit of activism is alive in our music); Aliza and Bernie Weinberg; Marc and Susan Talon-Mazer; Ari Mazer; Rachel Mazer; Joel Slatis; Ruth Slatis; and Evan Slatis.

Together, Dallas and Susan would like to thank: Jayne Standley and Cliff Madsen of Florida State University, for their integrity and direction in supporting and encouraging us in our work in using music as environmental design; Jay LeBeau; Arthur Harvey; Steven Halpern; Don Campbell; Joan Borysenko; Larry and Barbara Dossey; Jean Watson; Leland Kaiser; Nancy Moore; Harry Owens; Diane Bush; Harvey Zarren; Loretta Melancon; Bill Adamski; the Association of Healing Health Care Projects; Norman Weinberger; Sara Marberry; Wayne Ruga; the National Symposium on Healthcare Design; Barry and Gloria Blum; Ruth and Gene Glick; Pat Linton; Stephen and Fran Poe; Bani and Madhu Mahadeva; Eric Finkelstein; Debbie Koch; Becky Weinberg; Jeanne Gibbs; Barry and Gloria Blum; Reid Tracy; Christine Watsky; Jill Kramer; and the staff at Hay House.

Dallas would like to personally thank: George Corradino, Harry Schmidt, Albert Tipton, G. S. Sachdev, Ali Akbar Khan, Bertil and Helen Van Boer, Michael Irwin, Albert "Pee Wee" Ellis, Erv Munroe, Gert Wegner, Thomas Frykberg, Harry Severin, Bjorn Jason Lindh, David Carroll, George Ruckert, Max Rossmassler, and the late Jan Tangen, for making a difference in the world.

Susan would like to personally thank: Elyse Ilku, Velma Froude, Jan

Adrian, Joyce La Chuga, Margaret Kochendorfer, Judith Schmidt, Frank and Pat Terry-Ross, Dale Barco, Janet Harrell, Steve Fritzmann, Albert Tipton, Arthur Arian, Bill W., Anne Hardy, Lyon & Healy, and finally, Rose Arian, whom I miss so very much and but for whom I would not have found my life again.

Prelude

How We Began

D*allas:* My father has always been an inveterate whistler. When I was growing up, he whistled incessantly, spreading his good humor throughout the house. Every Saturday afternoon the radio broadcast of the Metropolitan Opera filled our home with dramatic classical music and a specific ambiance that distinguished Saturdays from other days. Some of those operatic melodies found their way into his whistling repertoire.

I also recall spending hours in front of my parents' old Stromberg-Carlson Victorola, enchanted by the clarinet solo at the beginning of Gershwin's *Rhapsody in Blue*. The heavy 78-RPM vinyl records would drop onto the turntable one by one, followed by the needle moving through the groove. As if by magic, the most amazing sounds flowed forth, the music punctuated by the records' characteristic clicks and pops. Interrupting my reverie every few minutes, the arm of the needle rose and another record dropped. In those few seconds when the music stopped, my awareness returned—I reverted to the living room of our farm in Alabama. My parents were doing their various chores, and roosters were crowing, clearly unaware that dawn had passed hours before. Then, when the next disk fell from its perch on the center spindle of the record player and the music began again, I was once again transported to another world.

Susan: Our front room seemed long and without fantasy to me; it had no roosters singing into its center, as did Dallas's living room. I was small and it was huge. Our old record console was unlike any other I had seen, a blond box almost as big as I was. It opened from the front and was closed before the music would resonate from the brownish-gray grill cloth face. I sometimes played beneath a card table covered with a sheet, in a space where my world closed in to hold me and my thoughts. The music would find me there.

On very special days, my sister and I became exotic dancers in the Arabian nights—to the accompaniment of Saint-Saens' *Danse Macabre.* We swayed our arms and bodies around the old hassock, creating another world, as children do. At those times, the living room was no longer the living room, the hassock no longer a hassock. It was a different time and place, if only because of the interrelationship between the music and our whole being. It was magic.

The Potential for Magic

Dallas and Susan: In any musical performance, there is always the potential for magic. It does not always happen. Even in the most brilliant interpretations of the most profoundly inspired compositions, there are no guarantees that magic will occur. Magic requires a step beyond technical perfection and harmonic sophistication.

When magic happens, the listener is born into a state of profound engagement with the music. It is an experience that takes place in "virtual time," sustained in the silence after the last note is played. The magic is sometimes obvious at the end of a performance, prior to an audience clapping, or in the stillness between the musicians' breaths. Philosopher Alan Watts called it "the expanded present."

As performers, we long ago realized that it was this very experience— a state of timelessness—that allows a listener to be transformed by music. We knew, as children, that the rooms in which we had our most profound listening experiences were somehow altered by the sounds we heard. If we could use music to design a space to be supportive, inspiring, and regenerative, to respond to the needs of the moment, then the sounds could enhance what was already good in the room, and relieve what was painful.

Similar Journeys

Dallas: I came to identify myself as a musician at a young age, not simply because I seemed to be talented, but also because, as an only child, music offered me intimate companionship. It became a safe haven in which I could find relief from the ever-challenging task of growing up. In the same way that certain animals "imprint" on the first moving thing they experience after birth, I seemed to imprint on music. There was always a melody of some kind going on in my head. My inner world was a complex orchestration of my thoughts and feelings, transformed into melodies and harmonies with each note magically played by my own imagination. Regardless of the power inherent in the spoken word, it became apparent to me from an early age that music was the easiest and most soulful way in which I could express myself.

My first instrument was the song flute, similar to a recorder, which all fourth-graders in my elementary school played. When I was 11, I began to study the clarinet, which I played until my junior year in college. Yes, I had to endure the junior high and high school band music, including the marches played in parades and at football game halftimes. My musical path eventually led me to receive a music scholarship at Florida State University (FSU) in Tallahassee.

My first two years at FSU were absorbed in music and academic activity. However, I also grew past the innocence of my high school years. By the beginning of my third year, I was no longer impassioned with my studies and was disillusioned with what I perceived to be the limitations of classical music in general, and the clarinet in particular. I felt disconnected from myself, from my music, and from my peers.

When the opportunity came to study in Germany during my junior year, it seemed to be the perfect solution to my musical and personal discontent. In order to finance my travels, I sold my clarinet, making a symbolic break with my musical past. While I did not originally plan it that way, I remained out of the country for three and a half years. In the process of learning to speak fluent German and Swedish, I was exposed to new experiences and cultures that forever changed my view of the world and my appreciation of the role of music in my life.

At the age of 22, two years into my personal pilgrimage, I traveled overland from Germany to India. It was here that the connection between music and the soul became most obvious to me. Being introduced to Indian classical music presented a new dimension to the aesthetic experience, complete with protocols, rituals, a hierarchy of mastery, and a highly developed spiritual dimension. According to traditional Hindu beliefs, music is a manifestation of God, and as such, is *inherently* healing. I learned to play the Afghan flute and then the *bansuri,* the traditional Indian bamboo flute. Their hauntingly beautiful sounds touched my heart. Enchanted by the silken fluidity of these instruments, I regained my musical passion and inspiration, ending the hiatus in my musical life.

Upon returning to the States a year later, I moved to San Rafael, California, in order to attend the Ali Akbar College of Music, where I began to formally study Indian music under Ali Akbar Khan, one of India's greatest musicians. My studies were infused with a sense of love, devotion, purpose, and discipline. Both Ali Akbar Khan and my bansuri teacher, G. S. Sachdev, taught in the oral tradition, playing for their students, who then attempted to mimic and master the subtle melodies completely "by ear" without the aid of printed music.

In the ensuing years, I sought to apply the meditative and devotional qualities of Indian music to my compositions and recording collaborations. I recorded meditation albums with keyboardist Steven Halpern, and singers Laura Allen and Sophia. Together with co-producers Teja Bell, Jon Bernoff, and Marcus Allen, I recorded *Petals* and *Summer Suite* (released on the Rising Sun label), which were produced for relaxation.

Concurrently, my musical explorations expanded into jazz, blues, pop, and rock; I played mainly on the silver flute, as well as the alto, tenor, and soprano saxophones. Despite my wide range of musical interests, the strict conditioning of my traditional Western classical training made it difficult for me to play the clarinet with the same freedom with which I approached my other instruments.

In the mid-1970s, synthesizers were just beginning to emerge as standard instruments on records and in the leading bands of the day. Although I was fascinated by the new technology, it was geared to either keyboard players or guitarists. I was unable to personally participate until a few years later, when I was introduced to the Lyricon, the first electric wind synthesizer. The Lyricon was comprised of saxophone keys mounted on an aluminum tube, connected by a cable to its tone module. It used breath pressure to initiate the sound and control volume. Although its reed did not vibrate, the mouthpiece was designed to feel similar to that of a saxophone. The Lyricon wind synthesizer was capable of a level of expressiveness that had previously only been possible on acoustic woodwinds. I embraced its wide range of tonal possibilities, which allowed me to move beyond being solely a melodic player; I became able to create symphonic textures. In due course, my introduction to the Lyricon proved to be as auspicious as my introduction to Indian classical music. It expanded my musical creativity to include the magic of both music and technology.

Susan: Music gave me a physical and emotional experience that was like no other. The feeling was a combination of wonder, the most intimate kind of spiritual connectedness, and definitive proof that there was more to my life than the events that surrounded me. I couldn't seem to find that mystery in anything else. I felt, perhaps, the greatest sense of myself, the most amazing fullness, when I heard a violin sing, or a piano play with the richness of a symphony, or a symphony reflecting sounds like the most infinitely brilliant rainbow.

Nonetheless, if I were to tell you that at the age of 14 my list of things to do in this life did not include playing the harp, you might understand why it took years for my role as a performing musician to become part of my identity. The opportunity came to me when I auditioned to become a music student at Cass Technical High School in Detroit. Velma Froude, the harp and piano teacher, auditioned me and asked if I would like to take harp as an elective. That was all she asked, an offer that forever changed the course of my life.

The harp was a challenge that would draw from me far more than my love of music. Unlike Dallas, whose musical talent was readily evident, mine was far less obvious. Because I didn't own my own harp for my first three years of study, it took several years for me to have as much confidence as I had passion. However, the fact that it was the most beautiful sound I had ever heard rallied my determination. When I finally owned my own instrument, I began studying with Elyse Yockey, the principal harpist with the Detroit Symphony. Working with her was truly the major event that forever bonded me to the harp, partly because she was such an inspiration, and partly because she assumed me to be a musician, a role I so much wanted to achieve.

By the age of 22, I had completed my master's degree in music at Stanford University, where I was a graduate fellow. I had also, by that time, studied and performed in Sienna, Italy with the North Carolina School of the Arts, and with the Detroit Symphony. Among my most memorable classical performances, there were many astounding moments, including performing with the English Royal Ballet in the some of the final performances of the late Rudolf Nureyev and Margot Fontaine. Despite my lack of obvious talent in my younger years and my chronic self-doubts, I had finally become a harpist.

Both Dallas and I questioned our musical identities at different times and in different places. While Dallas's crisis occurred when he was a junior in college, I found myself at a point of depression in graduate school. I had run out of music, passion, and inspiration. As the sole harpist among music graduate students, few of whom were performance majors, I felt socially and aesthetically isolated by the strict demands and unyielding boundaries of classical training. I did not play for almost nine months, during which time I had mononucleosis and wondered what I was going to do with my life.

In the same way that Dallas had to move beyond the clarinet, I had to move beyond the harp. Like Dallas, I expanded into jazz and pop music, and eventually into the world of electronic music. With some reluctance, I amplified my concert grand harp, developing a sound that allowed me to transcend the conventional harp and classical symphonies. Over the next 15 years, I expanded my repertoire and my interest in jazz.

Working as a solo artist at Harrah's in Lake Tahoe for 14 years, I had the opportunity to perform with world-class artists such as Frank Sinatra, John Denver, Ray Charles, Julio Iglesias, Loretta Lynn, Crystal Gayle, and Sammy Davis, Jr. All of these artists were masters, not simply due to their talent. Rather, their magic was evident in their capacity to respond to their audiences, in their artistic consistency, and in how they suspended time for those fortunate enough to hear them. Then I, like the audience, was suspended in a universe of perfection. In retrospect, perhaps my quest has always been about transformation, in whatever form it might happen.

Changing My Life's Direction

Susan: I do not believe that anyone strolls unconsciously or by accident into a life's work in health, healing, well-being, or any field dealing with the relationships between the mind, body, and spirit. It often requires a willingness to barter one's own pain for a life of service and spiritual philanthropy. I knew that my musical career needed to change focus and have a higher purpose.

For many performers, life is lived on two parallel tracks—personal and professional—each full, each unique, each with their own beginning, middle, and end. I was no exception. My public and professional life appeared to be intact to all who knew me. However, during those same years, I was also living my own private struggle with bulimia, a hidden backdrop to all that I did. While it may have appeared that I was a disciplined if not driven artist, and that I was physically quite normal, this private battle continued to plague me. Without going into great detail about the painful road that finally led me to a 12-step program, I will say that my battle became a blessing among blessings.

In 1981, I was in the midst of a very painful divorce and struggling with my bulimia. I had to find another way to live, which included a new purpose for myself and my music. Apart from my continuing to perform nightly, I began to play music for meditation and to compose my own. Not surprisingly, the new music began to show itself in all my performances.

At around the same time, my friend and former harp student, Margaret Kochendorfer, introduced me to the Center for Health Awareness in San Jose, California; they requested that I develop a workshop for nurses on the use of music in healing. The process of developing this workshop began my personal search for the foundation of what music does.

My goal was to give participants cognitive information, while also—and most important—creating that moment of magic that we referred to earlier, when time is timeless and only the present exists. Thus, the program took participants through a series of discoveries that cumulatively revealed the potential of the musical experience and its potential as a therapeutic protocol. Attending nurses who already loved music had questions not so much about *why* or *what* music does, but rather *which* music would do it best. I only had my personal experience to guide me, which had taught me that music was beautiful, lyrical, and rich in melody and harmony. Heard under the right circumstances and at the right time, it could generate a "healing" experience—one that enhanced the recovery process in a positive way.

In December 1983, two years into my recovery, I recorded my first album of original music, *The Fire in the Rose*. The theme was born out of a meditation that I played for my dearest friend, Rose Arian, who was suffering from heart palpitations. We had met a few days after her 73rd birthday, on the day that I made my first effort to seek help in dealing with my eating disorder. The music came from the elevated creativity and deepened surrender born in my recovery, and also from my deep love for Rose and a desire to offer tranquility, if only for a few moments at a time. This improvised musical meditation became the core of the album.

The Meeting

Susan: While recording *The Fire in the Rose* at the Music Annex Studios in Menlo Park, I remember seeing a record cover mounted in the hall of the studio reading "Steven Halpern and Dallas Smith." While Steven Halpern's name was familiar to me, it was the name of Dallas Smith that caught my eye for no apparent reason. Six months later, when Rising Sun Records began negotiating with me to license my album, they told me of the other artists on the label and gave me a copy of *Stellar Voyage,* Dallas's solo album.

Can one have a relationship with an album? Can the music be greater than any one composition or performance? Is it possible to connect with a soul on the auditory plane of harmony, melody, rhythm, and timbre? Today I might answer that question differently, but at the time, it took me by surprise. *Stellar Voyage* engaged me in a way that I still cannot describe—it was enchanting, brilliant, powerful, loving. Through a series of phone calls, I connected with Dallas's answering machine and he with mine. A truly technological romance, from vinyl to my ears to phone machine. . . . Our relationship began as it continues to be. The music is the river that carries us together through life.

> *Was it love at first sight?* Perhaps love at first sound.
> *How soon did we play music together?* Immediately.
> *Whose music did we play?* We improvised and created anew.
> *Was it magic?* It was magic.

In our first year together, we recorded two albums (*Inner Rhythms* and *Quest for Light*) and toured with jazz pianist Ahmad Jamal. *The Fire in the Rose* was released in 1984 on the Rising Sun label and became our first commercial album together. We composed new music and learned each other's compositions, working diligently to find our own sound, our own music, and our path to a future that neither of us could have predicted.

Dallas: From the beginning of our musical adventures as children and continuing past meeting each other in 1984, Susan and I have defined and redefined music and its role in our lives. We have found that for a musical experience to be a transformational event—to be life changing—it needs to be more than a technically perfect performance. Indeed, it needs to evoke personal meaning and depth of spirit. Thus, whenever someone tells us that our music is "healing," we know that the music has touched the listener in transcendent ways, certainly in ways that cannot wholly be attributed to technique, training, or even the sincere intention of our efforts.

In addition to its aesthetic value perceived by how it *sounds,* music transforms time and place. Therefore, using music to create life-enhancing environments shifts the relationship between music and listener from one that is content-based—that is, entertaining or distracting—to one that is contextual, expressing and supporting a purpose beyond itself. Ultimately, music accompanies the process of life, enhancing and enriching our capacity to live it.

Introduction

S*ound Choices* has been written to guide and inspire the design of the places and spaces in which you live so that they become the places and spaces in which you thrive.

We are musicians. Music, for both of us, is a path of the spirit—one sometimes paved with smooth granite, sometimes obstructed with huge boulders, and sometimes like a river of smooth, clear water. Together, we have cumulatively dedicated over 80 years to musical training and our varied careers. We have each moved through the worlds of symphony orchestras, jazz trios, big bands, solo performances, and recording studios, ultimately bringing music into health-care institutions. Within all this study and experience, the relationship between music and the audience was neither talked about nor questioned. It was silently held as a matter of public relations and stage presence.

In our personal efforts to understand the dynamic between music and listener, we found that, beyond its capacity to entertain and enrich, music gives structure and expression to both time and place, defining circumstance and meaning. Our task as artists, we determined, was to create music so engaging that time becomes timeless, reality changes, and life is created anew. Thus, what has perhaps not been acknowledged is that music creates an afterlife consisting of the moments and years following a life-changing performance.

The use of music as environmental design is not new. Rather, it expands the common use of background music from being an "add-on," or distraction, to being an intention. It also takes into account the whole auditory environment, just as the texture of the canvas becomes that of the painting. It recognizes all the sounds of life and uses music as a tool for design.

The Journey from Music to Health Care

For many years, each of us thought that mastering our instruments was the ultimate challenge of our careers; however, the transition from the traditional role of performing musicians into using music to design healing environments required more. Instead of simply demanding discipline, dexterity, and relentless practice, our new career led us to search for the meaning and purpose of music and how it actually functioned in our lives.

At the time we met in the mid-1980s, there was a philosophical dividing line drawn between musicians who performed professionally for a paying audience, and musicians who proclaimed themselves to be "musical health practitioners." It was not a friendly line, for the battle between music-as-art and music-as-treatment was one that threatened the integrity of the music. For the dedicated performer, the goal is not to talk about it, analyze it, or speculate as to its effects, but rather to simply play the music *brilliantly*. Creating music for any reason other than artistic valor, according to this narrow viewpoint, was for those who could not play as well, whose technical prowess was limited.

The question of why music does what it does, or, indeed, how it does it, has not been succinctly answered. Music, both historically and in the present, has been linked to the power to heal, control, incite, lure, seduce, celebrate the word of God, and spread the word of others. Thus, the relationship between health and music is not a new concept, although presently it is not without debate.

Currently, a vast array of philosophical and theoretical applications and practitioners utilize music as treatment. Some speak of music in terms of "vibration therapy" or "sound healing," and some proclaim its inherent power to affect our cellular processes. Others state that the true basis of music's healing power resides in the intention of the composer and the performer. The New Age movement believes that only certain music has healing properties, and that those properties are dependent on both musical and nonmusical criteria. Even as we write this book, the debate continues over whether Mozart, in his short and intense life span of 35 years, wrote the perfect music for all time and all people. At the other end of the spectrum, there are people who consider certain kinds of music to be toxic, endangering the health of those who listen. Others go even further and declare that certain musical genres are satanic, or representative of the anti-Christ.

In contrast to these varied theories, research in the field of music therapy applies stringent scientific methods to quantify the effects of music on listeners. Rigorous studies, documenting measurable physiological responses of specific patient populations under controlled conditions, indicate that appropriately chosen music can be of assistance to those who are suffering in specific ways. However, even the existing research results beg for still more research! Music that is soothing to one listener may have little or no effect on someone else. In fact, what may be "healing" for one person may be actually disturbing or even painful for another.

The Risk of Analysis

Susan: I remember taking an undergraduate course on the psychology of music that was both interesting and frustrating. As I plodded through the cumbersome, and, for me, foreign language of behavioral science, I found little that I could relate to, as either a performer or a listener. *My coveted musical experience is uniquely mine,* I thought, *hardly to be dissected, analyzed, and reduced to a psychological diagnosis that would make a contrivance of my experience!* I feared that this scientific inquisition might ruin the magic by implying that my emotional responses were actually manipulations acted upon me. It would be like revealing how a magic trick is done. If that were true, I could be left with only a musical trapdoor—one that would make my fears and stresses disappear artificially, as if the effects of music were some kind of smoke-and-mirrors sham.

Thus, in these early years of study and personal searching, the questions regarding the use of music as therapy became not only mired in confusion, but also greatly distanced from the process of actual music-making.

In spite of academic hypotheses and data about the impact of music, as performers we continued to believe that if our concert performances had any effect on our audiences, it was because the audience listened with open hearts and minds, and because we delivered a stunning experience. If music had *any* power in our lives, it was only the power we gave it as a direct result of our experience. Furthermore, *if* we allowed it to be so, music would alter our spatial and temporal orientation, making our lives begin again.

Our First Hospital

In 1989, Reno's Washoe Medical Center contacted us to present a weekend symposium on the use of music as therapy. They had begun to use music on the oncology unit with the encouragement of a volunteer whose personal goal was to use her singing talent in the field of music therapy. To join us as faculty, we invited Steven Halpern, best known for his work in music and healing; and Anne Hardy, whose renowned work treating adolescent alcoholics and addicts included specific music protocols integrated in 12-step recovery programs. In the course of this symposium and subsequent workshops, we continued to find that the direct needs and concerns of patients and staff involved more than the music, and that music was more than the sound it created.

We performed in the hospital and worked with the staff, realizing that the essence of the music was beyond the performance, beyond our instruments, and beyond notes and rhythms. Perhaps the core truth, we thought, was that music lives beyond itself in the same way that a painting affects the space outside its own frame. Playing music on the oncology unit, in the emergency room, and even in the hospital lobby made clear to us that these areas were not merely places for beds, blankets, and IV poles, nor were people here for a casual social call.

Rather, these spaces were where suffering met itself—the battlefield where disease challenged the essence of life. It was hardly an occasion for business as usual; rather, it was a place where ordinary people exhibited extraordinary courage in dealing with the trauma and fear of life-threatening illness. It was a place for which we could neither rehearse nor prepare, one that remained with us for hours beyond the actual time spent, and one in which the music seemed to be at once perfect and out of context.

From the first note, everything seemed to change. Music in the hospital setting was like an aural oasis—a distraction and an offering, entertainment and ritual. This environment demanded that we leave our egos at the front door along with our needs as performers. We were not going to have the benefit of the usual audience applause, acknowledgment, or any other tangible way of determining whether our music was sufficient. We had to accept the fact that for someone gravely ill, our presence might be inconsequential, the least significant event. At the same time, for those patients listening to the music drift down the long halls and into their rooms, our music could be the most important event of that afternoon.

Our sole purpose was to help patients and staff experience the clinical environment as *shiftable space*—space that can be transformed from fearful to safe, from strange to peaceful. Only then would it have the capacity to hold the wide range of emotional and physical events that occur in the transition from disease to recovery, from degeneration to regeneration.

Our music remains the unfolding manifestation of our collective efforts to combine the beautiful with the spiritual, the joyful with the soulful. Since finding each other in July 1984, we have driven over 300,000 miles across this wonderful country, carrying with us our harp and woodwinds, a sound system, and everything else we need for our performances. We have toured with jazz pianist Ahmad Jamal, performed in regional jazz and fine arts festivals, worked with thousands of wonder-seeking schoolchildren, and played music for patients and their families in numerous innovative hospitals around the country.

In order to respond to the need for musical resources for health care settings, in 1992 we introduced The C.A.R.E. Channel®, a 24-hour environmental channel that provides nature videos and instrumental music for broadcast over patient television; we also introduced its music-only partner, C.A.R.E. With Music™, for broadcast in hospital public areas and over telephone-on-hold. Provided through our company, Healing HealthCare Systems, The C.A.R.E. Channel is currently being broadcast in hospitals in over 25 states. A list of C.A.R.E. Channel artists and albums is provided in the appendix to serve as a starting point for exploring music to design your environments.

There will always be more good music than can be listened to by any one person in a lifetime. Therefore, this book is nonprescriptive and avoids offering a listening repertoire, which could imply a limiting judgment of all other music. Thus, any specific musical references simply reflect our personal tastes, experiences, and subjective valuations.

Sound Choices is written in two parts. The first six chapters, which comprise part I, provide a foundation of knowledge and understanding about music, sound, hearing, design, and environment. While it may seem that the information is common to all of us, the reality is that there are subtle and powerful ways that each of these factors determine how we interface with the world and other people.

Part II, chapters 7 to 12, gives practical, concrete suggestions for using sound in designing your environment—this is the heart of our message. After providing a means for assessing the environment, we then consider the home, workplace, health care, and learning environments. The afterword returns to the basis of the holistic experience, bringing together in few words the glorious possibilities available to all of us when we fully experience nature as the most perfect of all environmental designs.

Overall, *Sound Choices* is written to empower informed listeners to become informed designers.

"Words are the Music of the Mind.
Music is the Resonance of the Spirit.
Spirit is that which fills the space.
Music, Space, Mind, Spirit—
It's about design."

— Susan Mazer

Part I

Sound,
Space,
and
Spirit

Chapter One

Music and Healing

"They said, 'You have a blue guitar,
You do not play things as they are.'
The man replied, 'Things as they are
Are changed upon a blue guitar.'"

— Wallace Stevens (1879–1955), from *The Man with a Blue Guitar*

For Stuart, Monday morning started out very strangely. The last he remembered, it was Saturday and he had been snowmobiling on Mt. Rose. The weather was great and the snow even better. His experience using a snowmobile was less extensive than it could have been, since it was a relatively new sport for him. The last memory he had was of going down the magnificent snow-covered mountain, the white powder brushing his cheeks, the wind whipping around him from every direction.

Now he lay in this bed, in a room he did not recognize; he was unable to move. His eyes, expressionless, blinked. That was all. Nothing else of him existed. He was now a quadriplegic, paralyzed from the neck down.

We were informed of Stuart's situation because we were scheduled to perform music on the neurology unit. At the request of the staff, we set up our instruments near the nurses' station, which was centrally located to most of the patient rooms. This also positioned us directly in front of Stuart's room.

During the day, nurses went in and out of his room without comment. They kept the door closed. We were only a few feet from the door. It was one of those fluke tragedies that forever changed Stuart's life and the lives of all those around him.

Mid-afternoon, some of his friends started to arrive. Although they looked as though nothing was out of the ordinary, nothing was normal. One young man looked at us, surprised to see a harp and saxophone in the hospital at this moment, near this room. As if remembering something he had forgotten, the young visitor quickly walked back to the elevator and disappeared. Thirty minutes later, he returned with a boombox and some CDs.

The nurses talked to us throughout the six hours we were there, commenting on how sad the situation was. Then, upon leaving the room, one nurse came up to us and said that we should not feel bad about them keeping the door closed.

While other patients and visitors enjoyed the unexpected performance, and the nurses found it to be a welcome change from the normal ambiance, Stuart preferred to listen to his own music—hard rock from his personal collection—brought in by his friend.

Hard rock does not generally top anybody's list of healing music. But, then, who would have thought that music of any kind could have been comforting to a young man whose whole future changed in a single catastrophic moment? If anyone had asked what might be of therapeutic value to Stuart at this time, music might not have come up at all—at least, not in a medical model driven by technological protocols far removed from the essence of our human natures. However, even for those of us who claim to understand the way music moves our hearts and souls, hard rock might not be our first choice, or even our second.

While one might assume that our having performed in health-care settings would have enlightened us as to the ultimate therapeutic application of music, it would be more accurate to say that our life experience has made apparent the profound potential of music to affect the human spirit. In Stuart's case, if we had held on to the idea that our music was *the* formula, as opposed to *music itself* being the inspiration, we would have fallen short of appreciating its power to ease an otherwise tragic situation.

Nonetheless, specific questions regarding "healing music"—*What* is it? *Which* is it? *How* does it work?—continually arise, especially inquiries about which music is "good."

The word *healing* is ambiguous, defined by each of us according to our own experiences. For some, it implies a curative modality that will result in the permanent elimination of physical or emotional disease. For others, healing may be circumstantial, temporary, perhaps more felt than real, more spiritual than physical. For still others, it may have no meaning at all, because the concept of healing relates to a whole body of thought that would seem to be philosophical rather than scientific.

The concept of music may be even more ambiguous. As an art form, music exists on its own, distinct from any person, belief, or agenda. The *power* of music, however, is inextricably linked to the subjective, unique experience of the listener. While research has shown that music can stimulate or excite, it has not been proven that each and every one of us will predictably exhibit the same response to the same music under *objective* circumstances. In order to substantiate such a claim, requisite clinical trials—the same kind that all medical protocols are required to pass—would have to statistically indicate that you and I, and hundreds of others, would predictably react the same way to a specific kind of music. On the contrary, research shows that, under specific conditions, a well-defined listening population may respond in a variety of ways. Therefore, any expectations we might have that certain music might aid the healing process reflects our personal definitions, criteria, and experiences. Nothing can invalidate the healing that many of us have experienced when listening to certain special pieces of music; however, when we try to promise that others will have a similar experience, we find that the results are not quantifiable or predictable.

Unlike aspirin, penicillin, or any other pharmaceutical, the effects of music as an aural medication are not consistent or automatic. Rather, it is solely the response of the listener *at the time* that determines whether or not any piece of music is healing.

It is difficult to imagine music healing the soul or body of a person who neither relates to nor bonds with the sound of the music, the seamless whole created by the merging of melody, harmony, rhythm, and timbre. It is possible, however, that if one were determined to create the opposite effect, to cause pain or discomfort, one could easily select a piece of music that is so loud, dissonant, or distorted that it would be perceived as noise. Chances are that one would more easily accomplish the latter result on the first try, than be able to predetermine which piece of music would be the specific cause of healing for a particular group or individual. Nonetheless, it remains a fact that even music that most of us find unpleasant may still find unexpectedly appreciative ears among a cross-section of listeners.

Which *Music Is Healing?*

When someone asks for music that is "healing," they are suggesting an inherent distinction from music that is "pleasing" or "entertaining" or even "brilliant." Furthermore, they are most likely seeking an experience far beyond that of merely "liking" it.

Because our work has focused on using music to design therapeutic environments, we are often asked for a suggested listening list of the music we have determined to be healing. Out of respect for all the reasons stated thus far, and in deference to the seriousness with which the inquiry is made, we have consistently shifted the focus of the question from the music to the listener.

Music that is defined as healing is typically described as any or all of the following:

• soothing	• energizing
• relaxing	• spiritual
• uplifting	• intentional
• inspiring	• beautiful
• meditative	• invigorating

Stylistically, such music may include classical, choir music, organ music, Christian rock, meditative "space" music, and New Age music; it may be composed by Mozart, Bach, Yanni, Paul Simon, or George Harrison. It may emanate from harps, pianos, synthesizers, acoustic guitars, brass choirs, madrigal singers, violins, bagpipes, *ragas* from India, or the drumming of Native Americans.

We do not want to unduly limit our definitions, lest we leave out the specific kind of music that you have found therapeutic; therefore, let us say that healing music is "any music that renders us better than we were, improves our sense of self, raises the quality of the moment, or connects us to life anew." Healing, in this context, may include experiencing sheer pleasure, getting rid of a headache, crying long-awaited tears of grief, or being inspired to contemplate our existential state of being. In terms of recommended dosages, because there are no known side effects and its impact can be terminated at will, music can be used on an "as needed" basis—anywhere, anytime, live or recorded. We can even add that *liking* or appreciating a piece of music is *not a prerequisite* for healing. On the contrary, it has been our experience that to measure the healing quotient by whether one likes or dislikes a particular piece of music risks reducing the issue to one of preference or popularity, which may not be of any relevance.

Indeed, the listening circumstances may also participate in and contribute to the effect of the music. Attributing the healing to the surrounding conditions as well as the music does not invalidate either the reality of the experience or the actual value of the music. If anything, it speaks to the holistic environment and the fact that all things are connected, mind to body to spirit.

We spent many hours, weeks, and months trying to clarify for ourselves what had happened in the hospitals that was so different from other performances, but which truly seemed to capture the essence of what music does. We knew that it was not just "entertainment," although our music might have been entertaining to some of the patients. It was hardly a "concert," although some patients came out of their rooms to see us. We knew that, given the long hours we were there, the actual impact was not experienced as a "live" performance. Most patients heard us from within their rooms without being able to view us directly.

If anything, we felt that while we were performing music to serve the needs of patients, families, and staff, it was not "background music," for the objective was not to be generic or in the "back." Furthermore, music used in this context was different from conventional music therapy, because we were not directly treating patients. Rather, we were "treating" the spaces in which patients were placed, using *music as environmental design*.

Music As Environmental Design

Architecture is the art of designing fixed spaces according to specific functions, purposes, and values. Landscape architecture treats the outside aspects of the building, using natural color and form in plants, flowers, and so on to bring aesthetic beauty to the building. Traditional interior design adds beauty to function by using furniture, artwork, wallpaper, textures and fabrics, window coverings, plants, and the like. Acoustic architects plan the ways in which sound reverberates and travels through any space. That may include treating the walls, floors, or ceilings in order to control the movement of sound through rooms and hallways.

Environmental design goes beyond interior design by considering the wholeness of the space—the ways in which all the various elements work together, and the human outcomes that result from being in the space. It aims to create a palpable physical and spiritual context. Like gift wrap that protects and celebrates, environmental design makes obvious both value and meaning.

Actually, using music as environmental design may be how most of us already experience music in our daily lives. At its best, it is the purposeful use of sound and music to regenerate and inspire us. Music is used to condition the sound environment, adding intention to what often occurs by accident. Our work uses music to create, enhance, or otherwise enrich those aspects of our lives that emotionally and physiologically affect us.

Many books have been written about music—how to read it, how to play it, its place in the course of history, who composes it, who writes about it, and its power to both soothe and excite. This book, however, is about you and your capacity to create spaces that will enhance your own health and well-being. It is about *using* the music in your life and the sounds generated in the process of living. Indeed, it is about respecting your sentient capacity to hear, the complex relationship between what you hear and what you feel, and the ways in which music transforms generic sound into profound personal meaning.

Chapter Two

Some Basic Truths about Music:

What You Always Wanted to Know about Music, and Already Know!

"Great music is that which penetrates the ear with
facility and leaves the memory with difficulty.
Magical music never leaves the memory."
— Sir Thomas Beecham, British conductor (1870–1961)

A tale is told about Ravi of Calcutta, whose luck and good fortune had brought him both financial and personal success. His beautiful wife had borne two children. His business had benefited from his natural ability to manage such affairs, as well as the blessings that come forth in ways unbeknownst to most of us.

In spite of all his Earthly possessions, however, he still had within him the seeds of discontent, a hollowness that begged to be filled with greater understanding of the ways of the world and the ways of the spirit.

In India, it has always been an honorable occupation to become a seeker of spiritual enlightenment. Many renounce all their material possessions, *put on the simple dhoti (a piece of cloth wrapped as a robe), and take as their single possession the begging bowl, with full confidence that whatever is needed will be provided. Many spend years, if not a lifetime, on such a quest, seeking to know their life's purpose and how to fulfill it.*

One day, as if from a place unknown, Ravi was driven to begin such a venture. He took off his normal clothing and put on the dhoti. He told his wife that he was going to become a renunciate, take to the streets of India, and embark on a spiritual quest. She was quite distraught, knowing not what caused his discontent, but also knowing that she had no choice but to accept his decision and await his return.

In the many months that passed, Ravi traveled throughout the country visiting many holy places and praying for enlightenment. He met many others who were on their own path, and still others who were in the business sector and who reminded him of his lifelong spiritual shallowness.

After two years, he returned to his home, having found the answers he had sought.

"What have you learned, my husband?" asked his wife.

He brought out from beneath his dhoti an ektar, an Indian instrument that has only one string.

"I have become a musician," he said proudly.

With great disdain and frustration, his wife exclaimed, "You have left our children and myself for two years in search of enlightenment. You return with a single-string ektar, not even a tanpura with four strings, or a many-stringed sarod or sitar, or any other instrument that is capable of so much more!"

Ravi calmly explained, as he began to strum the single string, "Yes, my darling, all those other instruments have many more strings than the ektar. However, what has come to me is that all those musicians who play those other instruments are still searching for the perfect note. Here, with this one string, I have found it!"

— a traditional tale as told by Ali Akbar Khan,
one of India's greatest musicians

The perfect note, the perfect melody, the perfect nuance, the perfect moment. In all our years as music students, neither of us ever questioned either our own responses to a piece of music or our feelings about it. Nor did we ever question whether we would recognize "perfection" when we heard it. In actuality, most of us trust and use our intuition to select music to entertain, or to place a value on a song. The only time we may feel the need or desire to go beyond this initial experience is if we want to become more knowledgeable or acquire more acumen in making cultural decisions.

We all listen to music that we do not choose within the context of other activities: watching movies or commercials, eating in restaurants, riding in elevators, attending social gatherings, commuting to work or home—so many common, everyday events that we take for granted, in which music plays a critical contextual role.

Before we delve deeper into the practical application of music in the design of environments, here are 16 truths that will lay the groundwork for understanding where your own musical expertise currently exists.

1. *Your judgment, as a listener, is the only one that counts.* Regardless of what we may say here about any particular piece of music, or what other so-called experts in the field of music and health may profess, your listening experience is the only relevant test of its value in your life. Furthermore, the merit of any piece of music is solely listener-dependent on a one-at-a-time basis. That means that just because your parents may not like the music you like, its worth *in your life* is not diminished or otherwise changed. The reverse is also true: Just because you may find a particular piece or genre of music not to your liking, this says nothing of its value to others.

2. *Meaning is often a factor of familiarity.* Music that we are accustomed to often has an edge over music that is foreign to us. Author Robert Jourdain says that "early training teaches us to observe particular features of music. Thereafter we seek out like-minded music and acquire an even better ear for its traits." As a result, he continues, we can become "almost deaf to whole musical dimensions that were neglected in early experience." Thus, listening to classical Indonesian *gamelan* music may not be easy for those of us who were brought up on country and western, rock 'n' roll, or Beethoven. New music of a different culture is like a foreign language: While we might be able to pick out some of the words, we may miss the nuances, phrasing, and structure. For the same reasons, a grandparent whose childhood and teenage years were accompanied by the music of

Glenn Miller and big bands might find the tenor and pace of hip-hop, rap, alternative, or avant-garde jazz difficult to understand, let alone enjoy.

3. *If you have even once created a romantic evening with soft music, you already know the basics of using music as environmental design.*
Well, it's a start.

Music can make a wonderful, seductive atmosphere, but it cannot create a sexual attraction where one doesn't already exist. Neither will it resolve a dispute between eight-year-olds. However, it can enhance and facilitate an existing environmental predisposition to be romantic or relaxing, or be the perfect backdrop for a party. The challenge, of course, is to use music in other aspects of our daily living with the same commitment and determination.

4. *Movie soundtracks render us all emotionally intelligent.* If emotional intelligence is about *knowing* how we feel, then music is about *showing* us how to feel. Indeed, the power of music to portray emotion is demonstrated best in the brilliance and genius of film scores. Whether through the subtlety of a single bass drone, as in the music composed by Jan Hammer for the old television series *Miami Vice,* or the haunting melody composed by John Williams for *Schindler's List,* music reveals the meaning of what is going on, or foreshadows what is to come. Music can make funny what would otherwise seem tragic and sad; it can bring attention to what might otherwise go unnoticed.

Furthermore, film scores are written both to manipulate our feelings and to inspire them. Interestingly enough, in recent years, soundtracks have also been written to guide our understanding, to speak to a higher morality. For example, consider the movie *Saving Private Ryan,* which contains a somber theme written by John Williams; and the movie *Good Morning Vietnam,* which revived Louis Armstrong's old hit "It's a Wonderful World," layering lightness upon calamity. By juxtaposing military victory with Williams's solemnity or with Armstrong's lightheartedness, each sound track relayed a different story and message than might have been told by more traditional anthems and marches that glorified war.

5. *The benefit of a musical experience is dependent on time and circumstance.* Hearing the *wrong* song (the one you don't like) at the *right*

time (when it is most appropriate) can elevate it to being the *right* song. You just might like it!

Conversely, hearing the *right* song (one you love) at the *wrong* time (when it doesn't fit) reduces it to being the *wrong* song. "Silent Night" may be perfect on Christmas Eve, but may be difficult to listen to on the Fourth of July. Likewise, playing a John Phillip Sousa march for the church service would probably not work, just as loud, exciting, stimulating music would not be conducive to sleep. However, this type of music could be exactly what is called for at a birthday party for a 16-year-old. "Auld Lang Syne" may not be anyone's favorite piece of music, but it brings tears to the eyes of many on New Year's Eve. Circumstance is crucial in determining whether a song is *right* or not.

6. *The significance of a piece of music in your life is not fixed.* A song that may have brought you to tears in times past may not have the same effect on you in later years. The nostalgia movement in the music industry is an effort to acknowledge and market past times through music. The music of the 1950s, for instance, may revive memories of feelings and relationships from earlier times and places. However, it cannot return us to who we were or what was happening—to that lost innocence of bygone days. It is merely a vivid, aural hologram of our past.

The memory factor—the power that music has to evoke feelings related to the time and circumstances under which you may have first heard the piece or become aware of it—can render a clearer flashback of your history than probably any other kind of memorabilia. It can happen anywhere. A melody heard even in an elevator can bring up many feelings. Being cognizant of the nature of musical association can ensure that you are not inadvertently insensitive to issues of which you are unaware.

7. *If you don't like it, don't listen to it!* Being in control of your own environment means that you can choose the music, reset its volume, or choose *no* music! It further means that any of these choices are temporary, changeable, and at the mercy of your circumstance and preference. Sometimes we feel so victimized by what is going on around us that we ignore what can be altered. The power in design comes from *doing* it. Don't be afraid, in the middle of chaos, to be the one to change the auditory context in order to make everyone involved aware of the tone and volume of

their voices. Furthermore, in solitary moments, don't be afraid to add in a soothing companion by turning on a wonderful album of music.

8. *Music, noise, and sound are relentless—they will follow you like a puppy!* This is one more reminder that you almost always have the power of choice in your life. However, if you are victim to secondhand music, such as the kind that's blasting out of the car next to you or traveling across your neighbor's fence, you may have to make decisions as to what your choices are. For instance, requesting that the volume be turned down may not protect you fully. When we truly do not want to be afflicted by the sounds of a particular piece of music, turning down the volume does not wholly cure our discomfort. Neither may requesting that the music be changed result in a better choice. Furthermore, blasting your own music to cover up other music may result in a decibel battle that draws in and disturbs yet more innocent neighbors.

Be aware of how sound travels, lest it be *your* music that invades your neighbor's living room.

9. *Before you totally discard a new piece of music that you think you do not like, know that you might learn to like it!* We have all had the experience of disliking a piece of music the first time we hear it, only to find, upon subsequent listenings, that we have changed our minds. In one of our workshops, we set up a class of 45 eleventh-graders to be music critics. There were six pieces for them to listen to. First, we had them listen for about four minutes to each piece and write down their impressions—multiple choice: *liked, disliked, loved, hated,* or *bored by it.* After each selection had been heard once, we reviewed them one by one, playing them again and discussing their initial responses. Each piece, then, had been listened to twice—first for immediate response, and then to refresh everyone's memory. One student had been convinced that he didn't like a piece but said that on the second listening, he actually did like it. Our experience is that listening to new music can be compared to meeting new people—some you feel like you have known before, while others take more time. Therefore, be careful not to wholly eliminate the possibility that, at another time, under other conditions, you might develop an affinity for a certain piece.

10. *We all hear old favorites that we have never listened to before.* Have you ever wondered why some new songs sound like you've heard them before? Well, you're right—you *have* heard them. The current structure common to contemporary pop songs—verse-chorus-verse—is basically a shorter version of the *sonata form,* a classical structure made famous by many composers including Mozart, Beethoven, and Brahms. Their more expanded structure consists of melody (A), a different melody (B), and a repeat of the first melody (A). In the middle, we might find an improvisational section or variations on the original theme (called *development*). Classical and Top-40 pop songs both follow some version of this structure.

For listeners, this form is easy to grasp and falls well within our built-in auditory memory. After a very few listenings—sometimes just one—we can sing the melody. Repetition helps teach us the song. The part of the melody that seems to own our thoughts, known as the *hook,* is the key to every major hit song. Without it, any would-be pop song is bypassed in favor of one that has it.

Another familiar nonclassical song form is the 12-bar blues progression. It is based only on changes in the harmony and can use any melody or rhythm. Despite their diverse audiences, country, jazz, blues, and rock all use the blues form from time to time. Again, the key is predictability and repetition—it sounds like a familiar song that you have never heard before!

Twentieth-century classical composers have made a concerted, if not altogether successful, effort to stretch us beyond our 18th-century musical comfort level. Given that we are at the beginning of a new century, it is good to know that some early-20th-century composers have finally moved into acceptance. Claude Debussy and Maurice Ravel, for instance, are known to most listeners for such recognized classics as "Claire de Lune" and "Bolero," respectively. Other composers, such as Igor Stravinsky, whose premiere of "The Rite of Spring" caused riots in the streets of Paris earlier this century, still sound contemporary.

11. *"The Sound of Music" is more than a great title.* Having been conditioned by the 200-year success of the sonata form, music industry executives move our popular musical tastes with caution. Thus, in this generation, the biggest leap has been in the realm of technology rather than musical content. Some avid music listeners are still clinging to older vinyl analog recordings; they are repulsed by the idea, let alone sound, of electronic or

computerized music. Instrumentally, this generation has witnessed the development of the electric guitar, synthesizer, drum machine, and special digitally produced effects. Nonetheless, our musical tastes evolve at a slower pace.

Lest we judge ourselves too harshly, history has consistently shown that resistance to musical change is hardly new. Major composers such as Brahms, Tchaikovsky, and Rimsky-Korsakov, who each expanded the musical forms of their day, received pitiful reviews from critics who were not ready to take the leap. Les Paul, the first guitarist to use electronically generated echo and multitrack recording techniques, was the first to record a duet with himself, which could not be performed live. This innovative use of recording technology was praised by some and damned by others, being perceived as a "trick" masquerading as music, further justifying a defense of classical traditions.

In the same period, Elvis Presley was one of the first vocalists to use "reverb," or artificial reverberation, on his recordings for pure effect, introducing what purists regarded as musical "smoke and mirrors." A decade later, the Beatles were the first pop stars to include non-dance music on their pop albums, forcing the issue of listening upon a culture accustomed to dance bands, further inciting generationally biased criticism. Twenty years later, Michael Jackson, in his *Thriller* album, effectively demonstrated the virtuosity of computerized drums, igniting a contentious rivalry between live drummers and drum machines that continues to this day. And in all probability, the next major innovation will cause similar discomfort!

12. *Listening to new music, like tasting new foods, is a short-term risk.* While some of us are reluctant to try new foods, we sometimes find that different foods of the same family start tasting alike. Similarly, music of the same genre can begin to sound alike and have the same effect; after a while, a new song by the same old star is just not new or different. *New* music is genuinely a *departure* from the familiar, rather than a repackaging of established musical formulas. The music we listen to reflects who we are, so expanding our listening repertoire gives us a partner in growth. Thus, it is more satisfying to listen to different varieties of music and to become familiar with what you like and dislike, and to also be willing to venture into new territory.

Symptom of middle age: You don't know the names of current Grammy winners.

Symptom of old age: You don't *care* to know the names of current Grammy winners.

13. *"There are only two kinds of music: good music and all the rest."* This famous statement by Duke Ellington settles most questions regarding the *comparable* value of bluegrass versus Dixieland, Mozart versus Beethoven, or Madonna versus Whitney Houston; and the *universal* value of Pavarotti versus Prince, Kenny G. versus Itzhak Perlman, and rap versus blues. Today, there are more than 37 different musical genres offered by background-music companies such as DMX® or Muzak®. Many a good friendship has been threatened over the debate as to which style of music is better. The truth is that in each style there exists a range of quality—from poor to good to excellent to genius. Yes, there are even compositions of Mozart that never made it to your neighborhood music store, ones that were not his best. Time distills the listenable from the less-than-memorable tunes.

Asked about what constitutes "good" music, Ali Akbar Khan took a very broad view by stating that "any music that is *in tune* and *in rhythm* is good music." Composer Peter Schickele, the originator of PDQ Bach, opens his weekly syndicated radio program with the statement, "If it sounds good, it *is* good!" Thus, Duke Ellington, in attempting to answer the question of whether jazz was indeed music, expressed the very truth of truths.

14. *Songs that are addictive may have short life spans—the more you hear it, the less you like it.* Remember the song "Music-Box Dancer" or "Tie a Yellow Ribbon 'Round the Ol' Oak Tree," or "Celebration," or the theme from *Titanic,* or whatever song you couldn't get out of your mind last year? In the mid-1970s, there was no escape from the endless and relentless sound of "Yellow Ribbon." Tony Orlando and Dawn became so identified with this hit that they continued to perform it at every one of their concerts for at least a decade. "You Light Up My Life" and "Feelings" are other examples of popular hits that pervaded the airwaves—then just as quickly disappeared.

Consider this: When did you last hear these songs on the radio? Last month? Last year? In the last five years? We, the record-buying public, loved them to death; then we were done—we put them away almost forever.

As much as we love the repetition of pop-song mantras, we eventually get tired of hearing the same thing over and over. Peter Michael Hamel, in his book *From Music to the Self,* speaks of music that has too little complexity having a short life because it fails to engage us when there is nothing new to hear.

Songs that have stood the test of time are those that can be resurrected anew, or those that have enough depth and complexity to offer us new musical ideas. Songs by the Beatles have become classics because, musically, there is enough substance to withstand innovative packaging, a new arrangement, and new renditions by other performers. Jazz standards are written to be changed and seldom become so linked to one performer or one arrangement.

Note: Let us not ignore classical music in this discussion. The music of Bach has been well transcribed and arranged for countless new instruments and has also crossed over between classical and popular genres. Nonetheless, there remains a great debate among music scholars and purists about the authenticity, if not legitimacy, of music originally written for one instrument being played on another.

15. *Music is only one part of a larger auditory environment that is temporary and circumstantial.* The auditory environment includes each and every sound we make and each and every sound we hear. Everything—no exceptions.

Using music is one way to design and gain some control over the uncontrollable. It functions in the same way that the visual arts do: A painting is to a blank wall what a beautiful melody is to the sound environment. Sometimes, in the same way a blank wall may have some small cracks in it or otherwise be imperfect, music is heard in an auditory environment that may include other sounds, which may detract from our ability to enjoy it.

You may, of course, have some control over the sounds you make—that is, all except your bodily functions. You will have limited, if any, control over the sounds someone else makes. You have even less control over the erratic clicks and hums emanating from the machines around you. You may be forced to endure the distant roar of trucks on the street that seep through your windows into your bedroom. You may curse the wind when you are haunted by disconcerting rattles of your doors and windows. Although listening may be volitional, hearing is not so.

Eavesdropping, a pastime that few of us will ever admit to, is defined as "purposefully listening to conversations that are private." However, most of us are innocent bystanders, minding our own affairs, when words come to us that we were not seeking. Whether a heated argument between family members or an irate one-sided phone conversation we cannot ascertain, overhearing is most often uncomfortable. If people that we know and care about are involved, we may learn information that we are not supposed to know, putting us in a difficult position. These problems stem from an auditory environment that is too transparent, like a window into another's life that has no blinds.

16. *It's about "time."* Time is to a composer what clay is to a potter—to be molded, shaped, and transformed. Our sense of time, which can be considered a sixth sense, is so critical to our well-being that we can be rendered ill from having it either lost or distorted. However, the kind of temporal respite that music offers can remove us from linear clock time long enough for us to regroup and be renewed.

Unlike our other senses, each of which can be linked to a specific physiological organ or special cellular function, our sense of time has evolved culturally. Our day/night cycle, originally defined by sunrise and sunset, is now artificially altered by electric lights and black-out shades. Furthermore, work cycles stretch the issue with swing and graveyard shifts, either of which forces an adjustment in our body rhythms.

Even though time can be precisely measured by the use of clocks and watches, our *sense* of time does not necessarily coincide with those measurements. We use the phrases *a long time, short term, never,* and *forever,* none of which imply a definitive temporal measurement. "Never" is not necessarily zero minutes, and "forever" is not a literal eternity. Rather, all of these terms are experientially defined with circumstantial meanings that are influenced by the environment.

Noise is also temporal. However, unlike music, it is erratic, unmeasured, and thus annoying. Rather than helping us pace ourselves, it inhibits our natural rhythms, causing problems such as increased heart rate, increased blood pressure, irritability, or loss of memory. Noise, then, is an aspect of the environment from which we must protect and defend ourselves.

Stress is a response resulting from having to adapt to change in *too short a time.* The use of music as environmental design is based on its capacity to affect our *sense of time.* The potential of music to reduce stress, then, resides in its ability to create *more* time—at least, as we perceive it.

Slow music literally slows time, as fast music accelerates it.

The sound environment is a place within that begins without, a time that has a beginning and an end. It comes from somewhere else, penetrates our bodies through the complex organs of our ears, reaches our minds, and becomes the message that we either look forward to or dread. Every sound we hear has the potential to enrich our lives or disturb us. The design of the sound environment, then, must not be taken lightly. Rather, these invisible details of everyday life determine its quality.

In the following chapter, we look at diversity in listening styles and at how our predisposition and attitudes predetermine our relationship to the music we hear.

Chapter Three

Music, Music, Everywhere:
Many Styles for Many Audiences

"The important thing is not, 'Is it good music?'
(It's) 'what is the music good for?'"
— Folksinger Pete Seeger, quoted in Jourdain's *Music, the Brain, and Ecstasy*

Susan: I used to think that music was just music—that if I liked it, it was good music. It was one of those painful, shocking moments in my life when I discovered that I might be wrong.

Years of musical education and training brought me to a paradoxical realization that just because I liked a piece of music—found it to move my heart and do what I thought music was supposed to do—did not necessarily mean it was "good." I found out that a whole set of technical criteria have been established by scholars and musicians alike, which can be applied to determine if a piece of music is *actually* good. Furthermore, the final scholarly determination regarding the merit of any particular composition or performance did not necessarily have anything to do with what I heard, whether it moved my heart, or whether it had *value* to me personally. Perhaps the standard clashes between movie critics and moviegoers, between literary reviewers and avid readers, and between music critics and audiences exemplify the dilemma with which I struggled at an early age.

I write these words with due respect, for I am a tough, subjective, opinionated critic and have been that way for as long as I can remember. I recall years ago the dedication with which my sister listened to Elvis Presley. She would respond to his crooning with a passion that only a female adolescent in some sort of hormonal trance is capable. With both the Spock-like detachment and the unswaying wisdom of a ten-year-old, I struggled to figure out what she was hearing that I could not hear.

When the Beatles premiered on the Ed Sullivan show, I watched thousands of teenagers express levels of ecstasy that seemed to approach pain. Again, I could not hear what millions of others were clearly hearing. Years later, Jimi Hendrix's screaming electric guitar further exacerbated the challenge.

To Simply Hear What Others Hear

"Music is not a 'universal' language. The languages and dialects of music are many. Even within one and the same culture, it is the exception rather than the rule when a musical style is understood by all."
— Leonard B. Meyer, in *Emotion and Meaning in Music*

Susan: My continued search to hear what others heard became a social pilgrimage that encompassed far more than a critical opinion. I found out, of course, that musical taste is fundamentally personal. Subsequently, by being critical of a piece of music that has profound meaning to another person, I inadvertently put into question their values, judgment, and even more important, their experience. When it comes to music, what else is there?

Whether the music is by Elvis Presley or Frank Sinatra, The Grateful Dead or The Four Freshman, Santana or Segovia, whole musical genres and the artists that develop them become the personal histories of entire generations, rivaling in importance the most highly valued gems of classical music. It is what music is for us, regardless of scholarly criteria or any other measurement that may be applied.

Today, of course, all the artists listed above belong to times past, and new names and styles have taken their place in popular consciousness. It is the natural evolution of things. Popular music, in whatever form it takes, defines a moment in time that is ours, never to be owned by another generation in the same way.

No matter how any of us may perfect the basis of our opinions and critiques, a musical "moment in time" belongs to the listener rather than to the music—to the connected one, to the person for whom the melodies and harmonies have meaning. To assume that the power is in the music denies the unique sensitivities of the listener; the music is only brought to its full maturity by the meaning attributed to it. Conversely, music outside one's experience or one's genre of choice is sometimes rejected when one cannot seem to *hear what others hear.* Of what value is music if we cannot relate to it, but rather find it alienating and without meaning?

Listening and Meaning

Susan: In all of my years of training as a performer, the relationship between listening and meaning was one assumed and not questioned. Traditional music studies focus on specific genres, on listening analytically, and on identifying harmonic changes and similarities in musical styles. However, the most critical aspect of performance—being responsive to the audience—was left to the performer's intuition.

The question that haunted me was, how could a certain piece or genre be wonderful to one person and without merit to another? I was also intrigued by my own experience of *musical meaninglessness.* It was not that I just didn't like the music. Rather, I felt disconnected from those for whom the same music held significance. I experienced great distance between my generational peers and myself. Years later, this trauma would become a point of mutual compassion that Dallas and I would share.

Most baby boomers, and especially pre-baby boomers, grew up accepting as fact that *classical* music was the only *real* music. To this day, it is the accepted responsibility of the listener to learn to understand and love classical music. By contrast, it is the burden of popular-music writers, performers, and producers to assure that a pop song can be easily recognized, understood, and endeared forever in the hearts of its listeners. Classical music has such cultural clout that only someone with ample knowledge or arrogance would dare question its quality or relevance. However, music critics and listeners alike take great pride in mercilessly judging the artistic merits of popular music.

Diversity in Listeners

Music, when viewed as art rather than mere entertainment or distraction, draws various kinds of listeners who create a specific identity with the music in their lives. These types include the following:

— **Musical devotees**—the devoted fans—pride themselves on having taken the time and effort to understand music. To the best of their ability, they educate themselves in the fine art of musical discernment, lest they be subjected to music of a lesser standard. The devotee talks about music, embraces music in almost every environment, and at the same time, shuns commercialism. To their self-taught ears, the subtleties of performances are irrelevant. *Their personal meaning is derived solely from loving the music.*

— **Audiophile listeners** combine an interest in music with a critical understanding of the technology that reproduces it. He (since it seems to be a predominantly male trait to be into audiophile equipment) prides himself in listening only to music recorded at the highest technical standards, which exceed most people's standards. His critical listening to sonic details is so fine-tuned that he risks hearing the sound and missing the music.

— **Music lovers**—those who simply and innocently just love music—tend to be genre-based listeners. Because their love of music is emotional rather than technical, they will often apologize for what they do not know and leave the art of criticism to those with more comprehensive knowledge. Furthermore, being musically educated has never been, and never will be, of any importance, since their satisfaction does not require such cumbersome efforts.

— **Classical music buffs**—including musicians and those who confess to studying seriously only as children—may find themselves listening according to their early training. Burdened by almost too much knowledge, they are trained to focus on phrasing, intonation, details of interpretation, and other technical factors. Their level of devotion is high and lifelong.

— **Background-only listeners** use music to live *by*. That means they use it to exercise, wash the dishes, make the beds, drive to work, drive home, and help them get through daily tasks—simply to make life easier to endure. Frank Zappa said, "The manner in which Americans *consume* music has a lot to do with leaving it on their coffee tables, or using it as wallpaper for their lifestyles. . . ." These individuals actually count on restaurants, shopping malls, and office buildings to provide music to make the time pass. One wonders if music-on-hold was created specifically for them. Unburdened by the need to know exactly what piece of music is playing, these persons accept the melodic wash of sound as it is, unless the volume is so loud as to intrude on their activities or conversations. For this listener, a continuous-play radio at home and commercial background music at work suffices. Indeed, hassle-free listening is of greatest importance.

— We should not neglect to mention the **non-music listeners**—those who proclaim music to be of little importance in their lives. They tend to tune the radio to stations that cause the least disturbance, absorbing talk radio as part of their auditory diet. Furthermore, they listen to hours of music selected by commercial interests and agendas. Their lack of conscious listening makes them even more vulnerable to the consequences of an invisible auditory environment. These are exactly the individuals who might love the half-time celebration at the Super Bowl, but not count it as music because of the predominance of the sports and entertainment factor.

— The last group of listeners that we want to identify are the **musical bigots**—those for whom the very definition of music includes a blanket and unconditional dislike of one or more entire musical genres. Their bias may reveal itself in conversation by comments such as: "Country and western isn't worth listening to!" or "New Age music all sounds alike!" or "Classical music is so pretentious." In each case, the assumption has been made that all music of a certain genre bears the same weaknesses, is of little or no value, and is to be avoided at any cost. Those genres on the "hate" list are not considered music, but a poor *excuse* for music. I have been guilty of such bias, especially in my younger years. Now I acknowledge that for each commercial genre, there are thousands if not millions of dedicated listeners.

In recent years, I have lived with a musical omnivore—Dallas is willing to listen to a variety of different music, just as he tries many different cuisines. Therefore, I no longer allow myself to wipe out a whole class of music just because "I don't hear what others hear."

Music in Different Contexts

Regardless of which of the above roles one plays, using music as environmental design is neither foreign nor offensive to the particular purpose music serves.

In the same way that an original work of art can be either a focused or a peripheral experience, so can music be experienced in various ways. At any given time or circumstance, we may identify with any of the various listener roles, then switch to another. We may be avid symphony subscribers, and yet be totally satisfied to walk into a shopping mall in which the overhead speakers broadcast Mozart or Vivaldi in the background. When music is part of the milieu, we may suspend our personal preference and listen with different ears and priorities.

In chapter 2, we cited Duke Ellington's famous quote regarding musical judgments and biases. In a recent discussion about his life and work heard on National Public Radio, attention was drawn to how people *heard* his music, more than how they judged it. Ellington said that his main concern was whether they were *listening* or *analyzing*. He said that if people were analyzing his music, they were often left without the capability to truly listen. He felt that the capacity to experience the beauty and emotion in his music was in direct competition with its technical scrutiny. Analytical preoccupation could prevent the listener from experiencing the music as a moment in time whose meaning could be found in the heart, not the head.

Following years of training that had changed my emotional experience to an intellectual one, I had to regain my sense of abandon in feeling the passions of music. So often during my studies, it seemed that my fellow musicians heard only form—harmonic structure, phrasing, details of technique, minute details of the instrumentation—but could not truly enjoy and surrender to the beauty of the moment.

I was trained in a strict method of performance technique that focused on how I held my arms, what part of the finger actually touched the harp string, and what I did with my hands after the string was plucked. Therefore, I had to master and then further mature my technique in order to both play music and hear the subtleties of its sound. Dallas and I have both experienced the trap of perceiving our instruments instead of our music. After grieving from the burnout that resulted from intellectualizing what should have been moments of the sublime, music began to function in our adult lives as it had in our childhoods.

The Role of Technology

Audio technology affords us the luxury of constantly surrounding ourselves with music. Consequently, the dichotomy between two kinds of experiences—focused and peripheral listening—has become a critical factor in music performance and production. When early radio programming first brought music into the home, the relationship of music to the listener began to change. Early depictions of a family huddled around the radio or Victrola speak to the end of an era. From the occasional experience of a live performance, we moved into using music as a context for living. Being in the audience—actually seeing musicians make music—had been an important part of experiencing the music, if not the only means to do so. Audio technology removed the impact that a live performer had on what the listener heard. Therefore, there was more opportunity and more pressure for the music to stand on its own without the performer having anything directly to do with the listener's experience.

It did not take long to realize that radio—music coming out of a box, even a beautiful one—lacked the visual and acoustic experience that a live performance could offer. The pressure on the recording industry to somehow make up for the difference inspired a myriad of electronic effects, from stereo to surround sound, all designed to enhance the technologically based listening experience, and make up for the small imperfections that had been forgiven in the presence of the live performer.

Now, over half a century later, performers are expected to deliver a sound in live performance that matches the acoustic perfection created by the recording industry. One example of how technology holds the reins of runaway concert expectations is volume: How loud is loud? With the advent of headphones and state-of-the-art home stereo systems, live performances have had to increase their volume to match the experience of music "filling one's head." Volume levels are now dangerously high, with the public expecting music to deliver what had been neither possible nor imagined in previous generations. This only shows that the experience of music encompasses both music and sound, both performer and listener.

Having only audio systems that would now be considered primitive, Dallas and I knew, as children, that the rooms in which we had our most profound listening experiences were altered by the sounds we heard. We have allowed our memories of these profound events to inspire our work in using music as environmental design.

Chapter Four

When Sound Becomes
Noise or Music

"In the beginning was noise. And noise begat rhythm.
And rhythm begat everything else."
— Mickey Hart, drummer with The Grateful Dead

From the beginning of time, human beings have sought shelter from the elements. Whether in a cave or in a cabin, the pursuit of refuge long preceded the search for comfort. Thus, the first artificial or "built" environments were *security-based* spaces, leaving nature to fulfill our inherent need for beauty. This is the origin of what is now called *functional design*. There was no assumed separation between indoors and outdoors, since early built environments were only minimal barriers to protect us from storms, wind, and natural predators.

As clustered populations grew into communities, their economies began to afford the creation of spaces that were functional to community needs. Consisting of banks, stores, restaurants, and more, these environments were designed to be protective while serving other limited functions. Therefore, a bank did not have to have a bedroom, and a hotel did not have to have a public laundry. However, a bookstore needed shelves, and a restaurant needed chairs and tables.

Remember, we are still talking about functional design—creating spaces to support the activities that take place within them.

From Shelter to Environment—Beyond Functional Design

In the industrialized world, we no longer spend the majority of our days outdoors. Rather, daytime is spent inside buildings that now feel more "natural" than actually being outside in nature. Built environments have had to compensate for those parts of nature that were lacking and yet necessary. We created artificial light where there was no sunlight; we invented the "house plant," where no natural foliage existed; we developed various means of providing water. In addition to security and protection, this artificial environment had to provide the essence of nature, which remains essential for us to thrive.

Beyond all this, however, our environments reflect our values, mirror our priorities, and express our joys and fears. The structure called home is, then, the unique physical context in which we organize our lives, where our children embrace their sense of self, in which our relationships are harvested. Perhaps the beginning of music occurred when, once housed and protected, we could no longer easily hear the sounds of the birds, the wind, and the water. Thus, we began modeling nature into melody. Environments are living rituals—the dance of life in solid form.

Sound Defined

Whether surrounded by four walls or a forest of trees, we reach beyond ourselves with our hearing. Rain falls and makes rhythmic musical patterns on the roof. The old refrigerator motor abruptly stops, making its presence known. The microwave oven "pings," indicating that its cycle has completed. Or, a child exclaims gleefully when a tower of carefully stacked blocks falls to the floor. Sound is the spontaneous consequence of an event that our ears detect. We then intently interpret the sound by using our lifelong accumulation of aural memories.

The auditory event, then, includes both the sound and the listener. Consider the classic question: "If a tree falls in the forest and no one is there to hear it, does it make a sound?" The answer, according to the physicist and the psychologist, is yes and no, respectively. The tree falls and causes air to push against anything in its path at a momentum proportional to the magnitude of the falling tree. Even if the only obstacle to the fall is the ground itself, the "thump!" resonates the ground in a measurable vibration, so the answer is yes. However, the consequence *to you* of the falling tree would be determined by your distance from the tree. If the tree falls in Indonesia, and you are in the Arizona desert, then for you, the answer is no. So for us, sound is about place—where we are and what we perceive.

Nonetheless, whether we are referring to ancient tribal communications via drumming, to the sounds of audience laughter during an HBO comedy special, or to the sound of a newborn needing to be fed, we intuitively use our hearing to compensate for what we cannot see. It completes the picture. Therefore, when we consider how sound has functioned in our built environments, we have to return to the issues of protection and security.

Early log cabins had windows, but no glass. Survival was dependent on being aware of the outside for cues. Since we are social beings, the built environment was designed to protect, not isolate. As such, hearing other people, the sounds of children playing, and the various sounds of community, was an integral part of life. So, sound is a communication—this is based on the natural progression from an event (the tree falls), to the sound that occurs (thump!), and our ears perceiving it ("What was that?").

Today, the increase in population, the addition of technologically based sounds, and the stress of urban living define how sound functions in our environments. As a cultural phenomenon, our environments evolved so slowly from natural environments to ones so clustered with activity that the gradual increase in decibel levels did not require our attention until it became a problem.

The New Environmentalism

In this time of numerous political causes, environmentalism has been most identified with global issues: preserving the ozone layer, protecting the rain forests, controlling toxic waste, deforestation, and the sacrifice of natural resources in the name of development. Perhaps the greatest interdependence, however, exists moment-to-moment between the environment and ourselves—*where we are becomes who we are.*

Similarly, when we hear a sound, we cannot separate ourselves from the experience of the sound. It is said that if we each march to a different drummer, we each hear a different tune. The sound of a bell, for instance, is quite different to a young child, whose hearing is most acute, than it is to an elderly person, whose capacity to hear high frequencies is diminished. If the environment and its various components could be experienced in the same way by each of us, then all our perceptions—what we see, hear, touch, taste, and smell—would be identical.

The environment, then, becomes a critical extension of our inner selves—our experiences, perceptions, and feelings all filtered through our ears, hands, eyes, and minds; and mixed together with our interpretations, hopes, and expectations. For each of us, our experience of beauty and pleasure is distinct. If you touch the softest rose petal, what you are feeling is your finger touching the rose petal. The rose and your finger become one, each indistinguishable from the other.

In a similar way, music becomes one with the thoughts and emotions that it evokes. Perhaps the meaning in music is based on our individual capacity to merge with the melodies, harmonies, and rhythms—to become the music, if only for the moment. The use of music to create life-enhancing environments honors the relationship between you and the spaces in which you live. Music, then, is an aesthetic nutrient, satisfying the human need for temporal beauty, balancing the auditory activity of the mind and the need to reach beyond oneself.

Music Versus Noise: Subjective or Objective?

Since this book is about using music as environmental design, the blurred distinctions between noise and music are pertinent to consider. In addition, the auditory chaos in our daily lives places all music at risk of becoming generic sound—merged into the cacophony of people, machines, industry, traffic, and other technological wonders that characterize modern-day living.

Sound is defined by the *American Heritage Dictionary of the English Language* as "a vibratory disturbance in pressure and density . . . capable of being detected by the organs of hearing." By this definition, sound has more implied than direct meaning, since it is the result of something else; however, it does include the requirement that the vibrations can be perceived. Thus, a tree falls, the earth moves, and if we perceive it, it becomes what happens to *us*.

Noise consists of unorganized sounds, often occurring at random intervals and dynamic levels, and without significance to the hearer. The above dictionary defines noise as "a sound of any kind, especially when loud, confused, indistinct, or disagreeable." It can be best defined as "unwanted sound."

In contrast, *music* consists of sounds systematically organized within a culturally determined framework of tone and rhythm. It has a relationship to our subjective definition of beauty and pleasure.

The laws of physics measure sounds in terms of frequency and volume. These measurements, however, do not define what any culture designates as music. For instance, the standard musical interval of the octave is defined in physics as a doubling of the rate of vibrations per second of a given tone. It is not impacted by location, individual preference, ethnicity, age, or subjective opinions. An octave sounds the same to the ear whether it is heard in Iceland or New Guinea. The essence of music is beyond the physical definition of any interval and is embodied in its intellectual and emotional effect.

One Person's Music . . .

Some might say that noise's description as "loud, confused, indistinct, or disagreeable" could easily apply to any number of musical styles. Thus, the subjective aspects of noise and music are critical to understanding the impact of the sound environment. Another important characteristic of sound, regardless of whether it is in the form of music or noise, is that it does not require prior approval on the part of the listener. That means that a sound can occur without our consent, unavoidably affecting anyone within hearing range, as an accident or by-product of some other event.

Unlike our eyes, our ears have no natural capacity to compensate or adjust if endangered or otherwise assaulted. Our ears cannot blink, squint, or shut; they have no defensive maneuvers. Thus, we can be involuntarily subjected to either secondhand music or secondhand noise from which there is no immediate escape.

Music not only alters our sense of time and space, but can also be the defining factor of our environment. All the perceived properties of sound are married to the acoustic character of the space in which they are heard. If, for instance, you were by yourself in an empty indoor gymnasium and someone whispered to you from the other side of the room, you would probably hear them. If they whispered exactly the same words at the same volume in a room with lots of curtains, carpeting, furniture, and an air conditioner, you might have a difficult time either understanding them or hearing them at all. Similarly, when 20 teenagers play tag in the pool, their voices and the sounds of water splashing will echo enough that they must yell at each other to be understood.

If a sound is unimpeded, as in the gym, it will not only be heard clearly, but as it bounces around from one wall to the next, it will increase in volume and intensity. The louder the sound, the more energy it will have to propel and reflect off the walls. A sound that might begin the "size" of a ping-pong ball could, then, grow into a basketball! This synergy between sound and space determines what we ultimately hear.

The factors that distinguish music—melodies and harmonies made on purpose—from noise, or sounds that happen by accident, go beyond the cause of the sound. As mentioned in the last chapter, the immediate relevance and personal meaning within the context of our lives determines whether we will like or dislike any piece of music.

Music Beyond Measure

While sounds may be described in terms of pitch, volume, duration, and timbre, even the most sophisticated scientific measurements are unable to evaluate the essence of music as embodied in its intellectual and emotional effect. The psychology of music is a field that has generated formal research studies, which attempts to understand and quantify why we respond the way we do to certain musical elements. These studies examine everything from pure musical sounds to complete compositions, from how we perceive musical phrases to how long a phrase must be for us to comprehend it. It remains, however, a great mystery why some pieces that mean so much to so many can nonetheless be meaningless to others.

Likewise, the physical laws of acoustics that describe how sound reverberates fail to describe the listener's experience. Although we diligently search for it, "music" cannot be found within a loudspeaker, instrument, or headphone set, or inside the vocal cords. Music cannot be found in the grooves of an old vinyl record or within the shiny surface of a compact disc. It is neither inside a piano nor inside the most expensive audiophile stereo system. Its existence is solely within the experience of the listener.

We do not hear in a vacuum. Rather, we listen within an environmental and circumstantial context. For instance, consider the sound occurring as the result of two objects coming into abrupt contact with each other, such as two pieces of wood, or wood and a stone, or metal against metal. If we hear a screech followed by a crash coming from the front of the house, we would most likely assume that there was an accident. Our degree of concern would be based on whether our car was parked in front of the house.

We necessarily and automatically give meaning to every sound we hear. We will also determine whether the sound has something to do with our situation, our condition, or what may or may not happen to us. Noise, then, has meaning, relevance, and symbolism. However, every culture and family has its own dynamic, sound level, and style of expression, which can include elements of what others might call "noise."

Vive la Difference!

Susan: Dallas and I come from dissimilar backgrounds, have very different needs and expectations, and have divergent musical tastes. Dallas listens to music at full volume almost continually, sometimes with additional radios on in different parts of the house. To an uninformed visitor, it may sound like chaos. To Dallas, this is freedom; it is life, it is rich, and it is his environment by design.

I, on the other hand, often prefer hours without music, completely quiet, and I can only deal with one sound source at a time. If Dallas arrives home to an unusual level of chaos, he knows that I am most likely stressed, or otherwise in emotional disarray. Likewise, if I arrive home and the house is quiet, I worry.

Everyone has different definitions of what is normal. We use sound cues to comprehend our immediate circumstances because visual information is limited by our line of sight. Thus, the use of music to design environments adds intention to what is already a fact of life. Sounds that surround us are a direct and qualitative factor in how we feel, affecting both our quality of living and our capacity to respond in ways appropriate to our personal values and goals.

Sound is life—it is the sign of the living. So, our love-hate relationship with noise and silence mirrors the battle we have with life and death. Filling the void is perhaps easier than living with it. The Indian philosopher Jiddu Krishnamurti suggested that enlightenment exists only if we are able to move past the pain and discomfort of silence. While he offered that music can be used—and *is* used—as a distraction, we have found that it is also a vehicle for finding inner peace.

Only with the understanding of how we hear music and sound can we begin to understand the high stakes inherent in the sound environment.

Chapter Five

The Capacity to Hear:
The Basis for Our Musical Experience

"To the man who is blind, hearing is sight.
If he then hears only music, he sees only beauty."
— Susan Mazer

The five senses are our links to the world around us. However, sensitivities—levels of sensory awareness—vary in each of us. For instance, some of us see colors more or less vividly; others of us are ticklish, while others have an incredible tolerance for itchy wool clothing. Similarly, we each hear differently. With our sense of hearing comes an internal auditory RAM—our personal random access memory—which we use to recognize the voice of someone we have not spoken with for years, or to identify a sound that we heard only once as a child. The impact of what we hear on who we are begins in our infant years and lasts a lifetime. Furthermore, the ways in which we integrate auditory experiences into our view of the world are not simply cognitive. Rather, our innate attraction to beauty often bonds us to sounds we may not even remember.

Susan: Years ago, when I was performing in San Francisco, a charming young couple named Sally and Tom came in to see me perform over a long weekend. Sally and Tom were on their last "lost weekend" prior to the birth of their first child only days later. They listened to me for three con-secutive evenings.

Six years later, I was in the same performance setting, when they walked in with three little girls trailing behind them. The oldest girl, Jill, walked right up to me, dragging her chair right next to the small stage. Then she sat, almost swallowed by its deep upholstered cushions, and looked and listened as if she were observing the most astounding feat of magic. As I played to this young child, I felt as if she knew me.

When I completed the piece I was playing, she reached up to me and took my hand, very unwilling to let go. With a combination of shyness and familiarity, Sally and Tom then told me of our first meeting when Jill had been introduced to my music in utero. They further told me that from the time she had turned three, she had wanted to play the harp, although she had never seen one.

It may be merely coincidental that this happened. However, it may also have been due to the many hours of exposure to the sound of the harp just days prior to her birth when her hearing was so well developed. Subsequently, I arranged for Sally and Tom to find a harp for Jill, which she studied for years. Her first encounter with music, then, preceded her first breath of fresh air, her first experience of color or taste, or her first utterance.

Indeed, we experience our first sound environment before birth—before we see light, before we know ourselves to be alive. As we grow within our mother's womb, we hear our first word, our first song; we experience our first surprise. The event is so profound that, once born, we can soon recognize the sounds we have experienced and come to know. During gestation, an unborn fetus acquires fully developed auditory organs by the 27th or 28th week of gestation. Even prior to that time, sound can evoke erratic responses. Fetal ears are vulnerable to damage from too-loud sounds from beyond the uterus; the infant is sensitive to vibrations or long tones in the lower frequency range. In utero, the sounds heard include everything from the mother's heartbeat, to stomach and bowel sounds, to the swishing of the amniotic fluid. Furthermore, it has been determined that the actual skin and encasement of the mother's body around the infant acts as an attenuator, muffling outside sounds, but not rendering the womb soundproof.

Current research has examined the effects of loud music, specifically music that has the loud bass common in contemporary music, in relation to the unborn child. There are indications that infants born to teenage mothers who expose themselves to extremely loud music during pregnancy often incur some hearing damage. Part of the risk is due to the fact that, in the third trimester, infants hear only 15 decibels (dB) less than we hear. That means that if, for instance, the mother attends a concert that is blasting at 130 dB, the infant is exposed to 115 dB—almost as loud as a jet engine taking off.

Less than two hours after birth, a baby can differentiate its own mother's voice, and within four days, it responds to the *tone or texture* of its mother's voice. Within two days of birth, the newborn recognizes its own language and culture. For instance, an African-American infant will be able to distinguish an African-American woman's voice from a Caucasian voice.

As an infant develops, auditory cues become the key to language development and social interaction. Their own voices become their tools of communication, responding in kind to what they learn about expression and meaning. Older children can perceive a wider range of sounds without being frightened as they learn to interpret the world around them.

Likewise, within a very short time, the mother can distinguish cries of hunger from cries of pain or those that signal a wet diaper, as the infant uses the elements of pitch, rhythm, duration, and volume—all the components of music—to communicate its needs. The benefit of a birth mother speaking to her unborn infant and playing music, thereby evoking a response from the infant, is undeniable. So, not only is the sense of hearing substantively developed, but this sentient experience is primary in infant development.

In addition to having greater hearing acuity and less cognitive capacity, the infant sleeps at a much deeper level. We have all observed that most infants can nap through just about anything, just about anywhere.

When we understand how profoundly we are affected by our sound environments prior to birth, we realize how much they continue to affect us throughout our lives, on all levels, from the most subtle to the most overt. Therefore, not only can becoming conscious of our sound environments help us protect the infants and children in our midst, but it can also allow us to improve how we act, feel, and think as adults.

When We Don't All Hear the Same Thing and
Don't Know Why

Susan: My family is a loud family. It isn't that we scream all the time, but our conversation is simply much more loud and intense than other families—at least, much louder than Dallas's. I was brought up in a household where there was never a question regarding someone's mood. Anger was angry; humor was funny; sadness was sad. All of that being true, it would make sense that our experience of quiet and disquiet would sound different.

This is not a value judgment—I am not so sure that "quieter" families are more balanced, or better, or more intelligent, or have more or less fun than we did. I am just saying that the dynamics were wide—capable of quickly escalating from a sleeping house to one filled with the sounds of radio, television, piano, harp, and then everyone shouting over all of this. The irony in all of it is that my parents often used to say, "Keep it down up there," referring to our bedrooms.

My sister Aliza came into this world at a time when no one knew the effects of maternal rubella on fetal development. (Currently, immunization shots exist specifically for rubella.) When she was born, she was found to have a cataract on her left cornea that, due to the way it was handled at the time, left her blind in her left eye. It was thought that this condition was the result of my mother having rubella during her pregnancy.

During those early years, Aliza was disciplined many times for ignoring my parents' directives. She had the quirk of holding her head to one side, something that we all felt was just one of her childhood habits. Her experiences at school were not wonderful, as she was in "sight-saving" groups and was prohibited from participating in all but a few mainstream classes.

Her greatest area of success was her singing. Of all of us, she had the most natural talent and the greatest potential. She sang in school choirs and performed all the way through high school. Nonetheless, with her vision impairment and the corresponding needs requiring ever more attention, the social and academic challenges remained unresolvable.

Children are not kind to other children who are different. For my sister, school remained a painful experience from her first day through to her graduation from high school. She was miserable, had little success, and was offered literally no hope of her situation ever changing. None of us knew what to do, partly because we did not know what the actual problems were.

At 23, when Aliza was pregnant with her first child, her doctor discov-

ered that she was totally deaf in her left ear. When we found out, we finally understood what none of us, including my sister, had known—that what had been thought was disobedience was actually due to her not hearing what was being asked of her; that her difficulty in performing academically was the result of her neither hearing nor understanding what was being said at the front of the room; that her apparent social difficulties in mingling with her peers were, in major part, due to no one—even her—realizing that she could not hear, and therefore could not respond. Most social activities in school happen in the lunchroom (which can reach over 100 dB in volume) or the halls in between classes, which are equally as loud. Thus, because of being deaf in one ear in an already overly noisy setting, she was victimized by both her hearing impairment and the noise.

In response to her confusion both at home and at school, Aliza was angry, depressed, and physically and verbally aggressive. Consequently, the family relationships were strained, as none of us knew each other except through the responses and reactions to what appeared to be a problem child. Perhaps this was the highest of all price tags.

It is far from obvious when we don't hear what others hear. Neither is it obvious when others don't hear us. This is perhaps the best example of how powerful our personal auditory environments are, and how such sensitivities sculpt our view of the world.

This story is told with Aliza's blessings in the hope that understanding the impact of the undiagnosed hearing impairment will be of value to others. In adulthood, Aliza has been able to do almost everything that she was told she would never be able to do: finish college, drive a car, become an avid reader of everything she could get her hands on, and raise three wonderful children. She currently lives in Rehovot, Israel, and has for the past 15 years worked as an administrative assistant at the Weizmann Institute. The fact that she and those around her make accommodations so that she can hear and participate, makes her world and her life quite a different place.

Pervasive Hearing Damage

Clearly, a high emotional cost is incurred when communication is hampered, and literally no one is aware of the real cause. Considering the role that the auditory environment plays in our lives, the risks associated with undiagnosed hearing loss at birth go well beyond merely not hearing, and well beyond the behavioral issues that Aliza experienced. If stemming from birth, the inability to hear can become a developmental disability, resulting in poor language skills, both spoken and perceived. For instance, an infant whose hearing loss is not detected until it is two years of age will bear permanent developmental scars because its speech and speech recognition will have been affected. Similarly, a infant whose hearing is normal is affected by who speaks to them, what is said, tone of voice, and tenor of communication. Speech impediments are common to those who have hearing impairment or loss, due not to their inability to talk, but to their never having heard the accurate pronunciation of words.

Until recently, the only way an infant could be tested for hearing loss was by triggering the startle reflex: making a loud sound and observing the response of the infant, which should include blinking, facial grimacing, looking toward the sound, or some visible evidence that the sound was heard. After realizing that a high percentage of infants were being misdiagnosed, researchers sought a more sophisticated means of assessment. In spite of today's highly sophisticated diagnostic technologies, only 19 percent of all infants born have their hearing checked at all. *USA Today* reported on May 24, 1999, that "one in every 300 newborns has some hearing loss, with half of those children having moderate to severe hearing loss in both ears." Then, the report continues, if "newborns go home with significant hearing impairment... it will take 2.5 years for their disability to be discovered."

The Auditory Environment As Protector

Even if our hearing survives mishaps at birth, the auditory environment must still be protective. If we come into the world with perfect hearing, we still risk hearing loss at a later age because of our lifestyles and ignorance. Not unlike overloading an amplifier or speaker by increasing the volume beyond its inherent limitations, our ears can become damaged when we are exposed to sounds that exceed their capacity. The two most common causes of ear damage are either a sudden loud sound in close proximity to the ear, like an explosion, or long-term exposure to sound at high decibels, such as a four-hour rock concert performed at over 120 dB. We tend to incarcerate our ears, making them work long, hard hours while expecting them to serve us for a lifetime. However, their warranty is not unconditional. It excludes neglect, misuse, and self-inflicted injury. Unfortunately, damage to the auditory organs is cumulative, permanent, and irreversible.

Lindsay, a young graduate student at Stanford, was deaf in her right ear. It was not so apparent upon first meeting her. She made sure that you sat on her hearing side, sometimes physically leaning into the conversation in an effort to hear better. While she would if necessary ask for words or sentences to be repeated, she was left both uncomfortable and embarrassed. Being in a crowd of people was particularly difficult, as the conversations were hard to decipher.

As a student of linguistics and as one who had to deal with her own difficulty, Lindsay was particularly sensitive to the issues of the hearing impaired. She had become a masterful lip-reader and regarded English as a second language for the deaf.

Lindsay's hearing loss was not congenital and not the result of high fever or other illness. The permanent damage done to her right ear occurred several years earlier: During a celebration of the Chinese New Year in San Francisco, a firecracker went off immediately in front of her. Initially, she thought it was just a blocked ear, the kind that can be cleared by swallowing. However, it never recovered. The damage had been instant and irreversible. She had been rendered permanently deaf in her right ear.

If the celebratory events of the Chinese New Year had caused a few broken legs, an epidemic of chicken pox, or multiple cuts and bruises, there would have been more publicity about the matter. Hearing loss has gone unnoticed on a global scale, even with respect to World War II veterans who incurred hearing damage by shooting guns without ear protectors. Children are unaware of such potential risk, often screaming at high pitch in each other's ears. Unfortunately, we tend to handle the event as a disciplinary matter, not a health issue.

In his early 50s, decades earlier than men of past generations, President Clinton became the proud owner of two hearing aids. He plays the saxophone, is a music lover, and was subjected to all the noises of a typically hectic, public life. So, the damage was done over many years in the course of daily activities. Others of us in his age group could benefit from the use of hearing devices. Perhaps the most obvious symptom remains the volume levels at which we listen to sports, live music, and movies. Clinton listened to all the same music at the same volume as millions of other baby boomers.

What happens when our aural thresholds vary, when hearing damage is undetected? First, we continue to unknowingly scream at each other. Second, the audio industry builds ever more powerful sound systems, responding to a market-driven addiction to increasing loudness and intensity, but resulting in threatened hearing capacity. Third, our methods of communication become strained, as may our relationships. Finally, and perhaps exacting the greatest price, our worldviews become limited, if not biased, by what we mishear, do not hear, or ignore.

Stereophonic Hearing: Why We Need Both Ears

In spite of any claims to the contrary, stereo did not originate in the audio industry. It is built into the human organism—we are provided with two ears. The information that we receive through two ears is qualitatively better than that received by only one ear. In fact, the information our ears give us is far more than just content and cognitive meaning.

The ability to locate a sound—to determine the precise direction or location a sound is coming from—depends to a great degree on the equal hearing capacity of both ears. Sound, as it moves through the air, reaches each ear at a slightly different times. Our brains can, however, perceive these scant milliseconds and give us a sense of spatial orientation. Our ears are so finely tuned that we can tell the difference between a very loud sound that is very far away and a soft sound that is right next to us, even if the apparent volume of the two sounds is exactly the same. The accuracy with which our hearing determines the exact location of any given sound source has been measured to have an error rate of less than 10 percent.

In our visually oriented culture, we assume that our eyes are more accurate than our ears. However, the reality is the opposite. Our acute sensitivity to sound intensity or volume, combined with the way sound travels to both ears, makes our hearing more accurate than our vision in determining location, distance, and identification—if, that is, we have equal hearing ability in both ears.

In the event that we do not hear in stereo, our ability to discern different conversations at the same time may be impaired, and our ability to localize may be very limited. In crowded social situations, it could mean that if our name is called, we will either not hear it because it is coming from the wrong side, or we will not know which direction to turn—literally.

Most of us take for granted the ability to function comfortably in a room with multiple conversations going on, such as at a party or restaurant. Also, we don't have to worry about not hearing any kind of alarm, a baby crying, or a pager.

The auditory environment in the home is different for everyone who lives there. Because our homes serve multiple generations and a variety of needs for many years, the more we pay attention to the function of the auditory environment, the greater opportunity we have to support relationships and our overall quality of life.

We now live in a time when up to five generations can be in the same room at the same time. The desire and need for intergenerational dialogue has never been greater, nor have the relationships been more at risk. Along with the frustration of natural hearing loss, auditory damage incurred when young people listen to headphones at high volumes for hours at a time often goes unnoticed. The tally will be taken in years to come. However, in the total picture, when our hearing is at risk, so are intergenerational communication and relationships, a factor normally undetected and misunderstood.

A Limited Warranty: Age-Related Hearing Loss

An interesting dialogue in our families about hearing loss may be similar to yours:

Dad says: "My hearing isn't too bad. I can hear just about everything."
We say: "How do you know what you don't hear?"
Dad says: "What did you say?"

Personally, we long for the days when the issues of communication with our parents were about words and ideas rather than about physical capacity. At the point when denial wins, as demonstrated by the above script, hearing impairment seems to be the insurmountable barrier to maintaining quality relationships and being up-to-date in each other's lives. Furthermore, we can no longer be sure that the subtleties of humor and innuendo, so rich a part of a family's culture and banter, will be understood and appreciated.

The definition of age-related hearing loss has mistakenly been limited to loss of auditory acuity. The reality is that sounds are not only not heard, but also suffer from internally generated distortion, making words difficult to understand, specifically in the higher frequencies. Furthermore, sounds take a bit longer to process and words become particularly difficult to understand when surrounded by background noise. An article published by the *International Journal of Nursing Studies* further challenges the idea that hearing loss is a physiological condition by describing it as a direct relationship between the person and their living environment. Clearly, this kind of hearing loss is hardly an issue of not hearing *anything*. Rather, the frustration of those suffering from age-related hearing impairment, as well as those around them, results from not fully understanding that the nature of the difficulty is both physical and environmental, and the subsequent failure to find satisfactory solutions.

Hearing Aids Considered

Hearing aids, unfortunately, are not able to replicate the complex sensibility of the ear. A hearing aid is a microphone that is not, as yet, very "smart." Rather, it is undiscriminating and "hears" any and every sound that occurs. Furthermore, it magnifies the volume equally without differentiating between background, foreground, incidental noise, and other sound. Thus, hearing aids flatten or even eliminate aural "depth" perception, making it very difficult to discriminate between multiple auditory stimuli. Imagine that you are talking to your child in the middle of a supermarket or playground and every other sound is equally loud—how clearly would your voice be heard?

If we are born with normal hearing in both ears, our natural auditory reflex is so intelligent that we can look around and concentrate on selectively hearing particular sounds. For instance, you can be in a room with four conversations going on concurrently, look at someone across the room, and, like a boom microphone, tune in to that one particular conversation, simultaneously tuning out others. That is why we can have background music, computers, phones ringing, and the TV on, and still carry on a conversation.

To illustrate the issue, consider the difference between eyeglasses, which can fully restore us to 20/20 vision, and hearing aids. Vision provides, in many ways, similar complexities of information: We can identify what we see and estimate the distances between ourselves and the objects of our viewing. Depth perception is a function of two eyes. Thus, ideally we treat each eye as needed to restore each to equal capacity. Imagine how the world would look if you put on your glasses and everything looked as if it was right in front of you—steps, cars, people, walls—all so close that you thought you might be buried.

Hearing aids pose that challenge to their wearers. If there are four concurrent conversations at one dinner table, "soft" background music, and the clanking of knives and forks, then the person wearing the hearing aid experiences total confusion. Lip-reading helps, but the effort to participate becomes exhausting, and having to be in the line of sight in order to participate when you cannot determine what you are trying to hear is both cumbersome and exasperating. As such, it is not uncommon for the elderly to either not use their already-paid-for hearing aids, or to sit, as my friend Rose did, with a forced smile, pretending she is fully participating when she is just sitting in aural isolation. Each of our fathers struggles with hearing aids that they dislike. In fact, they are so uncomfortable with the devices that wearing them is worse than what they don't hear. The earlier script is played out on a regular basis.

Indeed, family relationships either thrive or languish based on how we hear each other and how we are heard. Understanding this concept is germane to successfully designing sound environments that enhance our lives and relationships. Taking seriously the fragility of our sense of hearing, and what is at stake for all of us, is equally important.

The design of the auditory environment, if it is to successfully support its inhabitants, must compensate for various hearing capacities. Whether at work or at home, hearing and subsequent listening are not isolated incidents. They are influenced both by the complex state of a relationship and by the environment in which it takes place. Impaired *hearing*—whether caused by physical disability or environmental stressors—results in impaired *listening*. So, the sound environment becomes a not-so-silent partner in all our relationships. After all, if we are yelling at each other to be heard, how can we adequately express or experience each other as sensitive, kind, caring, and loving?

Chapter Six

Exploring Our Sound Environment

"Music and dancing (more's the pity) have become so closely associated with ideas of riot and debauchery among the less cultivated classes, that a taste for them for their own sakes can hardly be said to exist, and before they can be recommended as innocent or safe amusements, a very great change of ideas must take place."
— Sir John Herschel, 1792–1871, English scientist,
quoted in Ronald Pearsall's *Victorian Popular Music*

Most of us would accept as true that listening to a romantic, sentimental song might make us feel . . . romantic and sentimental. If we take that one step further, we could say that if we want to feel romantic—or want to make someone else feel that way—one option we have is to play music with those qualities. Anyone who has staged an intimate seduction over a candlelit dinner understands the psychology and impact of providing soft, sensual music. Underlying this example is the question of whether music can be used to control and manipulate us. For example, if we hear a bombastic, confrontational, rousing military march, will we then feel combative, and go pick a fight? Or, if someone wants to cause us to act violently, could they do that simply by exposing us to violent or dissonant music, resulting in our unwitting compliance?

The very possibility that there is a direct or causal relationship between the music we hear, what we feel, and our resulting actions has long generated concern that music can somehow alter our morality, health, or emotional stability. There have been serious attempts to identify and avoid specific kinds of music thought to be unhealthy, while identifying and endorsing others for their "spiritual wholeness" or "health."

Music has been used both to "soothe the savage breast" (W. Congreve) and to express the "sound and the fury" (W. Shakespeare) of life. Whether we listen to Tchaikovsky's *1812 Overture* with its cannons and drums of war, the passions of Prokofiev's *Romeo and Juliet,* or the harsh lyrics of gangsta rap expressing the pain and anger of inner-city streets, it becomes very clear that not all music is created to reflect peaceful, healing, or uplifting human experiences.

The Orthodox Church in the 16th century, concerned about the consequences of misusing the power of music, banned specific harmonic intervals that were believed to incite unrest, eroticism, or some other unsavory emotional response. The experience of listening to such music was thought to be directly responsible for aggressive actions and negative or immoral feelings. It was believed that the effect of music was embodied in specific tonal relationships. Therefore, Gregorian chants, written to evoke spiritual devotion, are characterized by what are called "perfect" intervals, giving the chant a plaintive or meditative sound. The tri-tone, however, which is the "perfect" interval of a fourth or fifth altered by one half-step, was named the *diabla da musica,* the "devil of music." The fears of its potential effects were so strong that it was literally banned by the church.

Lest we think that such judgments are merely a quirk of history, under the fundamentalist Muslim rule of the Taliban militia, all secular music in Afghanistan is currently banned, permitting only the chants of the Mullahs.

The recent movement to put warning labels on recordings is evidence of the universality of this idea. At any point in history, each musical element—from rhythm to melodic intervals to lyrics—have been analyzed for their potential positive and negative effects, followed by attempts to harness such powers so that innocent listeners won't be unduly manipulated. Furthermore, the use of music as ritual has come from the fact that music affects us, often without our consent.

With or without scientific evidence, we have used, and perhaps misused, the powers of music in our efforts to control ourselves and each other.

We have found value in both the musical experience and its absence, in its use as either a means or an end, in both sound and silence.

History has time and again reflected this belief that music can inherently manipulate behavior, as well as physical, emotional, and spiritual health. However, regardless of any kind of cultural censorship or control that has been practiced, music continues to be used to incite and excite, to uplift and relax, and to be taken both seriously and frivolously.

Sacred and Secular Music

Before music notation and recorded sound were developed, music was passed down by oral tradition—from singer to singer and from instrument to instrument. For generations, there were basically two identified musical genres: sacred—a direct or symbolic connection to a Deity; and secular—for entertainment. To the listener, these purposeful distinctions were actually more relevant than more obvious differentiations, such as between vocal and instrumental music. Nonetheless, music of the sacred and of the secular developed concurrently. At the same time that French troubadours wandered from town to town singing words of current events and human interest, the sacred rituals of Gregorian chants preserved and celebrated the presence of the Church and the power of the Deity.

With the last 50 years of audio technology, and as we make the transition to the 21st century, we are witnessing more varieties of musical form and practice than ever before. The list of genres continues to proliferate, including classical, popular, acoustic, electronic, traditional/ethnic, Christian, rock, rap, blues, rhythm and blues, country, oldies, '60s, '70s, traditional jazz, avant-garde jazz, jazz-rock, fusion, bluegrass, Dixieland, soul, gospel, folk, and more. As we have said, the debate as to which genres are "good" continues to be passionately debated.

In the Moment

Although our auditory memories have a lifetime guarantee, an intimate communion with any specific musical experience may be momentary. Our infatuation with any piece of music is sometimes fleeting, dependent upon the particular time and place in which it is heard. Therefore, our attachment to a particular musical composition, experienced as love-at-first-hearing, may turn into but a lingering memory.

For many of us, learning to use music in our lives means an ongoing discovery of new moments in time, with our listening repertoire necessarily changing as we change. Each of us is an expert within our own domain—we each have the final word on what is "music to our ears." We are not monogamous listeners married to only one style, composition, or performer. Our emotional needs are varied, our circumstances diverse. Thus, the use of music in designing environments becomes an opportunity to apply what we already know about ourselves to expand our options and bring creativity into practical application.

Environment As Ritual

Every action we take to bring order and purpose into our lives is, on some level, a ritual. The form that our space assumes is the manifested ritual of our design. While it can be changed, in the moment, our space is an action frozen in time, acting upon us in powerful, invisible ways. Whether setting the dinner table, arranging seating for a meeting, or making sure that the head of the bed faces the door and is clear from a draft, our actions represent our intent. And just as rituals are often accompanied by symbolic artifacts and may require a specific dressing of the altar, so will the environment demand its own treatment, and everything we place in it will have significance. In more than one way, the design transforms function into purpose. The environment, then, becomes our proxy.

The sounds within the space, whether caused by ourselves or others, ultimately represent our intent. They are analogous to our breathing, which functions automatically and yet can be changed at will. We can breathe without thinking, or purposefully take a deep breath to savor the aroma of the fresh air. Similarly, every sound that graces the personal airwaves around us either directly involves an action on our part, or is indirect and requires some degree of response. What may seem an everyday act may be elevated to honor the wholeness of design.

Environment As Possibility

With all the attributes of a ritual, the environment becomes capable of inspiring actions. Whether we are considering natural sunlight—measuring the glare factor against the clarity that only light can provide—or the ways in which chairs are arranged, our actions become major variables that complete the transformation of the fixed space into one that is alive, dynamic, and breathing. Similarly, our words and their meaning are dependent on the context in which they are spoken and heard.

When we consider the environment to be a possibility, we are talking about the power of the space to affect our potential, our future, our actions, and our relationships. The auditory environment carries with it sounds as they travel from one person to another and from one space to another. Our relationships manifest in the messages that connect our thoughts and feelings to others.

Environment As Intention

Intention is what we mean to do; it is the conscious resolution and determination to reach our goals. Intentional design, then, can be defined as taking responsibility for our surroundings and the outcome. In chapter 4 we discussed functional design; intentional design is the next step beyond it, holistic in its goals and scope.

When we invite someone else into our lives, everything that is seemingly external to us—our homes and offices, the clothes that drape our bodies—become symbolically who we are. Aside from genetic and natural conditions that are clearly out of our control, every detail of our environment and being reveals to others our values, priorities, and motives. If it is not held as important, as vital, as representing both our relationship to ourselves and others, then it risks becoming the happenstance attic of the present.

Choosing the Right Environment

Communication is the transference of meaning from one person to the next. Everything in the sound environment—every word said and every sound heard—becomes the way by which another person comes to know us. Whether it is by the orderliness of things or by their disarray, whether it is the radio station we listen to or the profound quiet that permeates the space, the environment becomes the state of things in our life at the time. So, the environment becomes our proxy, our representative, often determining the way in which the future unfolds.

The verbalization of our thoughts and feelings partner with the circumstances under which they are shared. For instance, suppose we need to make a serious request for assistance from someone who we fear will be prone to deny the request. Electing to do so in the middle of a loud, noisy hallway would not support success or a clear understanding of our urgency. Loud, noisy places have the following effects:

- We are forced to talk faster, often too fast.

- We tend to speak louder, automatically straining our voices; consequently, we may come across as angry, anxious, or demanding.

- Listeners are prevented from hearing the subtle, unuttered meaning behind what we are saying. They can miss nuances of expression, and, at worst, misunderstand our words.

Dialogue is the music of relationships. Our tone of voice brings more meaning to the words than the words themselves. The melody of the message reveals the purpose behind the words. If you remember the last time you overheard an argument where you neither understood the words nor knew the context of the dispute, you were most likely able to determine at least the nature and extent of the conflict from the perceived intensity—the drama—rather than the content.

The quality of the sound environment, then, affects what is communicated from the standpoint of both listener and speaker.

The Power of Music

The power of ritual lies in purposeful action. The presence of music in an environment is assumed to be intentional and sets the stage for interactions between ourselves and others. In totality, the sound environment is fluid, temporal, potent, and pervasive. It yields to nothing except our sensory perceptions and interpretations. It manifests the dance of action and reaction—something happens, a sound is made, we hear it, we respond—like a ripple in the water that radiates from the source until its kinetic energy is dissipated at the water's edge.

Music-in-Residence

In 1989, we developed a Music-in-Residence program, beginning with Washoe Medical Center in Reno, Nevada. Our objective was to demonstrate to the hospital staff that the quality of the clinical environment could be healing by design. After much consideration, we decided that we would need to perform live for a period of eight consecutive hours for an average of 45 minutes at a time. Eight hours was a long performance, but we had determined that it would take at least two hours to overcome the entertainment factor, given that live music in that setting was so rare. We also decided that we wanted to perform through at least two meals and a shift change.

We did not consider the environment of the hospital in separate parts, with differing needs between units with different diagnoses or levels of care. Instead, we felt that patient-focused healing serves the needs of the patient rather than those of the disease. Our demonstration of how music can redesign environments needed to demonstrate holism, showing that all units could be transformed and that everyone could benefit.

Since the hustle of people, dinner trays, and the nursing shift changes were known to be unnerving to patients and families, we felt it imperative that even these times of increased stress and noise should be experienced as therapeutic. Ultimately, we wanted to be there long enough to become part of the environment and have everyone go about the business at hand. Thus, we performed on various units of the hospital, each for eight hours, each with the same objective.

Since patients and staff do not frequent the main lobby, it was not on our list for Music-in-Residence sites when we scheduled our program. However, we accommodated the request. When walking into the main lobby from the outside, we found ourselves in a large, open, seemingly wall-less space, arranged with several groups of clustered chairs. Adjacent to an open admitting area, the lobby was central to the elevators, led to the cafe-teria, and looked similar to a Marriott Hotel—nice chairs and sofas, plants, a television lacking viewers, and a volunteer desk with two kind and wel-coming faces.

We set up our instruments and sound system. On this Wednesday, it was not very busy. In fact, there were no people near us. We moved chairs to cre-ate room for ourselves and our instruments, knowing that we could be heard far beyond what our eyes could see.

Activity seemed normal—people coming and going, patients in wheel-chairs being escorted to their cars, obviously being discharged. If someone was not in an identifiable uniform or obviously a patient, there was no easy way to tell who they were or why they were passing through the lobby.

Although the carpeted lobby may have seemed similar to that of a hotel, no one was here on vacation. If anyone was sitting in this lobby, it was because someone they dearly loved was a patient. If anyone was passing through, they were hardly going shopping. This was a place to wait—not an easy chore. Even for a minor procedure, with a positive outcome assured, the fact remained that something had happened to make us mindful of how fragile life is.

Given that people were mostly just passing through the lobby, many not even glancing toward the source of the music, we assumed that those who most benefited from our performance were the staff. However, we were wrong.

At four in the afternoon, as we started to pack up our instruments, an older gray-haired gentleman started walking toward us. I remembered hav-ing noticed him earlier, sitting in an alcove at the far end of the lobby. He told us that he had been listening for two hours, and went on to say that his wife was in a coma. "Today is the day that we have decided to take her off life support. Somehow, your music has made it easier."

Waiting is itself a type of suffering that is perhaps eased only by its own termination. Time seems endless and distorted by the stress that accompanies it. For us, there was no way to know who was listening. Had we been asked, there would have been nothing we could have said that could have soothed the anguish of this gentleman. Nor was there a way we could have contrived our music to have the effect it had. Although it is difficult to know, intellec-tually, how the music "made it easier," we found that it seems to travel to those who need it, and is translated by them to be what it needs to be.

While the specific pieces we played on that day eased the gentleman's pain, more relevant than our repertoire was our use of music to design the environment of the lobby to be appropriate to the therapeutic process. So, unlike a commercial venue, we did not perform to accommodate the personal taste of our audience members; instead, we tended to the collective needs of anyone waiting in a hospital lobby—we designed the space *intentionally.*

The Role of Personal Taste

Personal taste is the generic justification that most of us hide behind when confronted with major criticism of what we like. "Beauty is in the eyes of the beholder"—or should we say that music is in the ears of the listener?

During the siege at Waco, Texas, one way that FBI agents tried to get the Branch Davidians to surrender was by broadcasting the music of Frank Sinatra for hours at loud volume. Similarly, when the U.S. invaded Panama in order to capture Manuel Noriega, the army broadcast loud rock 'n' roll around the clock. In both of these situations, there was an assumption regarding age, culture, and musical preference.

If you try to recall the first piece of music you ever heard, most likely you will not be able to remember. For most of us, music is so integrated into our lives that it's like taking our first step, which can only be remembered by those who were there, not by ourselves. Our histories, family backgrounds, religious affiliations and practices, the schools we went to, where we lived, and the economic climate of our youth are only some of the factors that contribute to our musical tastes.

Certain pop songs are related to periods of our lives. As opposed to classical symphonies that were composed for posterity, popular music is of the moment, with only the limited life span that commercialism and our memories afford it. If it lasts until our ten-year high school reunion, it's because it became part of us. The many distinct genres of contemporary music can each be distinguished, not only in terms of compositional style, form, and content, but also as a key to identifying with a specific social group, its values, and its needs.

In public settings, perhaps the most difficult challenge is to avoid inadvertently alienating or isolating certain groups and/or individuals by placing them in an environment pervaded by music that clearly represents others, and with which they cannot identify.

Those who have always and only experienced the music on commercial radio stations or other popular sources will not necessarily understand or be comfortable with opera, ballet, or symphonic music. Such personal opinions about music are strongly held, second only to views regarding religion and politics.

Personal taste, therefore, represents a complex web of personal and social history and culture. Design demands that we take into consideration all these factors, yet personal taste must yield to the more important considerations of whether a piece of music is appropriate to the moment and the design goal.

As musicians, for example, our music preferences are necessarily biased toward the genres that have molded our careers: classical and jazz. However, when the situation demands that the music function on a more profound level—to relieve fear or anxiety, or to alleviate pain and discomfort—our choices may be different.

In the hospital lobby, the gentleman whose life with his wife was coming to a close needed most to be in a *transformed present* in order to let go of past memories and future plans. It was most important that we *not* play according to his personal taste. Rather, we needed to offer another experience, one that would assist him in dealing with the painful task at hand.

The power of music to seduce one's attention is so strong that it should not be taken lightly. The relevant questions are: Who is in charge of the music? Who determines the objectives? Whose tune do we follow? The difference between the Pied Piper of Hamelin and the Sirens of Ulysses was only their audience. They each, even in myth, utilized the power of music to do their bidding. Delving deeper into folklore, we find Krishna's flute and King David's harp in the ancient stories associated with Hinduism, Judaism, and Christianity.

Unlike a cookbook, we can offer no fixed recipes with guarantees to satisfy the aural cravings of each of us at every moment. What is most important is to learn how to determine what will work specific to the time and circumstance, considering who will be affected. That is the ethic of design.

Feng Shui

Feng Shui, the Chinese art of placement, is an over-3,000-year-old tradition of designing environments to best serve, support, and nurture our health (physical, emotional, and spiritual); our productivity (creative and practical); and our prosperity (monetary and material). It is based on the belief that every environment requires harmony and balance, and brings with it a set of opportunities, both positive and negative, that affect the outcomes of relationships, work, health, and well-being. Feng Shui holds that the merging of intention and space inherently defines the substance of a particular environment.

According to this philosophy, the *Ch'i,* or energy of life, has predetermined properties that cause it to move through space in specific ways that are affected by not only the way a room is built—in terms of ceilings, walls, and windows—but also by objects within the space and where they are placed. Similar to a stream meandering down a mountain or the way smoke moves with the wind, how and where the Ch'i moves creates a set of *opportunities and possibilities* that can be either positive or negative, either fertilizing our lives or causing erosion.

The practice of Feng Shui integrates the interior environment—the inside of a building or structure—with the natural exterior elements that surround it. The conditions of one structure will affect that of an adjacent structure; that is, one room impacts, to some degree, the quality of another room, hall, or closet. Furthermore, Ch'i, which emanates from the core of the earth, moves through space much like air does, flowing from one room to another. The quality of the Ch'i is also affected by the combined physical relationships of the walls, windows, floors, and ceilings, and the shapes of the various objects in it.

Ch'i is optimized by a designed path that is guided by natural laws and translated into practical means for promoting health and prosperity. In earlier times, farmers would consider the Feng Shui of the land, looking at how the natural elements, such as the relative location of mountains and other natural boundaries, would either support or threaten the growth of crops and the long-term fertility of the soil.

Today, since most of us do not have full choice in the initial construction of our homes, we have had to look to solutions that would compensate for or counter the results of bad placement. These antidotes may include the use of mirrors to reflect good Ch'i or deflect bad Ch'i; the use of wind chimes or music to keep the energy moving; water elements; colors; and the careful positioning of various pieces of furniture in relationship to walls, doors, and windows.

Feng Shui and Sound

The application of Feng Shui principles to sound reminds us that sound is the result of actions and relationships whose physical natures alter how air moves. The principles of Feng Shui require that we take responsibility for the ways in which the sounds of our lives move, where they go, and whom they affect.

An understanding of the effect of material clutter can be extended to aural clutter—noise and gossip—as they, too, might result in stuck Ch'i, or a blockage in the natural flow of our life energy. In addition—since the practice of Feng Shui speaks to health, relationships, prosperity, and other qualities of life—controlling sound would include the containment of our own unnecessary or distracting noises.

Sound, according to traditional Feng Shui principles, either keeps the energy moving and fluid, or blocks Ch'i, making it stagnant. Therefore, the playing of a bamboo flute or wind chimes, or carefully selected prerecorded music, is part of the practice of Feng Shui. Similarly, clatter, bangs, noise, and music that is not in harmony with our goals are best avoided.

Feng Shui does not dictate or attempt to empirically distinguish life-enhancing music from that which would consume our energy. The principles of Feng Shui consider certain qualities of sound in a generic sense, but as we have seen, music is far more complex. Feng Shui calls upon us to be sensitive to the moment. It also addresses the *quality* of the sound—both its timbre and affect. Perhaps the complexity and seriousness of these issues is the very reason why there is no "Feng Shui Top 40."

With such a rich texture and weave of music to select from, the application of the principles of Feng Shui becomes ever more critical. In order to use music as one would use light or water or any of the other elements in nature, we must understand how our ears hear, how our sensitivities are affected, and how our cultural and personal histories become the filters through which our minds and hearts interpret what we hear.

The principles of Feng Shui assume the interconnectedness of all things. For instance, in considering the placement of furniture relative to windows and doors, Feng Shui recommends that desks should *face* the open doorway, yet also that opposing entryways should not be so aligned as to prevent the Ch'i from emptying from one room to the next. In transferring that to auditory issues, the etiquette of communication recommends that we not speak to another person with our back facing them, just as it is undesirable to be spoken of "behind our backs." The resulting message is that our eyes should turn toward the recipient of our words.

Using this same principle in designing a sound environment, we are forced to pay attention to how words and sound travel, and the meaning each carries. In assessing our sound environment, then, the penetration of sound from one room to another must no longer be an accident of physical design, but an act for which we are responsible. Healthy relationships support directness of thought and action, while honoring individual privacy and confidentiality. Thus, verbal communications and their meaning carry the Ch'i of the relationship.

Consider once again the door-to-desk issue: The desk should face the door so that we are connected to others, yet not be placed in a direct line with the open door, so we have privacy and a separation of the public from the personal. We can see that the containment of sounds emanating from a room is critical to supporting the integrity of the other rooms.

Sound, just like Ch'i, is freely absorbed and reflected from one room to the next. The distinction between good Ch'i and bad Ch'i invites a comparison to communication. Whether we are heard and our relationships are supported depends on our ability to be as sensitive to our tone of voice as to the words we say. Perhaps the most subtle powers of Ch'i are similar to our tone of voice, which carries the message often with greater clarity than words alone.

Striving for balance is best demonstrated in the yin-yang theory, which is part of the Chinese tradition on which Feng Shui is based. Yin and yang represent the opposing aspects existing in each of us that make us whole. Often described as the polarity between things, such as action and non-action, feminine and masculine, or hot and cold, it is said to be inherent in everything and everyone. In musical terms, these opposing aspects may be expressed as consonance and dissonance, silence and sound, soft and loud, or fast and slow. This kind of balance in an auditory environment supports the spectrum of dynamic communication, always seeking to restore harmony, using conflict and discourse as a medium of exchange without expressing unhealthy extremes.

In examining the tenets of Feng Shui, we find that the principles of balance, intention, and possibility are applicable to music and sound. As we move into a more in-depth understanding of the actual physical, emotional, and spiritual implications of using music to design environments, it will become clear that the personal nature of your own life, family, and relationships become your guide in applying these principles.

Creating Sacred Space

The objective of environmental design is to create spaces that facilitate health and well-being, creativity and productivity. This requires that the design provide a means for the environment to respond to changing needs, and also to be a source of energy and inspiration. While ancient cultures sought out and identified sacred sites on the planet as holding the core manifestation of the spiritual, today we know spirituality to be more fluid, a part of our thoughts and actions rather than a quality of the soil.

Inherent in Feng Shui is the power of *possibility*—the knowledge that we can elect to act and be appropriate to the interconnectedness of all things. Our experiences are a series of actions and reactions, the quality of which depend on our capacity to become our potential, be the best that we can be, and learn with as much grace as possible. The *I Ching,* the ancient Chinese Book of Changes, states that although everything happens in its right time, we can accelerate or decelerate that time frame based on our actions.

Lance Secretan, in *Reclaiming Higher Ground,* beautifully sums up the purpose of environmental design:

> Our opportunity is to create sacred soul spaces so engaging to people's spirits that we are as irresistibly drawn to them as we are to any place of outstanding beauty. . . . These are places to which we are drawn because their ambiance encourages us to recharge and invigorate ourselves—to regenerate. In these settings, our thoughts turn to creativity, inspiration, reflection, integrity, friendship, and love.

Feng Shui may tell us where to place our desk, but it does not tell us which desk to buy. Likewise, we think it is critical to individually assess the quality of the spaces in which we live and work so that each of us has the knowledge to make decisions about those spaces, and to then make the necessary changes. In essence, you become the designer, using music and sound to make palpable in time and space what is visible in bricks and mortar.

We often see our environment as a thing apart, separate from who we are, as if it were wholly external to us. Our individual sentient experiences of touch, taste, sound, sight, and smell unify our minds and bodies with the physical world. If the sky above exists to us, it is because we have elected to raise our eyes to see it. If the waters that nourish and cleanse our bodies are like liquid velvet, it is because we have been willing to swim. Also, if we see a blossoming field of wildflowers as a lush Earth-borne carpet, it is because we have used our minds, as well as our sight, to see, smell, and appreciate. So, while we tend to attribute beauty to things outside ourselves, our appreciation is internal and individual. The power of space, then, becomes ours only when we assume the responsibility of design.

Part II

Designing
the
Environments
of Life

Chapter Seven

Sound Choices:
Assessing Your Sound Environment

"The ever-increasing assault of sound upon us adds to the other stresses we face at home and on the job. This stress load can be lessened by bringing more relaxation into our lives. Unfortunately, our environment does not adapt itself to us. We must learn to adapt to it, or change it."
— Steven Halpern, in *Sound Health*

Since the Industrial Revolution, individuals and communities have struggled to reconcile the benefits of technology with the detrimental impact of an ever-increasing level of noise. Noise begets more noise as we raise our voices above the din to be heard. Striving merely to keep up with the pace of the day, transportation and communication highways generate still other layers of noise. And so it escalates, until the ultimate result is chaos. For each person who justifies the cacophony as the price of progress, there is another who claims a societal birthright to life, liberty, and the pursuit of quiet.

If all noise were bad and all people were noise-phobic, then design would be rather easy. We would just have to eliminate anything that made a sound we did not like. However, since not all noise is bad and we have fair-weather relationships with the sounds around us, the challenge is to match the auditory environment to the activities, people, and occasion.

All too often the auditory environment occurs by accident—a consequence, often unintentional, of actions and reactions, communications and responses, and people and machines. The power of design rests in its ability to move us from being *reactive* to being *proactive*. *Sound Choices* is about expanding our choice of sounds, and being empowered to make choices that are sound!

Beginning Your Assessment

The sound environment is comprised of various components that may include intense conversations, whining ventilation systems, pulsating mechanical noises, spurts of multi-rhythmic footsteps, and the droning hums of computer printers and appliances. Therefore, the first step is to listen to and identify the various sounds present.

Spaces are not isolated. There is always an inside and an outside—a next room, adjacent building, walkway, or window. In order to actually understand the whole space, you might move from one room to the next, checking to see what you can hear from adjacent rooms. Make sure that you stand in each room, testing the noise levels with the door both open and closed. If you are alone, you might put on a talk radio show and set the volume equivalent to normal speech. Listen from the hallways or corridors, and from adjacent rooms that share walls. If you are in an outside room or a building that has only one room, go outside and listen to what can be heard upon approach.

What do you hear? Are any of the sounds you hear annoying or distracting? Which sounds are optional or controllable? Are any of the sounds impossible to tame? If there is an overhead, central, paging/background music system, are there any built-in volume controls already in place? If you are not home, who has authority to take charge or implement potential changes? What specific problems are identified within the environment?

Night and Day

Sound dynamics vary according to time of day. When the space is the loudest, is its function negatively affected? Not all human traffic jams are bad. Lunchtime in the school cafeteria is definitely the loudest time, yet the kids all manage to feed themselves, so it can't be said that the increased noise detracts from the primary function of the room. However, in contrast, at a nurses' station of a large teaching hospital, the early-morning activity level can reach such a heightened pitch that it may be very difficult for some patients to rest or relax. In that case, the intended therapeutic function is definitely compromised by the increased noise.

Questions to Consider

"Silence must be comprehended as not solely the absence of sound.
It is the natural environment for serenity and contemplation."
— Norman Cousins, in *Human Options*

— *Is silence intended to be an integral component of the space?* If the goal is relative quiet, is that attained? When quiet is disturbed, is the function of the space equally disturbed? Is it possible to set up specific areas to be quieter than others, such as the school library? Do the staff, family members, or others using the space act appropriately to support the goal of the intended silence?

— *Does the design of the space support privacy and confidentiality?* There are two general categories of conversations within a space: public (those that can be overheard), and private (those we intend that no one should overhear). Is the design of the space successful at supporting both? Are people able to converse easily in the public areas without interference from external or internal noises? Is the space set up to provide distinct private areas? Is it possible to maintain confidentiality when necessary?

As water seeks its own level, so do "sounds find ears." Psychologists have documented that the capacity for a random sound to draw our attention or disturb us is fully dependent on its relevance to us. In other words, if you are in a crowd, you will most likely hear your name, your spouse's name, or anything else that may have personal relevance. It is also true that if you are dining in a restaurant and there is a conversation behind you about a topic that is of great interest to you, you may suddenly find yourself eavesdropping. In a home or office, everything seems to be relevant to everyone. Therefore, it is important to know whether one's conversations are heard only by those intended, or whether the conversations flood the airwaves, finding unintended ears hungry for the ideas being discussed.

Several years ago, we were doing a site visit at a hospital in the Midwest. They had recently renovated their main lobby, creating a very open, spacious, and well-lit space. It truly was beautifully constructed, incorporating inspiring stained glass, lush plants, and stunning artwork. When we first walked in with the hospital administrator, we stopped to listen. What we heard was this: In the middle of the lobby was the admitting area, an open counter separated by partitions. There, a new patient was being admitted—an older woman, whose health concerns were substantial. How did we know that? Within 30 seconds of inadvertent eavesdropping, we learned that this woman had a living will, that it was at home in the closet, and that she was willing to sign another to expedite her admittance. None of this information was meant for us. In fact, it was supposed to be completely confidential. However, sounds find ears, especially when unimpeded. In addition, voyeuristic curiosity comes into play, given that most of us are fascinated by other people's lives and concerns.

Assessing External Versus Internal Noises

Sometimes there are factors over which you have no control, like an ambulance driving by or an airplane flying above you. These are *external sounds* for which the only defense is to increase the insulation, applying the same techniques that are used to soundproof recording studios. However, if you are in the process of searching for a new home or office, remember that the proximity of an airport, railroad track, fire station, sports stadium, or other source of disturbing noise is a very important factor in judging the suitability of any particular location.

In treating the sound environment, it is usually much easier to address the *internal sounds,* those emanating from somewhere inside the space. Improving it may be something as simple as changing the volume of the phone's ringer or getting rid of that noisy dot-matrix printer. Or, it may be more complicated, such as the challenge of raising the awareness of a boisterous teenager who has no sense of sonic boundaries when enjoying his or her favorite music.

Chaos + Music = More Chaos

If the environment is already noisy and chaotic, adding music will probably just add another element to the existing cacophony. If the painter's canvas does not start with clean blank space (read *silence*), then it is very difficult to paint a new, beautiful picture (the intentionally designed sound environment). The following episode illustrated this point in a graphic way, giving us new insight into the challenge of influencing an existing sound environment.

On another scheduled Music-in-Residence performance, we were asked to include the hospital dining room in our list of sites. The director of dietary services was concerned about the stress and noise levels in the cafeteria, especially during the lunch hour. On the first of two consecutive days, we started our performance precisely at noon, when the lunchtime rush was already in full swing. Although our amplifiers were set quite loudly, our music could still barely be heard above the dull roar of clanking dishes and spirited conversations. It was disappointing to us that our music was not as effective at improving the environment as we had hoped.

On the second day, we made sure that we began playing well before noon, when relatively few people were in the cafeteria. As the noon hour approached and the main lunch crowd arrived, they entered a space where our live music, the primary event, was already in progress. The contrast with the previous day was significant. Although the same number of people filled the cafeteria to eat their lunches, the music was far more effective and successful in creating the intended ambiance. In addition, the overall noise level was substantially lower, never approaching the level of the previous day.

Attempts to calm a chaotic environment by simply adding sound or music are most often futile. It is like trying to cover hot red with pale pink, resulting in a hot-red smear. Likewise, adding calm music to an already high-decibel environment results in a thickening of the noise, but hardly induces quiet. Our experience performing in the cafeteria and in other settings has taught us that if the sound environment is in keeping with its purpose, then people generally respond appropriately.

Reverberation: The Sound of Space

In the cafeteria, neither the music nor the ambient sounds of dishes and discourse were heard in isolation. Sounds partner with the acoustics of the spaces in which they travel. In this case, noise from the food area—amplified by tile floors, hard walls, and low ceilings—spilled into the dining area, which had some thin carpeting on the floor. Even if not one word was said in the dining area, the noise threshold was still high because of the din emanating from the kitchen. Adding to the volume, however, was the *reverberation* between the two rooms.

Known colloquially as "reverb," reverberation refers to the reflection of sounds as they bounce off the floors, walls, ceilings, and objects within any space. In this case, the sound increased in volume as it bounced from floor to wall to ceiling, having a negative effect on the sound design. However, for certain specific purposes, reverb can be a positive, intentional quality of sound design; for instance, churches and cathedrals are renowned for their reverberative qualities, with majestically high ceilings and hard reflective glass, wood, and stone surfaces.

School gymnasiums are particularly prone to unintentional, excessive reverb due to the solid wooden floors and bleacher seats. In this case, the needs of the room's activities seem to be greater than the desire to make the room quieter. The bouncing of a basketball is then experienced visually, physically, and sonically, with the reverberation of the hard ball on the hardwood floor sounding like a drum of victory. The only difficulty occurs when other kinds of activities take place in that same room. Then, it would be advantageous to have some kind of sound-dampening materials, such as temporary baffles, so that dialogue can be heard with greater clarity. In certain concert halls, sound dispersion panels are hung above the orchestra to diffuse the sound and reduce the reverberation. These panels are temporary and can be adjusted as needed.

Industrial buildings often make extensive use of acoustic dampening in ceiling, wall, and floor coverings to minimize the existing natural reverb, which enables a relatively large number of people to efficiently work together in a smaller area. However, industrial kitchens, such as those in hotels, schools, and hospitals, suffer from very loud clanking and banging. For the sake of hygiene and sanitation, floor and wall coverings are basically hard tile, cement (which can be hosed down), and stainless steel. Solutions? It remains a challenge for the most experienced acoustic engineers. Neither headphones nor earplugs work well if the people wearing them must exchange directions or orders.

The most pronounced natural reverb is found in relatively enclosed landscapes, such as canyons or valleys, particularly if there is much exposed hard stone surface. Forests have their own reverberant sound, although the trees and bushes are much more absorbent than rocky canyon walls. Open fields have almost no reverb, since there are no surfaces to reflect sound back to our ears. Shouting in a flat, open landscape can make your voice feel very soft and weak compared to the immensity of nature.

In our living spaces, reverb too often becomes an unintended third party in our communication. Then, controlling the way sound moves becomes a two-step task: first hearing how the space responds to sound, and then making the correct adjustments. This may mean, for instance, that if the sound travels farther than we intended, we might speak more softly. It may also mean that we decide to move to another room, if privacy is desired. On the other hand, upon realizing that the current room is "quiet," or without much reverb, we might move closer to the person with whom we are speaking.

In our homes, the furnishings affect the quality of sound in a room. For example, a hardwood floor gives rooms a much "hollower" sound quality than a carpeted floor, which mutes the echo and gives rooms a warmer tone. We have all experienced how our voice sounds different in vacant rooms or buildings as opposed to ones that are carpeted and fully furnished. The reason we enjoy singing in the bathroom more than in the bedroom is because the hard tile's reflective surfaces create a strong reverb effect, which enhances the sound of our voices. The bedroom, filled with soft bed coverings and linens, absorbs any reverberation and deadens our voices.

Ultimately, music sounds best to us in a room that has more space through which it can move. A high ceiling provides multiple kinds of "reflections" that make our voices, as well as our music, sound rich and clear. This is why churches are built with "cathedral" ceilings, new home construction offers vaulted ceilings as a premium, and theaters purposefully make sure that each seat benefits from the surround-speakers mounted in the ceilings and walls.

The Sound Environment Assessment

Assessing the quality of the sound environment by using the following steps will offer you a complete picture of the aural space:

1. *Listen to the space:* Stop, listen openly, and let sounds reach you. What do you hear? Notice whether you find yourself listening "to" or "for" any particular sound—this indicates an imbalance in the general ambiance of the space. Notice, also, whether you overhear part of a conversation that was not intended for you, or if you notice an annoying rattle in the water cooler, or some other extraneous sound. When your eyes are open, your ears hear what they see. Listen with your eyes closed for a moment—your ears will hear without a visual bias. Unintended noises contribute cumulatively to the overall stress level of those who are forced to hear them.

2. *Keep an auditory log over a period of several days.* Given that spaces are used over time, it is important to know the dynamics of the auditory environment—how loud does it get, and when? Is it easy to conduct a personal conversation or talk on the telephone? When is the space the noisiest? The quietest? Become aware of patterns of noise congestion, their causes and timing.

3. *Assess the level of background noise.* Is the noise floor (the background noise level) high or low? It may be instructive to visit an office or a school after hours to compare the noise floor at night with the daytime level. Sometimes we forget just how loud the background noise level can be when a facility is filled with people.

4. *Note episodic noises,* or noises other than background noises—when they occur, what are they? How loud are they? Are they intermittent or predictable? It is also possible that the noise floor may be so loud that no episodic noises stand out. This simply indicates that the background noises require attention.

5. *Determine the nature of all sound sources,* according to the following categories:

- **External:** Sounds emanating from outside the space, such as construction, traffic, sirens, airplanes, etc.

- **Internal:** Sounds emanating from inside the space, such as telephones, computers, heating, air conditioning, appliances, etc.

- **Mechanical:** Squeaking chairs, doors, window coverings, etc.

- **Human:** Talking, laughing, overflowing conversations heard from room to room.

- **Quality of sounds:** sporadic or continuous, avoidable or unavoidable, desirable or undesirable, high or low frequencies, easily able to be masked or not.

- **Reverb:** Quality of any echoes, vibrations, or resonances.

6. *Assess the music:* Is there any music already present? If so, does the choice of music seem appropriate to the purpose of the environment? Is the volume level appropriate? Are there volume controls present for regulating the music in different areas? Does the music project throughout the space without being too loud in certain areas? If no music is present, would the addition of music mask some of the background noises and improve the overall ambiance?

When you have performed the environmental assessment using the above questions, you may become aware of sounds you previously ignored, as well as other stress-producing qualities in need of solutions. These steps can be used to evaluate any space, even prior to utilization. If you start thinking about a room and how it will be used, this assessment becomes the basis on which to design the sound environment so as to best serve its intended purpose.

Once you have gotten used to doing this kind of assessment, you will be able to do it in only a few minutes. You will hear more, your sensitivity to sound will increase, and you will understand its effect.

The purpose for any assessment is to improve or optimize the space. Using the results of the evaluation, determine which sounds positively contribute to your intention, which incidental sounds detract or prevent you and others from achieving your goals, and—very important—which sounds are both unavoidable and undesirable. The last determination becomes the first challenge—how to neutralize the sounds that, if ignored, become irritants or unwanted distractions. It may seem from our definitions that any noise is an irritant. However, we are now taking into account *levels* of irritation and our own capacity to prioritize our hearing. Perfection may be unattainable, but improvement is certainly possible!

If unwanted sound is generated from the outside, we might close the door or move to another room. We might move the sound source, like the hum of a copying machine, into a closet, or turn it off when not in use. If the sound travels and we want to assure privacy, we might use music to mask the sounds heard by others.

We will talk more about solutions in the coming chapters. There are often multiple options, and the art of environmental design lies in choosing and implementing solutions that will proactively support the outcome. Sonic Band-Aids, such as closing a door, are perfect to deal with an immediate issue. Long-term solutions, however, require careful assessment and informed decision-making.

Chapter Eight

Music As a Context for Living

"When I go into a room, I make a noise
just so that I won't be alone."
— Vince Guaraldi

An Unlikely Remedy

*U*ntil it burst into newspaper headlines in 1986, the city of Chernobyl was not unusually famous and had no great global significance. Although a thriving industrial center, it was not a tourist attraction. Its population and pace of life did not significantly differ from those of other cities of its size in the Soviet Union. Nonetheless, within its own local region, the presence of its nuclear power plants gave it some technological and industrial recognition.

Unfortunately, the most serious accident in the history of industrial nuclear power gave Chernobyl sudden notoriety around the world. It was necessary to evacuate the entire population, as well as that of surrounding villages, due to the residual levels of harmful radiation following the accident. A surreal monument to the hazards of technology out of control, Chernobyl was rendered frozen in time, vacated by its own population, and isolated by virtue of the radiation that will remain for thousands of years into the future.

On the television news program 60 Minutes, *reporter Steve Kroft described several interesting observations while touring the region around Chernobyl several years after the accident. The first thing that struck him was that there were no people to be seen in the surrounding countryside. Farmhouses stood devoid of their inhabitants. Children's toys left behind in the haste of evacuation lay abandoned. Barn doors stood open, many animals having simply been released to fend for themselves when they could not be evacuated along with the people. Milk and other dairy products from local livestock were too contaminated for human consumption, in any case.*

When Kroft and his camera crew entered the city of Chernobyl, they were confronted by an eerily deserted city, haunted by only two sounds: the clicking of the radiation detectors that the crew wore, and the sound of mournful Russian folk music being broadcast over loudspeakers throughout the city. Kroft inquired as to why the music was being played. The answer was that for those few essential workers required to work in the deserted city on the continuing nuclear cleanup, it was necessary to fill the void with music, without which the solitary workers would be unable to perform their jobs. The mournful Russian folk songs acquired a particularly poignant quality in that stark setting, palliative care for the stricken undertakers of a dying city.

The ways in which sound and music affect our lives are often taken for granted. Indeed, no one would have cited this incident in Chernobyl for anything more than dramatic commentary, because the use of musical soundtracks is so common. The application of music in this instance was reminiscent of the movie *Platoon,* a powerful drama about the Vietnam War that used the somber score of Samuel Barber's *Adagio for Strings* to accompany brutality and bloodshed, an emotional juxtaposition.

It was apparent, however, that to those few who were tending to Chernobyl, silence was unbearable. Music introduced the voices of the living, the past, and hope for the future. It helped the time pass and distracted the workers, transplanting their thoughts to other times and other places.

How We Listen to Music

The use of music as environmental design acknowledges that this art form occupies more than just the back of our minds, as might be implied by the term "background music." Rather, it elevates music to the power of context—enveloping people, activities, and goals. It creates the basis for action and response, inseparable from the fabric of life.

Hearing results from our ears perceiving sound and space. As long as we are awake, we cannot turn our ears off, because we do not "do" hearing. Rather, our ears are "on" all the time. To some degree, we have selective control over our listening. Our brains can prioritize disordered sounds as if in a queue, and listen to them in order, based not on chronology but on relevance.

The background music industry exploits this ability. It provides music specifically meant to be put at the back of our listening queue.

Elevator Music—the Music We Love to Hate

> *"The musically aware hostess no longer allows the butler,*
> *or her husband, to sling records onto the turntable in a*
> *haphazard way. She no longer risks the dangers of the soup*
> *being spilled by Haydn's 'Surprise' Symphony, or Mrs. Jones*
> *choking over the fish because an ill-timed bit of jazz trumpet*
> *has frightened her. She now supplies a ready-made background*
> *of elegant and suitable music to smooth the evening into one*
> *long feast of pleasure and unshattered nerves."*
> — Norman Weinberger, as quoted in *Music Research Notes*, MuSICA

While Muzak®, the most well-known commercial background music company, did not originate the genre called "elevator music," the two names have become practically synonymous. The term *elevator music* originally described the place where most people heard the first versions of commercial *background music*. The latter term is more generic and perhaps more accurate; it denotes a programming style designed to be heard but not listened to. The original format, first produced by Muzak during World War

II, took standard and traditional compositions and arranged them in a musical style characterized by:

- minimal dynamic or textural changes;
- moderate or slow rhythms; and
- predictability.

These musical traits have themselves become a style or genre that can be regarded as a blessing or a curse, depending on one's personal taste. "Easy listening," a radio programming format first developed in the 1950s, provided hassle-free, dissonance-free, challenge-free, and attention-free listening. The music included popular selections of moderate tempo, and either new instrumental or older standard songs orchestrated to fit the format. Perhaps you have found yourself walking in a shopping mall listening to a Rolling Stones or Beatles song, originally quite upbeat, but now performed at a slow to moderate tempo by strings, light percussion, and wordless voices.

Other formats have been created to respond to the need for a kind of "easy listening" with a jazz or pop flavor, as well as preselected classical favorites that, again, do not demand too much of the listener. Thus, we have "smooth jazz," New Age, and most recently, Retrospective ("retro"). All of these are mellow, contemporary, instrumental arrangements of old standard jazz and pop songs. All can be characterized as soft instrumental—the "easy listening" of the 1990s. Today Muzak, AEI®, DMX®, and other companies distributing background music all offer dozens of programming formats broadcast by satellite, cable, and other proprietary delivery systems.

Collectively, the qualities attributed to this kind of music could easily translate into the guiding factors in designing a sound environment. These would include:

- consistency in dynamic range;
- subtle rather than dramatic textural changes;
- predictability that limits the amount of potential distraction; and
- moderate tempos.

Environmental music is best designed to be a catalyst rather than a controlling factor. At any given time, the styles of music most commonly used for ambiance will not necessarily satisfy the need or desire for a more sophisticated or substantial musical experience. Indeed, from the schooled musician's point of view, as well as that of much of the public, easy-listening music is like nondairy frozen dessert, or any other wanna-be substitute. Ask most musicians, and they will quickly tell you that "easy listening" or "elevator music" is a travesty—a perversion of all the values that distinguish good music from bad, the lowest common denominator of American musical culture. Considered a synthetic contrivance, such music is seen by some as a symptom of the "dumbing down" of the American people—how could they put up with such drivel!

Nonetheless, what musicians and critics alike often ignore is that this format called *easy listening* reflects our need for music that is, literally, easy to listen to—music that is not demanding or distracting. Many created environments seem to benefit from music that is nonchallenging, preselected, formatted, and usually centrally broadcast. The key to easy listening, Muzak, and elevator music is familiarity—music tried and true in either the classical or commercial world. The criticism perhaps comes from those who have not yet accepted the fact that elevator music is a direct response to the need for music that is *meant to be heard, but not listened to!*

Truth Telling: Most of Us Are Closet Background Music Lovers!

Background music, far from an being an insult to our sensibilities, can be relaxing, soothing, and enlivening. It is often central to the design of a beneficial sound environment. So, the intentional lack of distinctiveness, regardless of the famous melodies it might contain, is the very quality that allows the music to reside in the back of our minds, rather than at the forefront of our attention. For some, like the musical devotee, music lover, or audiophile listener, this may seem an affront to all that music is. However, most of us, even musicians, hear the majority of the music in our lives as background for other activities. In fact, if each of us were to limit ourselves to only the music we have time to focus on—that is, do nothing else but listen to—the quantity of music in our lives would be dramatically diminished. In addition, it would require that we sit and stare directly at our stereos, since they are the "performers" that bring music into our living rooms!

In spite of our collective negative opinion of elevator music, the greater commercial market has delivered its verdict. The background music industry is a growing, multimillion dollar industry, indicating that the market continues to expand as our demand for music-to-do-life-by increases.

Although we, as a culture, have assumed that the use of music as background diminishes its value as art, the truth is that this need has been continually filled by an avalanche of producers, musicians, and composers of instrumental music. Radio station formats that broadcast soft instrumental music include The Wave, The Quiet Storm, The Breeze, and formats known as adult contemporary, smooth jazz, cool jazz, and space music. Norman Weinberger, a professor at the University of California at Irvine and author of the Website at **www.MuSICA.com,** lists the many ways in which background music has facilitated positive outcomes in learning, buying, or in general behavior.

Recent research supports the growth of the background music industry. A study using college students as subjects measured their retention of memorized materials after having been exposed to different styles of music while studying. Positive if somewhat ambiguous results were reported by those students who listened to the music of Mozart. These preliminary results, indicating improved memory retention, have been seized upon as a phenomenon called "The Mozart Effect," a specific improvement of brain function attributed specifically to exposure to the composer's music.

Subsequent research findings contradicted the previous results, which could not be consistently replicated, and led to a broader definition of the benefits of background music as articulated in Don Campbell's book, *The Mozart Effect.* Campbell's expanded definition includes *any* music, in addition to Mozart's, that has a positive effect on problem solving, brain function, enjoyment, and stress reduction.

Some commercial background music companies have claimed since inception that their bland, nondynamic, nondescript formats have improved everything from productivity to health and wellness.

Regarding actual documentation concerning the impact of music on behavior, *The Journal of the National Association of Music Therapists* reported findings from observing aggressive behaviors in the public areas of a psychiatric facility. The study compared the use of two kinds of radio formats—hard rock and easy listening—and used the absence of any music as a control or baseline. The study showed that the easy-listening music resulted in a reduction of aggressive behavior by 80 percent. It further found that a complete lack of music actually resulted in a higher incidence of aggressive behaviors than did easy listening.

Another study showed that playing soft music in the dining room of a nursing home reduced agitation, a common symptom associated with Alzheimer's disease and dementia.

Using Music by Design

Most of us determine whether music is of the background or foreground type based on volume, as opposed to the qualities discussed earlier. In addition, if we are not subjected to commercial radio stations or Muzak, our choices naturally tend to be our "favorite" pieces, those we have elected to purchase and make part of our personal collections. However, this perfunctory method of using our own "greatest hits" as background without considering other factors may reveal certain challenges. For example, even at lower volumes, our ears may go on a search-and-find journey when we hear any part of what has once been important to us, such ᴀꜱ a theme or lyric that we know very well. Part of our brainpower may then be diverted to sing along with our favorite songs, which is not inherently bad, but may not help us concentrate on tallying a list of accounts or composing an important letter.

Our neurological system works in such a way that we have the capacity to experience multiple and dense amounts of sensory information. We can have a conversation with one person, have the radio on, hear the doorbell, and then know when the microwave alarm goes off. That is, we can do all of that when none of these tasks are particularly demanding.

We continually prioritize the focus of our attention, separating the sound of the air conditioner, for instance, from the sound of a strange automobile approaching our house. We can even separate dialogue that is of no concern to us from a conversation in which we are intent on participating. Most of the time, we are successful. However, if we attempt to read or listen to one conversation while we are hearing words coming from another external source, the difficulty increases. The two levels of conversation—foreground and background—compete for our attention and force us to constantly choose which one is more important. For these reasons, instrumental music more readily succeeds as background than do songs.

In either case, music that is overly dynamic is not always easy to push to the back of our auditory minds. Our ears perk up whenever a substantial change in tone or texture occurs; therefore, commercial background services that offer classical channels draw on the compositions of relatively predictable composers, such as Haydn and Vivaldi, to the exclusion of more dynamic composers, such as Bartok or Stravinsky. Complicated musical forms and styles require our undivided attention to be appreciated. For this reason, the jazz channels of commercial services typically feature the music of smooth-jazz saxophonist Kenny G., but do not include dissonant avant-garde jazz artists such as saxophonist Pharaoh Sanders or the Art Ensemble of Chicago.

Dallas: Next to the language challenge, familiarity also means automatic expectation. This is particularly the case if we choose to use very dynamic music, simply played at a low volume. In my own case, one of my favorite classical pieces is Maurice Ravel's ballet, *Daphnis et Chloe.* This impressionistic, instrumental, orchestral work consists mainly of relatively soft, abstract music, much of which might serve well as background. However, the suite also contains several rousing climaxes, including the grandest one at the conclusion of the piece. So, regardless of my efforts, I am bound to be distracted by Ravel's masterful music, if only when it reaches one of those dramatic peaks. Worse, I know well in advance when those high-energy sections are coming, since I've listened to the piece countless times. Therefore, as much as I love *Daphnis et Chloe,* it does not serve me effectively if I attempt to use it as background music.

If you think about your favorite pop song, you will most likely remember the chorus, or a few catchy phrases that are repeated—the hooks we discussed in chapter 2. The tendency, then, is to subconsciously hear the chorus, if we hear nothing else. It *entrains* us, or psychologically chains us to its rhythms. Again, our ability to concentrate and focus is challenged. *Entrainment* is the phenomenon identified throughout nature, where two separate entities will eventually become synchronized with each other. Fireflies will start blinking in unison. Infants placed near each other will eventually breathe together. The rhythm of a piece of music will cause us to tap our foot, and eventually this will influence our heart rates and respiration levels. We feel rushed when a fast, rhythmic piece of music is heard. This is not a mere emotional impression; it is an involuntary physical response.

As individuals, we all have particular idiosyncrasies based on our personal histories, cultures, and preferences. Since we are now assuming the role of designer, we are best served by a wide palate of colors and textures in order to not be trapped by our own profiles. Eclectic guitarist/composer Frank Zappa said that music is "a type of sculpture. The air in the performance is sculpted into something." Similar to how the best art draws from many mediums, effective environmental music necessarily moves beyond the limitations of any single musical style or genre. Rather, it requires that the environment created by the music be directly and intentionally designed.

About Broadcast Rights

Since we are talking about accessing the vast repertoire of prerecorded music, we feel we should also include accurate information about the conditions under which you can legally use music that does not belong to you. When you purchase a CD, you purchase the right to use the music in your personal setting—in your home, on your Walkman, or in your car. However, broadcasting music in commercial or public settings requires written authorization.

Copyright laws were written to do three things: first, to ensure that art will eventually be owned by the public; second, to give incentive for artists to create new works; and third, to set up a means of protecting the original rights of an artist from being violated. Primarily, the law created a timetable for any work of art to enter the *public domain*—that is, to be owned by all of us. The current law protects the rights of the composers and their heirs until 75 years after their death.

Copyright laws also created what is called a "compulsory license." This says that once a song is performed or recorded, another artist can record it by paying a statutory royalty, which is established by law. This both ensures that the composer of a work owns that work, and impedes that person from preventing its lawful dissemination. The top one-half percent of all musicians—such as Madonna, Kenny G., and film music composer John Williams—earn the lion's share of royalties paid. Most classical music is in the public domain, but recordings of these pieces may be protected.

Like thousands of other composers and recording artists, we have based our careers on creating new music and recording it so that those who cannot attend our concerts will still be able to hear our music. We receive royalties from companies that provide commercial background music, and also from television producers who use our music for soundtracks. Artists who contribute their music to The C.A.R.E. Channel and C.A.R.E. With Music, which are noncommercial programming formats, receive a nominal royalty and promotional acknowledgment for their artistry and generosity, allowing hospitals to provide this service at no charge to patients.

Broadcasting music in commercial or public settings requires written authorization from the copyright owners, or their agents—Broadcast Music, Inc. (BMI); and the American Society of Composers, Authors, and Publishers (ASCAP). These two are the authorized agents for virtually all of the recorded composers whose works you can readily find. To make it simple, you can acquire your written permission from them. If you can locate the artist, you can also get permission directly from them.

Remember, you pay only for your personal rights of use when you purchase a CD or listen to the radio (the radio station pays for their right to broadcast). Further licenses are required only if the music is used for public or commercial use.

Chapter Nine

Designing Your
Home Environment

"Music washes away from the soul the dust of everyday life."
— Berthold Auerbach

It's been said in many ways. *Home is where the heart is. Be it ever so humble, there's no place like home. Home sweet home.* For most of us, home is where we regroup ourselves, where our relationships thrive, where the results of our work in the world become manifest. Home is where the art of living begins. It holds us like a cradle as we recover each day from the stresses of daily living. It is almost impossible to separate our homes from ourselves, since they mirror our values and goals.

Home is also multigenerational, often having micro-generations of children between the ages of birth, age two, age four, and so on through almost every year of childhood and adolescence. These years are defined by improving language skills, increased memory capacity, and cognitive participation in life and relationships. In these well-defined and familiar chronologies, home holds our past, present, and future.

Learning to design the spaces in which we live requires paying attention to factors that have profound effects on us. Everyday situations are dramatically impacted by the insidious power of aural chaos. Normal chatter and discourse necessarily escalate in intensity due to the relentless drone of telephones, televisions, and radios. Circumstantial listening impairment—when we cannot hear each other for the deafening sounds around us—leave us in auditory overwhelm.

Unlike other design elements, sound has traditionally been dealt with from the standpoint of lifestyle and moment-to-moment activities. Music has been a matter of either survival of the loudest or "whoever pays the piper calls the tune." Local laws do not distinguish between noise and music—disputes between neighbors are settled by addressing such conflicts under nuisance laws.

Home improvement usually connotes a major, comprehensive project such as remodeling kitchens, adding rooms, interior decorating, painting, roofing, or landscaping. Attention to music and sound, however, is generally limited to buying a new stereo or building a new entertainment center. But in reality, intentionally designing a sound environment is far more comprehensive, involving both hardware and software—the delivery system and the music—as well as the room itself.

Design is the purposeful arrangement of all parts based on a desired outcome; it is not simply playing a compact disc or housing the CD player. Intentional sound design can, for example, protect our elderly family members from being assaulted by contemporary volume levels, while also protecting the teenager from being subjected to their grandparent's soap opera, which may be set extremely loud to compensate for hearing loss. Intentional sound design may be the only way we can ensure that we hear each other and are heard. Music is utilized as the most fluid and malleable design element.

Unlike the bricks and mortar that make up a house, the auditory environment of a home is living, dynamic, and changeable. It includes speech, household appliances, telephones, televisions, the sound of water rushing through the pipes, doorbells, furnaces, air conditioners, and fans. Added to this list may be the cries of an infant, the laughter of a child, the conflict between teenager and parent, or the intimacies between husband and wife—every argument, every loving compliment, every expression of sadness and joy. Thus, the auditory environment serves family connectedness, individual privacy, a wide variety of activities and interests, and multiple populations and generations.

Inescapable in any form, the auditory environment penetrates to the corners of every room, knows neither loyalty nor bias, and carries communication, purpose, and action—of both person and machine.

Functional Construction

In conventional construction, rooms in most homes are both built and identified according to their function: a dining room is to dine in, a bedroom is for sleeping, a family room is for family entertainment, and so on. Although functional design has been with us for a long time (see chapter 4), since the mid-1960s, architects and psychologists have understood that the environment impacts the behavior and relationships of its users. In chapter 6, we discussed intentional design: where we strive to make our spaces holistically support all the diverse ways that we use our home spaces. The relationship between the space and the individuals who reside within it is a primary alliance. Thus, when we speak of "home," that includes not only the individuals who reside there, but also their interpersonal relationships, their collective and individual potential, their productivity and growth, and their capacity to learn and heal.

While the concept of privacy is not a part of every culture, in the West it has become a symbol of bold individuality, to be valued and protected. Homes, therefore, must satisfy the diverse needs of individuals. In modern times, they have been designed to serve both the need for family connectedness and the need for individual privacy. However, balancing separateness and togetherness involves more than walls, floors, and ceilings.

As we have discussed, sound knows no social boundaries, only acoustical ones. That means that although a door may be tightly closed, if the music is loud enough, it will penetrate the closed entry, seep into the next room, and invade the rest of the house. The volume may not be equal in all these spaces; nonetheless, the music will be heard by those who otherwise would not choose to listen to it. The design of a home environment is complex and must consider the physical and relational factors at stake. Here are some steps to take:

1. *Determine the conditions under which you want to live.* Clutter comes in two forms: physical and aural. While you may want the overall feeling in your home to be orderly, activities and people may move things

around. The kitchen may be in total disarray as a result of having cooked and served a festive meal. Beds may go unmade for a day because you left early for work. However, you are able to return the environment to the orderly state to which you are accustomed.

2. *Design resilience into your home spaces.* In any home, there are a variety of rooms: living room, family room, dining room, kitchen, bedroom(s)—and sometimes a playroom, library, or workshop. Although we give names to the spaces according to function, each of these rooms may at any time be used for something else. Perhaps the kitchen is the best example. Functionally, it is the place for food preparation. Realistically, at least in our home, it is also the place of the greatest traffic, social activity, and intense personal discourse. It becomes everything because it is the center of the house. On occasion, for those of you who have the option, you might have dinner in the formal dining room, but more often, for your closest friends and family, the kitchen is town center.

When we talk about the resiliency of any space, we are referring to the ability to move easily between varying levels of sound and action. Activities and their accompanying decibel levels may be very dynamic—sometimes totally quiet, at other times almost raucous. For this reason, a space is best designed to have the capacity to accommodate.

The family room is perhaps the home's first and most active "multi-purpose" room. The term is what it implies: a place for families to gather to do a variety of things together. At one time, the room may be used for a quiet, concentrated game of chess; at another noisier time, Monday night football may dominate, as we take popcorn and beverage in hand. Similarly, bedrooms may be personal and separated by doors, yet hold children's games and study materials.

Children's rooms are best when they can be totally chaotic, filled with the manifested curiosity and energy of a child, with toys covering every visible square inch of floor—and then, when needed, be restored to a spacious, centered, peaceful, quiet space where a child can be read to or can listen to music, and regroup their energy to begin again.

The auditory component is very much like the material component. It can be orderly or chaotic, noisy or quiet. It needs to be able to *adapt* to the course of daily life, not *cause* the course of daily life. Being resilient means that the sense of healthy balance is present at every dynamic level, and that the sound of the room is not so live or "boomy" that even the quietest conversation becomes louder than intended.

Several years ago, we were working with 50 third- and fourth-graders in a school on Detroit's East Side. It was an old facility—actually a classic. The auditorium had been built decades earlier, with concrete walls that had been painted innumerable times, wooden seats, high ceilings, and classic incandescent lights attached by long poles. As with most auditorium seats, these folded up. However, having been built so many years earlier, they made a rather loud snapping noise when they were either raised or lowered. The noise was only a problem because the reverberation in the auditorium made one seat sound like ten. Every whisper was not only heard, but bounced easily from one wall to the next, gaining intensity. Even two children sounded like ten—and 50 sounded like 200! The room was so "live" that it was impossible to achieve quiet. Also, the louder we spoke, the less we were understood. It all became a mush of sound.

Another example of this kind of environment is an indoor swimming pool, where sound reverberates much too easily and is basically uncontrollable. This is the best example of a nonresilient space—it's either totally quiet or noisy, with little in between.

Solutions to this kind of overly reverberant space lie in the areas of either decision-making or physical conditioning. If we cannot completely remodel the auditorium, due caution should be used in planning activities that take place in this space to avoid a mismatch between the character of the room and the desired outcome. If the budget is available, then using temporary acoustic panels similar to the ones used in concert halls (see chapter 7), could very well improve the acoustic character of the room. Current school design specifies and measures acoustic properties and uses materials appropriate to the purpose of the room.

Most home settings today, with carpeting and drapes and padded furniture, are far more manageable. However, recreation rooms are often built with tile floors, hard walls, and minimal furniture. Thus, the level of resiliency may be far more limited than one would imagine. A new home with high cathedral ceilings and hardwood floors may be as difficult to control as the auditorium. Adding in some wall hangings, furniture, and area rugs will help, but don't expect to easily have either privacy or softer social gatherings in this kind of a space.

3. *Design your personal environments for change.* If we accept that any room is a multi-purpose room, then we can support its inherent flexibility on an aural level. Using music to create healthy, productive environments requires that we be *event-specific,* which may mean, for instance, that if the family room is being used for study, then the entertainment center can provide music appropriate for that, reserving the television for another time.

Entertainment is an event, an activity. Although it is how we often lump our musical experiences, in this book we are talking about using the right music to support our activities and goals in the moment. Given the diverse population and preferences of most families, programming the home environment to support immediate outcomes is the preferred criteria for choosing music, rather than trying to appeal to personal preference. For instance, when there is a group event, such as a family dinner, it becomes more appropriate to select the music and set the volume level to support, rather than inhibit, communication.

Usually, some parts of our rooms remain able to accommodate changing activities and populations, despite unchangeable attributes such as walls, ceilings, and large pieces of furniture. Whether it means using room dividers, in the case of a large living room, or setting up reading corners distanced from the television, don't be afraid to build in such flexibility or create it. It will expand your social options and also offer a way to renew the social energy.

4. *Treat yourself like a guest.* In designing home spaces, it is important to take seriously that the sound environment is an up-to-date, to-the-minute mirror of who we are. Mirrors can intensify the objects they reflect. Likewise, the sound environment can either lower stress by design, or exacerbate it. The sound environment needs to be designed and utilized with purpose and flexibility.

Preparation of the space includes evaluating the current objectives, including who is populating the environment, what activities are to take place, and what the desired outcome is. The kinds of music we might use to prepare dinner may not be desirable when it comes time to eat dinner. Music that may be perfect at 6:40 A.M. may not sound as perfect at 11:00 P.M. It is a mistake to assume that any one kind of music, regardless of how much we love it, will be appropriate on every occasion.

Be a discriminating listener. Assume that you will need to have several choices, since moods and preferences of the moment are as changeable as the weather. There may be some musical favorites that you can count on to always work if you need to be cheered up or calmed down. However, those will only be discovered after trial and error.

5. *Remember that noise begets noise—loud begets louder!* The volume at which we speak is dependent on how we hear ourselves. Probably the clearest evidence of this is how loud people talk when wearing headphones. The Lombard Effect says that we must speak 15 dB louder than the background noise to understand each other. Therefore, as loud as the mechanical sounds are, the spoken dialogue will be that much louder, which will then generate an even higher level of volume as a continuing response to the escalating noise level.

If the environment is quieter, then the overall volume level will be set by the natural dynamics of communication. As such, there is a symbiotic relationship between noise and conversation: the louder the noise, the louder the conversation. The louder the conversation, the more strain and stress in it.

We have both traveled thousands of miles by car, carrying our instruments and sound system with us. We have owned several vans, each well used by us. One challenge of traveling cross-country is the necessity of spending of many, many hours in the car. The time, which we have found to be very enjoyable, is an occasion for concentrated music listening. As you can probably guess, we share control over the music we hear.

The first year we were together, however, I realized that the music could, if not monitored carefully, become a third-party antagonist in our relationship. This is what would happen: Dallas would select one of his favorite jazz recordings. Given the roar of the road, the relentless drone of the motor, and Dallas's personal volume preference, the music would be relatively loud.

For the first few minutes, the volume would be fine. However, if we had anything to discuss, the conversation would be that much louder than the music, which was already blaring. Within a short span of time, it would feel like we were screaming at each other—because we were! Then, it would feel as if we were having a fight, when we weren't. Finally, I would turn the music off, and we would both realize that the tone of the conversation, the volume level, and our attitudes had all been changed for the worse due to the louder volume at which we had been forced to speak to each other.

6. *Design the space to support the relationships that occur within it.* How we hear each other—whether at work or at home—is not an isolated factor. It is a combination of the state of the relationship and the environment in which the relationship takes place. If we are yelling at each other to be heard, how can we adequately develop or experience interrelational sensitivity?

Hearing and listening are qualitatively different. One is by accident, the other is on purpose. The environment plays a critical role in either case. A consequence of impaired hearing—whether caused by physical disability or environmental noise—is impaired listening, which results in miscommunication and consequent misunderstanding.

Sensitivity training, which was in vogue in the '70s, taught individuals how to be emotionally receptive and responsive to each other. Since then, however, the threshold of sensory impact of one person on another has dramatically changed. Some of the more subtle ways in which we could speak to each other, and the value of soft-spoken discourse, have been buried in a sea of loudness. Children today often maintain their tendency to scream long past the early years when it is accepted or ignored. Parents assume that it is their job to compete with the sounds of technology.

Relationships are born in and defined by the environments in which they take place. Until two people truly know each other, the space plays an important role, affecting how individuals see and hear each other. For example, where people meet often gives them circumstantial information about each other. Meeting at work offers some evidence of values, education, and intellectual capacity, while removing the often intimidating anonymity of meeting at a bar or bus stop, or in the middle of the street. The so-called chance meeting is nothing of the sort, since being at any particular place is set up by circumstances that are hardly "chance." Whatever commonality that exists with respect to the meeting place becomes the first point of relating.

Since most of us prefer to begin a relationship with some predetermined set of parameters, social establishments such as restaurants and bars must make some accommodation for strangers to interact. If you picture the standard lounge scene, there are many people, an abundance of liquor, and lots of sound and loud music. The result is that the individual gets caught up in the mood of the crowd, which is controlled by the noise level predetermined by the music. At closing time, however, the music is turned off and the lights are turned up; the ambiance dissolves, and the magic is over.

The typical model of a commercial establishment has not evolved by accident. The entire "staging" is by design. The model has been developed over many years, using carefully collected information to benefit most patrons who need to feel that they are having a good time, to see and be seen. Others require special facilitation to create relaxed social discourse when the relationships themselves have not authentically moved to that level. Throughout the world, the rules of environmental design are the same—evidence of their success. All dance establishments make sure that the music is loud and the lights are low.

One of the best examples of an environment successfully designed to impact social behavior is the gambling casino. The objectives include keeping people stimulated, making them think that they are having a good time, losing their inhibitions, loosening the reins on their wallets, and helping the patrons forget about time. The intentional design components include: loud machines and music, free liquor, and 24-hour lighting that never changes—literally smoke and mirrors! Nothing changes—day after day, hour after hour. The noise floor is loud even if no one is there, with machines going off, overhead music, and glitter everywhere. The lights are always up and the bar is always open. If only we could design our schools to be as efficient in impacting behavior and outcomes as we have our gambling establishments!

In our homes, it is most important to consider the relationships, the events, the communication, and the outcome. Only then can we design the space to accommodate the best result. If the motive is to resolve a family dispute, loud music as a backdrop is counterproductive. If soft music is playing but the tenor continues to rise, turn the music off. Common sense plays a great role here.

The auditory environment is temporal and temporary—it can change instantly if we want it to! For example, if you are listening to upbeat music and the mood shifts for the worse, then change the music!

7. *Remember that volume sensitivity can also be a function of musical preference.* While it is not so unusual to find someone who likes the same cuisine that we do, it is a mistake to assume that we each hear music in the same way. Preferred listening volume is not a function of objective measure, but of sensitivity. Volume, especially with respect to commercial music, is an important part of the style. Rap, for instance, does not seem to have the same impact if it is heard at the same volume that might be common to

Mozart. A rock 'n' roll song can actually sound different when played soft-ly. Therefore, if one listener is more sensitive and hears sounds more loud-ly than another person might at the same volume, then trying to reconcile the perception gap is a challenge.

We tolerate music that we like at loud volumes, but at any level, we have little tolerance for music we don't like!

Dallas and I were almost newlyweds, married only a couple years. We traveled so much that our time at home was perhaps the only time we real-ly felt married. Of course, it was the time when we really had to get used to each other—our habits, quirks, and differences. I remember when it hap-pened—when the first challenge to the peace of our relationship occurred. It was a morning like any other. We had been up late the night before, recording a new album. So, when I got up a little later than Dallas, it was not unusual. I was taking a shower, trying to come to grips with the morn-ing that had somehow come too soon. Then I heard the pumping bass, the passionate saxophone, and the swinging snare of the jazz drum set. Under other circumstances, I might have reacted differently, but it was like having tuna fish and pickles for breakfast. It just didn't fit my mood or my physical capacity to ante up to the energy in the music, and it felt like fingernails on a chalkboard.

Dallas was in heaven. He had begun his day in this same way for years. And, of course, when we were on tour, he could not indulge himself. However, my response surprised both of us. While I don't see myself prone to wide mood swings or melodramatics, had you been with us that day, you might have thought differently. I became irritable, contrary, and not clear about what was so out of sync for me. Dallas, who was quite cheerful, could not understand where the storm came from—it seemed truly out of the blue to him. At some point mid-morning, we both decided to turn the music off. Then, it became quite clear that it was better for our marriage to find other wake-up music.

We have since negotiated our morning programming, settling on NPR's *Morning Edition,* which seems to satisfy both our preferences. If we get up too early, then classical music seems to be suitable for both of us. However, the menu of music for breakfast was one we had to work out. We did—and you can, too.

8. *Be respectful of varying tastes, and try to transcend the issues that will cause conflict.* In the early '90s, we presented a workshop on the therapeutic environment as an intervention to a group of mental health professionals. We suggested that if the objective was to see how teenagers and parents manage conflict, one could simply play the music of the teenager.

Without a doubt, the fastest way to unveil the power of personal preference is to play music at a volume that makes it hard to miss. Sharing a musical experience is a kind of intimacy. Genres are often matched with personality, ethnic groups, economic standing, age, geographic location, and more. Thus, it would follow that each of us probably has a strong opinion about the kind of music we like or dislike.

Certain musical genres are less obtrusive than others, with the most important factor being volume. Most of us can listen to a variety of music in public that we may not listen to at home, regardless of the volume.

If you want to encourage conversation, avoid songs with discernible lyrics at even a moderate volume. Our brains do have the capacity to separate relevant information from the irrelevant; however, trying to distinguish some words from other words is difficult. Therefore, both talking and focused listening become difficult. There is no point in making anyone strain when you are supposed to be entertaining.

9. *Using music as environmental design is different from using music as entertainment.* Entertainment serves the individual or groups based on exclusive preferences. The greatest entertainers make each member of the audience feel that they are being singularly addressed, making personal what might otherwise feel impersonal. In contrast, music as environmental design supports us in accomplishing our goals. Entertainment focuses on the music; environmental design focuses on our goals. This distinction is critical to understanding how to create a space that serves multiple opinions, preferences, and needs.

Environmental music plays a subtle yet comprehensive role in *supporting* other activities, rather than *being* the activity. Perhaps the best analogy is the difference between a painting and wallpaper. A painting uses measured space; its size is quite intentional. It is placed in a particular location to have a singular, specific impact. In contrast, wallpaper or another wall treatment becomes part of the whole room. It is not as focused in its intention, but is, by design, ambient. Similarly, environmental music is both softer in volume and larger in impact. It is designed to fill a room for a longer duration, rather than demand focused attention for a short, concentrated period of time. Furthermore, and perhaps most important, it is selected and utilized to be appropriate to a purpose *beyond* itself.

If the objective is to create a space to hold a diverse listening population, then it is important to avoid musical partisanship. Favoring one kind of music over another can literally create a bias toward those who prefer that genre and against those who do not. Unless that kind of musical favoritism serves the overall objectives, it can create an unintended estrangement that may then have other consequences.

In his book *Fatherhood,* Bill Cosby said, "Nothing separates the generations more than music. By the time a child is eight or nine, he has developed a passion for his own music that is even stronger than his passions for procrastination or weird clothes." Even accepting that as fact, it has been our experience that people entering a designed space respond to the environment, which tells them where they are and how to act. Even teenagers accustomed to a quiet dinner table have the capacity to separate the music that they may prefer in their own age groups from music geared to the family setting. So, creating the environment as ritual can support the capacity of family members to be appropriate to the moment.

Several key factors, including the politics, technology, and social practices of the times, determine the music of each generation. As discussed earlier, Elvis Presley and the Beatles seemed extreme in their times, but now seem quite mild when contrasted with current rap, hip-hop, alternative, and the like. However, we reveal our age and our position in the generational ladder by even addressing this issue!

10. *Both hearing and listening capacities are age-specific.* Homes are multi-generational, housing parents, children, and sometimes grandparents. Occasionally, the needs of one generation must supersede those of others; these needs encompass the sound, music, and decor of our space. Homes with infants are marked throughout not just by rockers, cribs, and playpens, but also by the sounds of music boxes and rattles. Later, the presence of young children may be evidenced by a plethora of toys and snacks, and the sounds of *Sesame Street,* Barney, and Raffi. As the children grow up, home activities may include entertaining friends with still more sophisticated television programs and computer games. The toys, which at one time adorned

every cranny of the living room, may finally be confined to one or two rooms. Eventually, they become the responsibility of the child to whom they belong. Their boom boxes may finally be relegated to one room. Television time may be monitored and limited. A few short years later, teenagers generate still another dominating ambiance, characterized by music that only they find beautiful, emanating from bedrooms that can barely be walked through.

After all those stages, the children leave home, and the parents eventually return to living as a couple. They indulge in non-childproof cabinet doors, food that serves a purpose other than nourishing the boundless adolescent appetite, and music of their own tastes and sensibilities.

As these years pass, the couple becomes concerned with taking care of their aging or infirm parents, which becomes yet another challenge in home design. Subtle, romantic lighting yields to brighter lights to compensate for diminishing visual acuity. Stairs are often avoided by making sure that most vital needs are met on the first floor. Bathrooms are sometimes equipped to accommodate those who can no longer negotiate fixtures that used to be so easy to manage. Radios and televisions are turned up louder for reasons entirely different from those that serve adolescent ears.

Each of these generational stages not only has different modes of musical expression, but also varying hearing and listening capacities.

The Teenage Years—Risky Solutions

Parents have a formidable task. They must cope with and try to comprehend the music of their children. However, the reverse is also true: Children must cope with their parents' music. Due to family dynamics, battles typically center around the music of the younger generation. Looking at the challenges facing young people and their pace of life, it would be naive to assume that their music would sound like the innocent days of the 1950s, or the disco days of the '70s. Each new generation has broken through past aesthetic boundaries, responding to fast-changing circumstances and an innate yearning for a unique identity. However, the real question is how to teach both young and old to listen to a wide variety of music and use each piece to support their personal needs.

In our work with high school students, we have consistently avoided any judgment about whether loud, inciting, and even angry music is healthy or appropriate. Rather, we have sought to provide additional options and tools for students to use when using music to relieve stress, or otherwise supporting their personal goals. Without exception, we found that having more options seems to lead to better decision-making. The more diversity one has in listening repertoire, the better the choices are when music is sought to soothe the frustrations of adolescence.

Research has not directly linked music to drug use and lawless behavior. Rather, it has shown some relationship between those who use drugs and are at risk of violent behavior, and a preference for volatile music such as hard rock, rap, and other similar styles. The difference between these two assumptions is critical. We all know too many well-balanced, productive teenagers who love rap and alternative rock to even insinuate that the music is the *sole* cause of certain types of behavior. Nonetheless, we feel it's imperative to offer a variety of musical options so that when loud, exciting music is not appropriate, there are other choices at hand.

Technology—Not Without Risk

Setting aside any issues regarding judgments of the merit of young people's music, there are other concerns that deserve attention. The listening habits of teenagers have been honed by a technology that is wonderful but not without its perils. Too often, sheer intensity of volume is a defining component of contemporary performances. Loud music is a large part of the culture of adolescence, but it places young ears at great risk.

Playing loud music is not a capital offense, but imposing it on other people is considered a public nuisance and can lead to a citation. In Fort Lupton, Colorado, the community created the Music Immersion Diversion Program, requiring youthful noise abusers to listen to loud music *that they do not like* for an hour. As a result of the program, violations diminished from an average of 17 per month to zero. If any of the music to which violators were forced to listen exhibited any appeal at all, it was immediately removed from the "aversion" hit parade.

We would be remiss if we didn't speak about the ever-growing danger of irreversible damage incurred when a teenager (or anyone) listens to music at high volume for extended periods of time. With the advent of head-

phones, teenagers are able to listen for hours on end without being monitored or interrupted by anyone. While it may seem that this is a good solution for the musical battles that are prevalent between parents and teenagers,
there is a high price to pay. Currently, rock concerts—which involve many
musical genres—are broadcast at over 128 dB and can last several hours. A
little-known statistic that has been consistently ignored is that at a sound
pressure level of 126 dB, permanent ear damage begins after only 1.87 minutes of exposure!

The rock group Motley Crüe announced several years ago that they
were going to be selling earplugs at their concerts rather than compromise
their artistry by turning down the volume. Speaking of contemporary rock
bands, we wanted to make you aware that the headphones worn by their
members are not for their protection, as is often thought, but are actually
connected to loudly blasting monitors that enable the musicians to hear
themselves and the drumbeat above the din. Unfortunately, most bands,
even those playing at local establishments, play music loud enough that the
Occupational Safety and Housing Administration (OSHA) finds it necessary to set a policy regarding noise exposure of bartenders and waitresses
who work close to the bandstand.

The two risk factors critical to measuring healthy hearing—decibel levels and exposure—come into play when teenagers elect to listen privately.
So, if we depend on headphones to defensively soundproof our adolescent
population, there may be a long-term price tag attached.

Ultimately, the healthiest and most gratifying environmental solutions
are ones that offer balance and flexibility. That might translate into moderate use of headphones balanced by listening at other times through room
speakers at moderate volumes. Different kinds of music work for different
times and circumstances—the more experiences we have with matching our
feelings and intentions with the music we hear, the more adept we will be
in the design of our environments.

The Elder Years

We know that our hearing changes with age. We have also mentioned
that while our personal music tastes may remain consistent, the rest of the
world moves on. What do we listen to when the current fad isn't to our lik-

ing? What if it has been more than a decade since we had a favorite song? The answer has to do with what we call *nostalgia*.

Longfellow described nostalgia as "a feeling of sadness and longing that is not akin to pain, and resembles sorrow only as the mist resembles the rain."

English poet Eliza Cook said, "Oh, how cruelly sweet are the echoes that start when memory plays an old tune on the heart!"

For those of us who think we are too young, the attraction and aversion to nostalgia shows up sooner than we think. It evokes the thoughts and feelings of a past never to be relived, and with it, a reminder that the world has changed. However, it can also make us feel good and comfortable. As implied in the above sentiments, nostalgia has had mixed reviews.

As musicians, we perform for many groups of many ages. Our experiences may offer some insight into the danger of making assumptions about the musical tastes of our elders.

From 1987 to '91, we performed on cruise ships, averaging about five weeks each year. The average age of passengers was over 70. The oldest passengers were in their 90s. The entertainment included a big band that played Glenn Miller and other music of that generation, a dance review that recapped music from the Broadway theater, and one or two headliners, including a male and female singer. We were categorized in the the "classical duo" slot, although we were not actually playing classical music.

On our first cruise, we included standard classical pieces in our concerts, while also introducing our original compositions. The response was revealing: The old standards were well received. The new music, however, inspired a standing ovation. A similar response occurs when we perform at senior centers or at hospitals. It is clear to us that nostalgia—revisiting the past through the use of music or other mediums in order to reminisce—has both its place and its limitations.

As performers, nostalgia means yesterday's song list—the piece you played for your first recital. Today, even pieces that we might have played frequently in past years must be played anew, as if for the first time. Each listener deals with past musical loves differently. We own 1,000 vinyl records (collected over several decades) and hundreds of CDs. We have purchased only a few re-releases of older recordings. We don't listen to music from the past unless it has meaning in the present.

Musical nostalgia can be fun or soul-satisfying, light or intense, positive or painful. It has a place and a time. However, under circumstances that place the future in question, such as a health crisis, the past takes on a different meaning. It can inspire intense sadness and anxiety. As a result, musical nostalgia should be applied with care, balanced by new experiences to avoid getting trapped in thoughts of the past, and being unable to be fully in the present.

Chapter Ten

It's Off to Work We Go!

"One of the saddest things is that the only thing that a man
can do for eight hours a day, day after day, is work.
You can't eat eight hours a day nor drink for eight hours
a day nor make love for eight hours—all you can do
for eight hours is work."
— William Faulkner (1897–1962),
interviewed in *Writers at Work,* ed. M. Cowley, 1958

Dallas: Although I had worked summers in the post office and for Bekins Van Lines, my work experience was hardly extensive at the age of 21. During my studies in Kiel, Germany, I had limited funds, not unlike other students. I also wanted to practice my language skills and learn about life beyond the protective borders of the university. These were the incentives that brought me to the Arbeitsvermitlung, the student employment office.

Those students desiring work would assemble there early in the morning, and various companies would hire day-laborers. These jobs involved unskilled, often tedious, physically exhausting tasks. Since my lifelong goals were still being formulated, I tried to identify with and respect those for whom these places of work constituted lifelong occupations.

I did construction work, loaded and unloaded delivery trucks, spent a day at the slaughter house dragging bloody cattle hides from the skinner to a cold storage area (my least favorite job), and spent three months as an orderly at the local hospital.

On one particular day, the Eiche Brauerei, the "Oak Brewery," needed a worker, and I stepped forward. I took the streetcar to the other side of town, which seemed far from the university, deep within the industrial section of Kiel. From where the bus stopped, I had to walk about 100 yards to a huge stone building with large windows. It was old and well worn, a tribute to its long tradition.

As I entered the building, I left the natural sunlight behind to enter the cavernous brewery. Overhead industrial lights hung from long thin metal poles suspended from the vaulted ceiling. The filtered daylight shone through dusty gray windows, bordered by dingy gray walls and concrete floors.

Clearly, the brewery was its own world. The most disturbing aspect of the setting was aural: Clanking, creaking, and banging resounded from the conveyor belt as it transported its bottles along a convoluted path, spewing them into the collecting area. The seemingly endless rows of glass bottles bumped against each other with a persistent rhythm. They obediently moved from the washing station to the filling station, on to the capping station, the labeling station, and finally to what was to be my position for the next eight hours—the end of the line.

My job was to take newly filled beer bottles off the assembly line and place them into plastic crates for stacking and shipping. While the conveyor belt was running, conversation was impossible; I could not practice my language skills or get any sense of who my co-workers were. With the relentless din of the machines and the endless stream of bottles coming toward me without pause, my eyes were riveted on the task at hand. My co-workers were likewise constrained by their jobs, barely glancing at each other until the belt suddenly lurched to a stop for the lunch break.

Only then, in the sudden quiet, did I realize that my whole body had been adjusting to the endless drone echoing and accumulating with intensity over many hours.

As William Faulkner said decades ago, we spend a greater percentage of our lives engaged in work than in any other activity. On a typical work day, you arise at 6:30 A.M., leave for work at 7:30, and start work at 8:30 or 9:00; you then leave work at 5:00 P.M., arrive home at 6:00, and retire at 10:00. If this is the case, then you spend 2.5 hours per day in your car, 5.5 hours at home, and 8.5 hours at work. So, more than one-third of every

24-hour day and more than 50 percent of your waking hours are spent at your place of work. If you add the weekends (when you are not *supposed* to be working) then perhaps the "50 percent" would be somewhat reduced. However, many of us run around getting errands done, doing the laundry, seeing our loved ones, paying bills, and going to church. As a result, all of these various and requisite tasks replace our jobs, becoming perhaps a second job for all of us.

Furthermore, this equation may not go far enough, since only some of us are able to put work totally out of our minds at quitting time. For those of us who are self-employed, hold down two or more jobs, or have careers that require lots of preparation time, such as farming or teaching, work is never done, over, out of sight, or out of mind. How many of us feel as if we work *all the time*?

If you are honest about how much time you invest in your work, it will become obvious that it is impossible for your workplace *not* to affect you. Indeed, it is a predictor of the quality of the rest of our lives. If work makes us "sick," then the burden is on our home life to make us "well." The place in which we earn our living mediates and negotiates the conditions of our life. It makes us feel better or worse, shifts our mood either positively or negatively, and its design—whether accidental or intentional—makes a critical difference in our health and well-being. With all of this in mind, a fair question and concern is this: Do we design the environment in which we work with as much care, pride, and purpose as the environment in which we live?

Your Mental Image of Your Workplace

Whatever you do as the "work" in your life, think for a minute about where you do it. Could you be productive in a garage or attic without altering the space? Would you have to insulate it, paint it, ventilate it, or light it? Would you have to add chairs, air it out, put in a fan, or rid it of clutter? Would you have to build or otherwise create an entranceway that would be safe, inviting, and respectable?

Most places of business are designed to facilitate the tasks required. Whether that requires putting cash registers on long thin counters, planning Saturday evening dinner parties for six, or providing high tabletops for clients to paste up their work prior to copying, the details required for a business to accommodate its clients and customers are extensive and specialized.

If you are in the kind of business that requires many hours to complete the jobs for your client, but those hours are actually spent alone, then the question remains: What does this work environment need to look like, be like, sound like, and feel like in order to increase the quality of your work and decrease the amount of time it takes to do it?

So far in our description, the only thing missing is *you*. If we assume that the tasks get done and the place is convenient to the outcome, what happens to you? For any of us to thrive in our lives, we must also thrive in our work. It is vital for us to be able to handle stress, to recover and regenerate, and to be able to maintain our creativity and enthusiasm. Even if your job includes "good" professional stress—the kind that comes with success—the working conditions must be designed to be appropriate to the challenge.

The Two Flavors of Stress

Current discourse tends to use the word *stress* to connote a wholly negative condition that should be avoided or immediately remedied; however, there are actually two kinds of stress.

Productive stress is the result of hard work, of performing at the highest professional standards. As the stakes get higher in either economic or professional arenas, the stress increases accordingly. This is positive stress—motivating, exciting, and stimulating. Few people complain about the "sounds" of accomplishment, such as inspiring discussions, the bustle of productivity, or the rewards of healthy relationships. Rather, these sounds are more than tolerable—they are desirable.

Unproductive stress, however, is just that: strain and anxiety born of frustrated efforts to adapt to circumstances that detract from your primary goals. Joan Borysenko speaks of "joyless striving"—the result of a conflict between inspiration (what you *want* to do) and obligation (what you *have* to do). It can also occur as a symptom of burnout—exhaustion, depletion, and depression. Events that dominate such an environment may include political rifts between co-workers, frustration caused by a computer's crash, inefficient and oppressive working conditions, job insecurity, or fear of failure.

Unproductive stress has its own sounds—and not only are they intolerable, but they worsen the situation. Whether the auditory culprit is an unwarranted and invasive phone solicitation or the rattle of a noisy air conditioner, our tolerance threshold lowers with time and exhaustion. Psychiatrist Gerald Grumet reported in *The New England Journal of Medicine* that the price we pay in a noisy environment is that we tend to focus on mechanical, rote tasks and concurrently become "less engaged, less caring and less reflective [or] show increased aggression and annoyance."

If our work environments are to be places in which we are creative, competent, and inspired—from which we are sent home healthy—then they must be malleable. All of us strive to survive the stress that accompanies various tasks we do. Our environments must do the same in order to bring us back to a healthy state of productivity. They must regenerate us on Friday and inspire us on Monday. The fact that we spend more than half our time in our places of work is good reason to design them to both build on the success of the past and facilitate the goals of the future.

Home Versus Work: Are the Issues Different?

In chapter 9, we discussed home environments, learning how to assess them and how to support our individual and family health and well-being by design. As we examine places of work, we will again learn *how to assess them, and how to better design the places in which we work to support health and well-being.* Sound familiar? In fact, what works at home fully applies to the work environment, in terms of respecting diverse needs and different people performing a variety of functions in one space. If there is a difference, however, it is that we spend more than 50 percent of our waking hours at work, and that time sets us up to be able to do everything else in our lives. Certain conditions that may be short-lived at home, such as episodes of high-level noise, become critical health risks when exposure is increased, especially if it is on a daily basis. Using the following suggestions, critically evaluate the sounds that accompany your work setting, which at the least, can annoy you, and at worst, can put your hearing at risk.

1. *Listen to the space:* More than other settings, a work space must serve those responsible for fulfilling focused, defined goals. The space may involve one or more people, as it could be one person's office, an open office filled with many people, or a space where you meet your clients.

Each of these situations should be dealt with, even if they all occur in the same physical place. Whether you experience intrusive sounds from without or words said at normal volume that have traveled beyond their intended boundaries, both situations can easily be addressed.

2. *Keep an auditory log that reflects the pace of the workday and work week.* Listen to where you are. Note the time of day. Are the circumstances typical for the normal workday? Spaces must be resilient, able to adjust to a variety of levels of activity and accompanying noise. Make sure that the log reflects the pace of the workday, which may reveal periods of more or less activity when the sound levels vary substantially.

3. *Assess the level of background noise.* Notice the hours when the noise levels noticeably change. Background noise predetermines how loudly we must speak to each other to be understood. If an office is adjacent to a copy machine with a fan, or motor noise that echoes within a narrow hallway, it can easily affect the tenor of conversations—both in person and on the phone.

4. *Note episodic or occasional noises.* Episodic noises can include noisy carts, doors opening and closing, traffic noises that may be louder during certain times of day, increased traffic due to meeting schedules, and other sounds. When they occur, they can impede work, disturb both intra-office and telephone conversations, and, at the least, create a distraction that lasts longer than the event.

Truth and Consequences

Dallas: Too often, work environments place employees' hearing at risk. Unfortunately, the German brewery that I discussed at the beginning of this chapter was not out of the ordinary. Not only did that sound environment isolate the workers socially from each other, but it actually may have caused cumulative hearing damage. In testimony to the OSHA Standards Planning Committee in 1994, Dr. Alice H. Sutor described the problem in this way:

Anyone who has suffered a handicapping hearing loss, or who has had a close friend or relative who has, will understand its implications. Like other neurological deficits, hearing impairment degrades, even destroys the quality of life. Helen Keller used to maintain that the handicap from deafness was worse than that from blindness, because deafness separates you from people, whereas blindness separates you from things. Hearing impairment interferes not only with the ability to hear music and the sounds of nature, but, more important, with the ability to communicate with family and friends. This is especially true of the attempt to communicate in groups or in noisy backgrounds. The handicap of hearing impairment eventually leads to withdrawal from social situations and dependency upon one's spouse or another family member for virtually all communication needs. The result is often loneliness, isolation, depression, and lowered self-esteem.

The implications of this statement are that, first, our hearing is critical to everything in our lives, and second, we may be at jeopardy and not know it. We often think of dangerous sound levels relating to construction jobs or other heavy industrial settings. However, we should be aware that today, all of us are risk.

Measuring Noise Levels

Monitoring hearing levels means getting a digital decibel meter (around $50 at most audio stores), and using it. It will allow you to measure noise levels anytime, anywhere. We carried a newly purchased meter on a streetcar in New Orleans on a quiet Sunday afternoon. There were only three other people on this car. On a Sunday, with an almost empty car and little traffic, the meter read 80 to 85 dB. We were only on the car 20 minutes. The driver, however, was exposed to those sound levels for eight hours a day.

Several years ago, Nevada casinos began putting Plexiglas baffles behind the bars located in front of the entertainment areas. They also aimed the speakers out to the audience, not down toward the bar. Why? Because OSHA said that without it, the employees risked hearing damage. Furthermore, the casinos set up decibel meters and began regulating the music volume. None of this was done as a Good Samaritan effort. Rather, as occurrences of noise-induced hearing damage were identified as work-related injuries, OSHA officially established safe standards. It is obvious that the decibel levels of live performances in discos, casinos, and other sites have risen faster than could have been anticipated. As a result, casinos were confronted with concrete evidence that working conditions needed to be evaluated, specifically the auditory environment in which their employees worked for hours at a time. Unlike other entertainment settings, casinos faced a challenge because bands were performing in competition with the constant ringing of slot machines, the rowdy crowds around the craps tables, and the sheer volume of people.

The unprecedented power and volume levels made possible by innovations in audio technology have contributed to a general social dynamic many times louder than that of previous years. So, dangerously intense aural levels have become the norm. Furthermore, the reality that one person's place of entertainment is another person's place of work is held without regard. In every cocktail lounge, dance club, karaoke bar, or dinner theater, there are many people who work there five nights a week. Their risk is the highest. Decibel levels in school cafeterias, hospital and hotel kitchens, laundries, fast-food chains, and other service industries can also surpass safe listening levels.

Hearing damage is based on two factors: loudness of the sound and duration of our exposure to it. You may work in a quiet setting, but this gives you little immunity from incurring damage somewhere else. For instance, you would not want to spend your lunch hour in the boiler room or in a restaurant where the music is so loud that your ears ring afterward. Most communities are involved in some kind of redevelopment, so being around a construction zone is not so unusual. Remember, while *you* may not be "working" all the time, your ears are! That means that they have no vacations, coffee breaks, or any other time when they are not operating at full capacity—so take care of them!

Preventive care is the easiest to do and the most difficult to *want* to do. Today, there are many different kinds of earplugs, protective headphones, and other devices to help us preserve our hearing. However, in the same way that some motorcyclists reject helmets, so are earplugs shunned by many of those who love loud music. Yet, both helmets and earplugs can literally save one's life, or one's hearing. How much higher could the stakes be? Hearing damage is cumulative and irreversible. As we have said over and over again, hearing doesn't just relate to music, it relates to *everything* in life.

Proactive Solutions

A hospital recently conducted a study of the decibel levels generated by commonly used transport equipment. A particular transport cart measured in at over 85 dB, which edged close to dangerous levels for the operator exposed to this sound for many hours. An escalator in the front lobby was so loud that it could be heard all the way into the surgical waiting area at the top of the escalator. By adding rubber wheels, the transport cart became quieter than most other pieces of equipment. The sound of the escalator, however, will require some work—perhaps reconstruction—to minimize its current loud and continuous drone. Northside Hospital in Atlanta, Georgia, recently reduced their overall noise level by modifying over 300 pieces of equipment.

Carpeting, drapes, acoustical ceilings, felted room dividers, blankets— all these common materials make walls sound absorbent, helping to lessen reverberation, which causes sounds to automatically gain intensity and obstreperousness. Go into your office and stand a moment, and listen for conversations happening on the other side of the room or way down a long hallway. If you hear something not meant for your ears, it means that the hard walls, hard ceilings, or vacant corridors are amplifying the sound. Being proactive in the design of the sound environment means instituting preventive measures by keeping the noise levels lower, before any noise becomes apparent. Even foot traffic, motorized transport carts, elevator bells, and escalators all have their own noise even before people are added into the picture.

What can you do if you are in a small office that is quite loud? "Passive" noise control can be designed into the room. Window coverings such as drapes or valances absorb sound, as does carpeting. In addition, you can obtain carpet squares from your local carpet store and place them in a decorative pattern, or use them as a kind of wall liner, adding both visual and auditory design components to the space. Also, small 4' x 6' rugs (or larger) can make very nice wall hangings. The benefit of using acoustically functional components is that it allows you to bring art and color into your office while "conditioning" the sound environment.

Sound Masking in Large Offices

One of the primary challenges of large offices is that they serve more than one person. Privacy and confidentiality are elusive when multiple conversations take place simultaneously, as no one can control who listens to what. Nor can we withdraw into some private space in order to protect our ears from hearing what we are not supposed to hear. Remember: Sounds find ears.

Sound masking occurs when one sound literally covers up or "masks" another—not unlike placing a veil over a piece of furniture. You still see that the furniture is there, but you may not see the detail. Sound masking will not make a noisy office silent; that is not its goal. Rather, it makes the words less perceptible by placing a protective veil over conversations and making them more private.

The most typical noise-cancellation system consists of "white noise"—broad-spectrum noise reminiscent of the "whoosh" of an air conditioner—broadcast by satellite loudspeakers strategically placed throughout the work area. That is simply high-tech sound masking. Invented in the 1960s, this technology is becoming more popular because of the current trend toward open office environments. It contributes to speech privacy by reducing the understandability of conversation to an unaware listener, who may be sitting at the next desk or across the room. That means, for instance, that if someone says your name, instead of your ears perking up to hear what is being said, you may hear a sound but not recognize it as your name. Thus, distraction is averted. Promoters of sound-masking technology claim that in an open office environment, employees are more able to concentrate, and are, therefore, more productive.

Most people whose work is confidential—such as lawyers or physicians—work in closed offices. For them, privacy means protecting their own conversations from outsiders. However, in most open office settings, the situation is the reverse. Privacy does not mean keeping your voice in; it means keeping other people's voices out. For example, who would not be annoyed by a worker in the next cubicle arguing over the phone with someone?

Employees in open offices are used to concentrating despite repetitive electronic noises of office machinery and air circulation systems; however, *other people's voices* are more distracting, and thus remain a major stumbling block to concentration and productivity. What is worse, the sound-absorbing materials used in open plan systems may partially absorb background noises, but not speech, allowing every detail of your next-door colleague's intimate conversation to come through loud and clear.

Active noise abatement is most often used in large, open-floor-plan offices, but sound masking can also be used in closed offices, particularly those constructed with walls only to the ceiling and not beyond. Realistically, some degree of sound will travel both into and out of walled offices, unless they feature expensive drywall construction through the ceiling, heavy doors, and minimal use of glass. A combination of active sound masking and other passive elements—including carpets, panel materials, panel configuration, and ceiling and floor tiles—is the best speech privacy solution.

Larger office spaces are more likely to use noise-cancellation technologies; smaller offices use background music as the primary means of sound-masking. However, this is solely a defensive strategy; it is not proactive in improving the productivity or satisfaction of employees or customers. It is, rather, aiming at a *zero*—neutralizing the impact of one conversation on another. The use of background music may support several purposes, including sound masking. However, music can do more than avoid distraction. Using music as environmental design is more comprehensive than putting on background music. It can support the mission and culture of the organization, while functioning as an acoustic treatment.

The all-inclusive sound environment of any business represents the ethic of the company. For the employee, it affects everything from productivity and accuracy to self-esteem and endurance. For the customer, it reflects the quality of the products and services, predicting the long-term treatment they can expect.

Your work environment affects both your finances and your health. If you find yourself screaming at your co-worker or customer, unable to easily hear what is being said to you, or overhearing conversations you would rather not be subjected to, be proactive in evaluating and making change. The stakes are high.

Offering More Than Zero

A lawyer, a hotel manager, a dentist, and a musician were all trapped in an elevator on its way straight to heaven. While they were awaiting res-

cue by whoever attends to elevators that go that high, they introduced themselves to each other.

The lawyer spoke first, saying that he had been a senior partner in the highest-profile law firm in his community, with an office that overlooked the Washington Monument and that had floor-to-ceiling windows.

The hotel manager explained that his position had been of the greatest importance, that he had served some of the world's most famous people, had been able to offer them the most luxurious suites with the best city views, had served the finest foods on the most expensive bone china, and had provided the elegant sounds of string quartets for afternoon tea.

The dentist stood quietly and spoke not a word until asked by the other two gentlemen. "What did you do, and where did you do it?" they asked him in unison.

Thoughtfully, he said, "I worked in a small room with only one chair, high-pitched machinery, bright lights, and metal tools just within my reach. I had to wear rubber gloves and a face mask. I had windows in some of my rooms, but seldom looked beyond the sill that could have used some paint and color. But I must say that I would not have traded my position for either one of yours."

The musician, who had stood listening quietly, finally piped up and said, "Regardless of where you all worked during your lives, I am still collecting royalties. I am trying to convince St. Peter that elevator music will put all of you in a better mood. Actually, this time the results are better than I could have hoped . . . for while you've been in this stuck elevator, you forgot that you'd died and hadn't yet gotten to heaven!"

In our discussion about sound in the workplace, we have looked at unproductive noise as a villain seeking to disarm its powers over us through design. However, as we saw in this story about *real* elevator music, music as environmental design can be used both protectively and proactively, transforming the power of the auditory environment from a potential deficit into an asset.

Music to Design the Office

Music will do for us what we program it to do. It can improve productivity, reduce stress, and protect the integrity of relationships and communication. The cognitive and the auditory are closely related. What we hear has an immediate impact on what we think and feel. Also, it can affect our ability to communicate, comprehend, and respond. Music, as a means of conditioning the sound environment, can serve to increase focus, provide insulation from outside distractions, and bring intention into an otherwise generic space. The most common question we get asked is, "What music?"

However, in designing environments, the primary question is, "Who's listening, and what are they doing?" The secondary question is, "Who *else* is listening, and what are *they* doing?"

"Who's Listening, and What Are They Doing?"

Since employees and staff are the permanent residents of any place of business, they are the "who" in this question. Because of the controversy that arises from asking, "What music?" many places of work use either *no* music, commercial background music, or they bypass the issue by allowing individuals to bring in and listen to music of their own choosing.

If you are able to use your own music and have control over your own work area, we recommend that you take all the steps we've discussed to design your own space. To select music that will work for you, you must pay close attention to the effect different pieces have on your productivity and stress levels. Selections may change from day to day, and your use of music may be more beneficial by adding variety and options.

If you are using music to affect a large environment, several options exist. We have already described *background music,* which is generic, genre-based programming that makes every attempt to be ignorable. We also defined *environmental music* as ambient music that supports the intention, goals, and immediate needs of the moment. In the case of a work environment, the following factors will give you a great head start. Use music with the following qualities:

- *Instrumental music* to avoid distraction yet provide all the positive benefits of appropriate music.

- *Moderately paced music* to avoid detracting from the work at hand.

- *Music in the appropriate genre:*

    — Classical music has been used to support concentration
      and productivity (such as Mozart, Haydn, early Beethoven,
      Mendelssohn, Schubert, etc.).

    — Appropriately selected noncommercial music bypasses per-
      sonal preferences and avoids distraction by association (try
      Fred Hersh, Liz Story, David Benoit, Pat Metheny, etc.).

    — Try easy listening or smooth jazz if it is appropriate for the
      intention, clientele, and employees.

    — Film scores may serve as environmental music
      (for example, soundtracks by James Horner, John Williams,
      Jerry Goldsmith, and so on).

    — Finally, try specific music and musicians listed in the
      appendix.

Susan: The music present in any space, as we have said before, carries its own message in content, volume, and character. Years ago, I performed at an Elizabethan restaurant in the Cannery in San Francisco called the Ben Jonson. The Elizabethan theme was presented in a variety of ways: decor, costume, menu style, ritual of service, and music. The background music was a continuous recording of 16th-century Renaissance music of the time of the playwright Ben Jonson (a contemporary of William Shakespeare), after whom the restaurant was both named and designed. While the tape was several hours long, the day-to-day feel was consistent, almost as if the music were one continuous song. The extent to which the owners, Lawry's, Inc., designed this restaurant was extraordinary. The room's ceiling panels, walls, floors, bars, and other furnishings had been imported from England and all dated back to the time of the playwright. Period costumes were worn by all employees, including myself.

The harp sat in front of an elaborate fireplace, looking as if it, too, came from England. Each night I began the evening with an arrangement of the old English melody "Greensleeves." It allowed me to ease the transition from prerecorded music to my live performance. However, my repertoire for the evening included current pop and jazz tunes on the acoustic harp (this was before I amplified my harp). I represented the merging of old and new—the sound of the harp was traditional, and the music was contemporary.

One day, a supervisor from the main office in Los Angeles decided to modify the background music for the sake of commercial appeal. When I arrived that night, instead of the subdued historical environment, I got a dose of contemporary commercial background music. It was a complete reversal of the Ben Jonson theme. I was so thrown by the dramatic change in character that I had difficulty deciding which piece of music to play to begin the evening. The new music lasted only a single day before being changed back to the original music of the period; in the ten years following, the issue never came up again. Neither did any of the employees complain about the music not being their personal favorite. Rather, they remembered the day the atmosphere was violated.

♪   ♪   ♪

The consequences of either the wrong music or no music further illustrate the critical impact of sound in the work environment.

The decision to use music or any other kind of sound conditioning should be based on who is present, what is being done at the time, and how best to support or improve the outcome. The balance between task and environment is one that should be continually reevaluated as needed. The decision has two parts: One refers to the task being done, such as writing a contract, serving customers, or creating a new architectural drawing. The second part, however, is the mission behind the task: creating long-term sustainable relationships; providing the highest standard of customer service; or envisioning a building that will support the values of the community it serves. The chosen music becomes the context in which both parts are accomplished.

In 1939, at the Hawthorne Plant of the General Electric Company, there was a study to determine what would improve worker productivity. The company experimented with many things, including changing coffee-break times, introducing new schedules, and other protocols. The confusion came when one change caused an improvement, and then, after a period of time, reversing the change also created an improvement. Researchers determined that the positive change was not due to the particular modification, but rather to the employees perceiving that they were the focus of attention— henceforth known as The Hawthorne Effect. The outcome pointed to the benefits of taking notice of employees so that they don't feel like anonymous worker bees.

Regarding music, designing change and flexibility into a space may have the same effect. Playing music in a workplace 100 percent of the time will have a different, if not diminished, impact compared to balancing variety with consistency. Paying attention to the pacing will be more effective than taking a set-it-and-forget-it stance.

Therefore, we encourage you to be active in alternating different types of music with silence. Take advantage of music's ability to change the mood and effect of spaces. Also, use shifts in lighting and other variables to reenergize yourself and your environment.

Who Else Is Listening, and What Are They Doing?

Let's start with the people you can't see.

A national company that serviced the majority of its clients over the phone had a work space that was one large, open office area, speckled with desks and computers and brightly lit with overhead fluorescent lights. (The cavernous area had a substantial echo.) There was a casual dress code, a snack area, and a water fountain. Music, compliments of a local radio station, was broadcast from a small radio trying to fill the entire space. Unfortunately, some customers started reporting that the employees seemed to be calling them from the local bar or pool room. At least, that's what they *thought* they heard over the phone. Since the company acquired, served, and maintained their client base over the phone, they mistakenly assumed that they were as soundproof as they were invisible. The company ended up eliminating all music, and six months later, we received a call requesting information about sound environment design.

Telephone-on-Hold

The telephone system has become an environment in every sense of the word; it is no longer just a communication device. Critical personal and business relationships are cultivated, decisions are negotiated, and opinions are formed over the telephone. Since the onset of "music-on-hold," the environment has become one of design, not just one of convenience. While we may find it annoying to be put on hold, it was pointed out to me that without some kind of sound, no one would know if we had been disconnected. Being on hold seems to be better than getting a busy signal. It is not uncommon to hear music, promotional sales information, office hours, referral numbers, and a directory of employees extensive enough to take up more time than the actual phone call.

The hold system can be an important marketing tool. As such, the style and content of any message or music provided to the caller should reflect the feeling and image that the company desires to project to the outside world, as well as to itself. Unless there is a separate phone system for public relations, vendors, and employees, everyone enters into the same system prior to being directed to their particular area of concern. Therefore, if the telephone system is used for advertising, then we should be aware of the risk that the caller will feel trapped, assaulted, or taken advantage of as a captive audience forced to wait for the attention of a live person. If an employee calls, will the message instill ever more pride in being a part of the organization? Many people appreciate a method of skipping the recording and being able to expedite their reaching the person to whom their call is directed. If one is put on hold, however, the system becomes a *remote waiting area,* for which care should be taken just as we attend to any other facet of customer/personnel service.

Office Waiting Areas

Depending on the kind of office, there may or may not be a waiting area. We have often called this a "holding area," since it seems that one is being detained at the convenience of the office. Actually, that is how most people feel, unless the waiting environment presents another perspective. Most waiting lobbies are functional, with some offering token conveniences such as a television. The problem with only addressing the function of a space is that there is a missed opportunity to promote the client/customer relationship. After all, most of us, when given the opportunity and nothing else to do, pay considerable attention to what we hear, what we see, and where we are in general. Then, we come to basic conclusions about the environment and people as a result of these observations. Whether we are waiting for a physician, beautician, lawyer, accountant, or teacher, the conditions under which we are greeted (and then wait) become part of our total impression and experience.

Sound Systems

While it may seem that the greatest challenge involved in designing a sound environment is choosing the music, selecting the delivery system is equally important. It is not difficult to match the sound system's size to the space in which it is being used; however, it has been more difficult to justify the expenditure on a "good" system versus one that seems more cost effective. In today's marketplace, small sound systems are available that look far better than they sound. Home stereo-system speakers broadcast the sound in a 45-degree radius, not wide enough to cover a larger office area. Also, they tend to be low-powered, which limits their volume capacity. Using a small system for a large space, then, can overdrive the unit, resulting in distortion, crackling, and unclear sound. While all of us have heard such distortion, listening to it for hours at a time can increase stress and irritability, and decrease productivity. Small systems are ideal, however, for small rooms where they are not expected to broadcast over a long distance. In the appendix, we have provided an overview of how to choose a sound system for the home, which would also be applicable for a small business or home office.

For larger offices, dispersing the music evenly—making sure that the sound at one end of the room is the same as it is in the middle, for instance—is a challenge. Music (and paging) is louder in the vicinity of the loudspeakers and softer at the greatest distance from the speakers. Usually, if the music is broadcast at a volume sufficient for the area farthest from the speakers (potential dead zones), then the music is too loud directly under the speakers (the hot spots). If the loudspeaker happens to be the traditional cone-type design—like most overhead speakers—the sound is heard in a confined pattern similar in profile to the light from a spotlight. Being in the hot spot, directly below the speaker, is like being blinded by a spotlight, and being in the dead zone is like being left in auditory darkness. Stepping away from the speaker, off-axis from the hot spot, the volume and clarity of the sound diminish. In most buildings where paging speakers like these are used, increased volume is used to compensate for the lack of even dispersion. That means that, potentially, the speakers are too loud in the hot spot and too soft in between. Then, distortion and accompanying annoyance can result. Ideally, the sound environment is seamless, allowing the staff and visitors to move throughout the space without being aware of where speakers are located.

Evaluating the Effectiveness of the Design

In comparison to walls, ceilings, windows, overhead lights, and other more fixed components, sound is quickly altered and easily modified. Sound and music are fluid and changeable. Even our capacity to hear or be heard can be immediately altered by closing doors or windows, or otherwise changing the auditory space. Thus, we have the opportunity at any given time to evaluate and redesign—mildly or dramatically—the auditory environment.

If we assume that our objective is to design meaning and purpose into our work spaces, then taking responsibility for the sound environment allows us great flexibility in definitively responding to changing situations and circumstances. We invented doors, for instance, to provide the ability to instantly alter the auditory and visual access between a room and its surroundings. Privacy, confidentiality, protection from distraction, and other momentary individual preferences are determining factors in why we might open or close a door, whether we speak louder or softer, and whether we are able to be completely candid. This kind of flexibility needs to be applied to the auditory component as a whole.

The most effective use of music as environmental design, then, is not about overlaying one sound over all others. It is about balancing the needs of the moment, mitigating some of the challenges that arise with a space that is either too quiet or too noisy. Most of all, however, it is about making the auditory environment a proactive part of the work objectives.

Environment As Mediator

The topic of many seminars, communication skills are well known to be critical to good working relationships. In such discussions, the auditory environment often becomes the unidentified third party. Whether we refer to computer printers or the hum of heater vents, these and all the other ambient sounds of the workplace become the context of all communication. The sounds we hear necessarily impact how we speak to each other. Our tone of voice, the volume at which we speak, and our capacity to accurately interpret the words and their meanings are collectively determined by the environment.

Designing the environment to help mediate interpersonal disputes in the workplace is an art. It requires due consideration and respect for those involved, and satisfactory resolution for all parties. It also means that the space needs to provide a place for healthy, accurate, and respectful discourse.

Traveling to Work: The Automobile Commute

It would be a combination of denial and neglect not to address the time and energy spent commuting to work and back. For those who drive farther than five or so miles, this is as critical a part of their life as the hours actually spent on the job.

No doubt, the automobile is a miraculous invention, affording far more comfort than its horse-drawn predecessor, but its inherent joys can be enhanced by realizing that it is a portable environment that moves us from one place and time to another. The degree of stress we feel when dealing with traffic increases or decreases depending on the environment in which we drive.

More than any other setting, the automobile renders us captive. Indeed, automobile sound systems have improved not because they are a nice thing for manufacturers to offer, but because they are a marketable utility. They have become critical to the experience of the driver and passengers, and to the marketplace that uses the time trap as an opportunity to sell their wares.

Through the ever-improving automobile music system, we are offered a varied auditory menu. In addition to having our own CD or cassette player, we can tune in to talk radio or local traffic, news, and weather reports. We can also be entertained by verbose disc jockeys trained in the art of distraction, and numerous varieties of music, sometimes lined up so closely that we cannot hear the end of one piece for the beginning of the next.

During the long commute, which could total as much as 10 to 15 hours a week, we are subjected not only to the relentless drone of road noise, but also to screeching brakes, honking horns, and other erratic sounds. Depending on your speed and the conditions of the road, the rumble can reach 75 to 85 dB, even with adequate insulation and the windows closed.

Therefore, take seriously the impact of the music you listen to, the cell phone that may distract you, and the conversations that take place. Prioritize the events that occur in this environment so that the outcomes are appropriate to what is actually happening and not merely a response to sounds out of control.

When You Commute by Air

If taking a business trip by air, we might find that we have a low tolerance for dealing with the hassles of parking, luggage, and so on. However, most of us just grit our teeth and fly, because it is the best way to get from one part of the world to the other. Regarding auditory risk, airports are notorious for being hostile atmospheres. People, taxis, planes, and more planes. Even during local political debates regarding airport licenses and expansion, noise has become a major bone of contention.

Flying is the only activity in which we [the authors] consistently use earplugs. At first, we were so accustomed to the noise that they seemed unnecessary. However, as soon as we used them, we experienced less fatigue; could better manage the stress of the trip; and could read, write, or sleep with far more satisfaction.

In case you've never noticed, the first-class cabin is at the front of the plane and farthest from the sound of the motors. The back of the plane is the worst, where the jet engine noise is the loudest. So the pilot's and flight attendants' voices can be heard over this din, the speakers in the plane broadcast loudly, in spite of being only inches from passengers' ears. The open-ear headphones provided for on-board movies and music must also be played loudly enough to be heard clearly *over* the noise of motors, speakers, and other passengers.

All told, planes are risky places. We suggest that you use ear plugs that reduce the noise by at least 15 dB; they are available at any drugstore. You will still be able to hear, but the rumble and the overall roar of the plane will be reduced from a roar to a whimper.

Making a Living

We started this discussion of work environments by saying that we spend more time working than engaged in any other activity. Whether at work or at home, boundaries blur when we realize that our health and well-being are impacted. "Making a living" becomes living a life; the outcome of one begets the other. How we survive work determines how we live in our homes, and how we experience our homes becomes the predictor of how we function in our workplace. Therefore, tend to each with great care, for no less than the total *you* is at stake.

Chapter Eleven

Creating a Healing Health-Care Environment

"Art and its countless expressions are more than important adjuncts to medicine; they are the heart of its successful practice."
— Hunter "Patch" Adams

High-Tech versus High-Touch

Susan: I was six years old when I contracted scarlet fever. I was probably one of the last people to ever have this potentially fatal and highly contagious disease, although I don't remember it as such. What I do remember is having a fever and being confined in isolation to my room at the back of the house. My sister Aliza and I had shared a room, but I don't know where she slept during this time. My dad told me that when he was a child, he'd had scarlet fever and lost all his hair. My mom would explain to me, after I was better, that any toys I had played with were going to be burned to avoid contagion.

On the day the rash first appeared, my parents called Dr. Budson. He was a good doctor, but I was always afraid of him for some reason. I don't think that he was an intimidating person; perhaps it was the situation that terrified me.

I remember lying in bed and hearing the doorbell ring, followed by my mom's not-quite-audible conversation. As I heard the doctor's footsteps and my mom's approach down the long hallway, I became even more frightened. Then Dr. Budson came into my room, carrying his black bag. He walked over to me and spoke to my parents as he felt the swollen glands in my neck. He took out the cold metal stethoscope, and after asking my permission, with his even colder hands he pushed my pajamas up and listened to my heart. I coughed on demand as he tapped on my back. Then he took my temperature, chatting with my mom as we waited: 104 degrees—from what they all said, I gathered this was high.

Dr. Budson went into his black bag and took out what was, to my six-year-old eyes, a huge *needle. After filling it with what I found out years later was penicillin, he walked over to me and said, "Turn over, Susan. This will not hurt."*

That was when I forever learned that the language and rules of health care were different from my own.

In recalling my experience with scarlet fever, my most vivid memories were only the image of the hypodermic needle, the sound of footsteps down the long hallway, and having to be in my room by myself. Everything else related to the actual illness has passed into the limbo of nonmemorable experiences. For most of us, illness is both a physical and circumstantial experience.

When my father suffered a stroke 15 years ago, he demanded that we bring him his own pillow, which we did. His next complaint was the bland walls—he said that it was like a prison. He has never since spoken of his stroke, from which he fortunately recovered. He has only spoken of "that room," a place he is committed to never revisiting.

Recently, a health-care educator told us that she was uncomfortable in hospitals. When she'd had to visit a friend, she dreaded having to walk into the building. She was in double jeopardy: If well, she works in a hospital. If very ill, she either gets to stay home or becomes a ward of the hospital. In either case, the environment does not represent, to her, either health or care—only a place to be avoided and one to which she is daily required to report.

An illness offers two major challenges: first the clinical diagnosis, and then what Florence Nightingale called the "sick room." She said, as long as 150 years ago, that the environment of care was as critical to patient survival as any other therapeutic protocol. She further said that if we want to know why infection occurs—why some patients suddenly die or why children get sick—we should look at the house, school, or place of work for clues.

Health Care in Centuries Past

"In a dark place the sick indulge themselves too much in various fancies, and are harassed by imaginings devised in an alienated mind, since no external phenomenon can fall on the senses; but in a bright place, they are prevented from being wholly in their own fancies which are rather weakened by external phenomena."
— Aeclepiades of Bithynia, ca. 50 B.C.

The Aesclepian temples of ancient Greece were legendary places of healing that used all the components of care known at the time, including diet, exercise, and the healing arts. To care for the sick, the Greeks used art, music, theater, humor, prayer, and spiritual rituals, all in a setting that provided the most powerful and beautiful elements of nature. It was believed that the body healed itself with the help of the god Aesclepius.

Centuries later, yet less than 100 years ago, trained physicians practiced medicine with only what they could carry in their small black bags, traveling from patient to patient by carriage or on foot. They took their skills and dedication to the patient, wherever they were. The doctor was part of the community and provided health care in the home.

The isolation of the ill was an attempt to prevent recurrence of the plague and other epidemics that caused the deaths of thousands. From the dismal conditions common to early institutional care, it would not be unfair to say that the mission of containing illness was equal to that of healing the sick.

It was during the Crimean War of 1854 that the "Lady of the Lamp," Florence Nightingale, was able to institute environmental protocols, sparking a new interest in the actual design of the "sick room." She raised to the level of clinical imperatives such common components of daily life as nutritious food, fresh air, natural light, flowers and plants, warm blankets, stimulation for the mind and spirit, and careful attention to the impact of sound on the patient.

Nightingale's new practices resulted in reducing the mortality and morbidity of wounded soldiers in Crimea from 42 percent to 2 percent. Her environmental protocols became the foundation of modern hospital design. The values she espoused remained the prevailing standard until the advent of modern technology that itself demanded environmental considerations.

The Sounds of Healing

Relentless in her advocacy for the ill, Nightingale held that every aspect of the environment either aided the natural process of healing or worsened the disease. She recognized that sound—whether noise, word, or music, direct or indirect, intentional or inadvertent—was critical to the condition of the patient. She believed that words either carried messages of hope or instilled fear, which could, on its own, threaten the very capacity of the sick to survive. She was most critical of insensitive and stress-producing actions that she believed threatened the very life of the patient. In her *Notes on Nursing: What It Is and What It Is Not,* published in 1859, she said:

> Noise that creates an expectation in the mind is that which hurts the patient. It is rarely the loudness of the noise, the effect upon the organ of the ear itself, which appears to affect the sick. How well a patient will generally bear, e.g. the hanging of scaffolding close to the house, when he cannot bear the talking, still less the whispering, especially for it be of a familiar voice, outside his door. . . .
>
> Unnecessary noise has undoubtedly induced or aggravated delirium in many cases. I have known such. . . . in one case death ensued. It is but fair to say that this death was attributed to fright. It was the result of a long whispered conversation, within sight of the patient, about an impending operation . . . the strained expectation as to what was to be decided upon.

So, noise was long ago acknowledged to have a powerful impact on health and healing, as well as pain and suffering. Nightingale felt that while pain may be part of the healing process, suffering need not necessarily be.

Morbidity was, she felt, most often caused by the way in which a patient was cared for and the state of the sick-room environment.

Welcome to the Medical Center of the Present

Susan: In an article called "Sing a Song for the Sick and Tense," I used the following description to convey the feel of modern hospitals.

> The two sets of smoky glass doors slide open automatically, widening onto a blank corridor of sterile linoleum. The walls are nondescript, with overhead fluorescent lights and painted arrows on the floor. The sounds are a combination of crying, laughing, talking, machinery, beepers, and loudspeakers, all mixed together with an ominous silence. Upon entering the aloneness of the hospital room, the sounds continue to intrude from far beyond the four visible walls. Noises are exaggerated, distorted, unending. The din coming from everywhere soon blends into the still-nondescript walls, never yielding to the fear it creates, and enrolling all present in its relentless chorus.

A hospital is where we go in hopes of relieving physical pain, of transforming illness into wellness. The above description is not one of health care. It portrays the environment in which health care is delivered and could apply to any modern urban hospital—if not in whole, then in part. Health-care facilities can feel both impersonal and institutional. Even with her most forward vision of hospital design, Florence Nightingale could not anticipate that technological innovation would make hands-on nursing and direct person-to-person care a premium rather than a standard.

When We Have a Choice

Dallas: The process of dealing with illness cannot be rehearsed. Most of us are unprepared and ill equipped to deal with hospitals. One of the most telling revelations about the power of the care environment occurs when a physician becomes a patient. For the more than 40 years that he practiced medicine, my uncle, Dr. George Bertling Smith, was the consummate physician to my immediate and extended family. He provided generous treatment in his office, at the hospital, or by making house calls at any time of day or night. When Uncle Bert was diagnosed with bone cancer, he was well aware of the implications of his diagnosis. He also knew that the progress of the disease might be treated most effectively in the hospital. Nonetheless, late in the evening on the day he was told of his acute and terminal condition, he demanded to be transported home. Indeed, the hospital environment in which he had worked for so many years was foreign to how he lived. Knowing that medical treatment was no longer useful to alter the outcome, he had neither the patience nor the willingness to subject himself to institutional care any longer. He spent his final days on his porch overlooking the lake he had built, surrounded by his family. His chosen environment for living became, itself, palliative.

The modern hospital room bears little resemblance to the home "sick room." However, the needs of the ill have not changed since Nightingale's time. If we are sick, we want to be well. When we are acutely ill, under the influence of both our physical condition and medication, our perceptions may be distorted. Ultimately, we may be unable to manage situations that otherwise would require little effort. For these reasons, the environment of care becomes either part of the disease process or a direct means of relieving suffering.

What's at Stake?

Whether at home or in a hospital, our lives change when our health is at stake. Regardless of planning and long-term goals, unexpected illness can be a rude intruder. Apart from the joy of celebrating a birth, visiting a hospital is rarely a pleasant experience, the kind you look forward to or want to repeat. No family hopes to spend a holiday at the local emergency room because of its stimulating atmosphere.

A health-care crisis is not unlike other major life events, except that the risks are greater. It can be the catalyst for a family reunion or the impetus for major life changes. Indeed, physicians' offices, emergency rooms, acute-care facilities, and urgent-care clinics can become the most sacred of spaces when the health or survival of ourselves or a loved one is at risk.

At first glance, hospital lobbies and waiting areas do not reveal the fact that no one enters the building on a lark. Often, there are vending machines sprinkled throughout the hospital with food and drinks that seem to ignore any particular dietary requirements. Televisions are plentiful—many of them tuned to popular talk shows or news programs—without the slightest indication that the viewers are not there for entertainment. All of these factors—machines and people—become part of the auditory environment.

Different Perspectives

Equally pertinent in defining the environment is the fact that the perceived experience can be totally different depending on the condition of the individual and their reason for being in the hospital—whether they are patient, visitor, or staff member. In 1998, our friend Eric, one of the finest and most popular drummers in the Reno-Tahoe area, had open-heart surgery. Perhaps his experience best demonstrates the impact of the auditory environment and the difference between the perception of the patient and that of the caregiver.

Eric had a congenital heart condition. At age 33, the condition had rendered him unable to walk from the living room to the kitchen without becoming out of breath. During the diagnostic process, the medical opinions he was given did not allow for many options. He decided on an experimental technique. After all, he was young and in good health—a perfect candidate. Unfortunately, in the end he had to have his heart valve replaced, but that is not the end of the story.

Eric contracted septicemia, a hospital-borne staphylococcus infection. His condition was so acute that he was forced to remain in the hospital for 32 days, 14 of which were in the intensive care unit (ICU). At one point, he had to be intubated, a procedure where a tube is inserted into the throat to assist the body's respiration.

During his time in the recovery ward, the constant sounds of monitors disturbed Eric the most. Because he is a drummer, he tried to find a rhythm that might help him deal with and pace his waking hours, but none of the sounds were in sync with each other. The various beeps and buzzes reminded him of the sonar of submarines he had heard in war movies—beeps traveling into the void, responding to no one and signaling nothing.

At one point, he begged a nurse to turn off some of the monitors. He had managed to do so with another staff member, who admitted that many of the offending monitors were not attached to any patients, but were in cubicles where the beds were empty. This time, he had to work harder.

"Please," he begged, "please turn them off!"

"Turn what off?" the nurse asked.

"Those monitors—they go beep, beep, beep . . ."

The nurse stopped and listened earnestly. After a few moments, she said sincerely and apologetically, "I don't hear anything."

The difference between Eric's and the nurse's perceptions had little to do with what they actually heard. Not unlike how any of us might become habituated to the hum of the refrigerator or the air conditioner, this most diligent and experienced nurse had been subjected to the din of the monitors for so many weeks and years that she literally could not hear anything but the alarms. As a patient whose priority was his own critical condition, Eric experienced everything in the ICU as either friend or foe. The nurse, in contrast, filtered the environment for the information necessary to determine the condition of each of her patients on a moment-to-moment basis. Any sound that was not an alarm, then, was irrelevant and went unnoticed.

Lest you think that Eric's perception was unusually sensitive due to his musicianship, consider the July 2, 1999, article in the *Reno Gazette* describing the death of an 80-year-old, which quoted that gentleman as saying that if you think you will have to go to the hospital, you "might as well get yourself pinched and check yourself into a nice, quiet jail."

The relationship between one sound and other sounds, or the domination of one voice above others, or one conversation among many, is referred to in the visual world as *figure-to-ground.* Our ears in many ways are much more accurate than our eyes. Our ears provide the *auditory scene,* the three-dimensional physical picture of the environment that our minds create from the sounds we hear. We are able to selectively listen and separate one sound from many others, based on what we are doing and the focus of our attention. The picture our ears presents gives us very specific information—not only about *what* is around us, but also about *where* everything is in relationship to ourselves.

One facet of the experience demonstrated by Eric's story is the fact that the patient spends far more time than the caregiver in the *sick room.* Details of the environment that are unnerving to the ill are often unnoticed by those passing through. As a patient's advocate, Florence Nightingale warned of the sounds of footsteps, the rustling of skirts, and squeaks in the floors. She was so concerned about the effects of external sounds that she demanded that a patient be carried to a top floor rather than have to endure the sounds of footsteps on the squeaking wooden planks that would otherwise be heard from the floor above. Had she been forced to experience the relentless drones of monitors, beepers, buzzers, overhead pagers, and cell phones, she would have undoubtedly put them at the top of the list of patient hazards.

Many hospitals that were originally built on the basis of Nightingale's work have become distracted by technology that has its own environmental requirements. For instance, computers are sensitive to temperature, static electricity, moisture, and other elements common to institutions. Innovative surgical techniques, once unheard of but now commonplace, are accompanied by stringent technological requirements that have taken priority over the comfort or perceptions of the patient.

One hundred years ago, the common health-care environment could have been either the hospital or the home, as both were considered viable options for the sick. Whether treating the patient in the bedroom or a converted parlor room, the physician practiced medicine according to where the patient was, not the reverse. It was not unusual for both birth and death to take place in the same room. Interestingly, this trend is once again gaining popularity.

Adapting to the Environment

In contrast with other species, human beings have survived due to our ability to adapt to changing environments. We live and thrive in a wide variety of climates—from the heat of the tropics to the cold of Alaska—and we move easily from one setting to another. That is, we do when we are well.

Depending on the situation, the less "well" we are, the less our adaptive capacities function. In fact, the roles reverse, and either the environment is intentionally changed, or we suddenly fall victim to settings that may be otherwise benign.

As patients, we are more easily overwhelmed by sensory input and have less capacity to respond. We may have a greater sensitivity to light, a lower tolerance for noise, a shorter attention span, and/or a short temper. If we are nauseated, we may be unable to tolerate the luscious smell of otherwise delectable food. If we have a fever, the touch of even the lightest blanket may be unbearable. Similarly, our personal musical preferences may change, possibly rendering us unable to figure out what we want.

In each moment, and certainly over longer periods of time, changes occur—not only in the patient, but in the room, the caregiver, and the family and visitors. The more flexible the environment, the more able the patient will be to tolerate the confinement. Florence Nightingale spoke vehemently about the need for art, color, flowers, daylight, and fresh air. She asked, "What is the difference between four yellow walls that never change, and a prison cell?"

Mental anguish, fear, trepidation, frustration—all of these feelings seem to own us when we are not well or when our sense of well-being is threatened. Furthermore, the long series of events that comprise the health-care drama demand of us different kinds of responses, and will raise different fears. Since our sensitivities increase with acuity, the impact of music proportionately increases. Therefore, the question of which music we listen to and its impact on us becomes ever more critical.

The Nature of Time

The definition of *waiting* encompasses many factors; however, in the health-care setting, it refers to only one thing: time. The only universal currency, time comes in various denominations, is nonrefundable, and often mimics the stock market in its fluctuation of value. It is the least negotiable aspect of illness and its accompanying processes, and can be either cherished or wasted.

Whether at work, at home, or in the hospital, it's probable that waiting consumes the majority of the time we spend dealing with health issues. We wait for the aspirin to work. We wait to decide if we are sick enough to call the doctor. Put on telephone hold, we wait for someone to tell us if the doctor is in. When we are finally on the other side of the pre-illness scenarios, we spend time waiting in the health-care arena: having lab work done, filling out papers, filling them out again, and on and on.

Healing does not necessarily begin during any of the waiting times we just described, but occurs instead on a schedule somewhat like that of the tooth fairy, that wistful entity who somehow makes losing a tooth an exhilarating event for a child. Healing happens when no one is looking. We cannot see it, harness it, or modify it to fit into our neat understanding of what might be reasonable. It cannot be forced to appear—yet we always know when it has occurred.

If we expect that our recovery from a serious illness or injury will be long and drawn out, then our capacity to deal with time may diminish. Minutes become elongated, with 20 minutes of nausea seeming like 20 hours, 5 minutes on hold seeming like 30, and the four to eight hours in the emergency room feeling like a month.

Music is a great organizer of time, altering our internal clock in ways that can ease the endless moments consumed by illness. It is that place of "virtual time" that we spoke of earlier—that place where we can just *be*. To design healing environments, we use this aesthetic manipulation of time in order to ease the recovery process.

Music Therapy

The practice of music therapy has been a licensed profession since the 1950s. In addition to musical training, music therapists undergo many years of diligent study and certification, not unlike other types of health-care professionals.

One of this profession's primary contributions to health care is in the field of research, providing evidence that documents the positive effects that music can have when administered according to specific protocols appropriate for the patient. Research has demonstrated that music can be used to lessen pain and anxiety. It has been shown to both reduce the amount of medication required and increase its effectiveness. Alzheimer's patients, whose memories have been dramatically impaired, have responded to songs from their past. Other studies have shown that listening to music has lowered blood pressure and improved respiration in post-operative heart bypass patients.

What's #1 on the Hit Parade for the Sick?

When we are asked what the perfect healing music is, we often shift the question to reflect a broader understanding: "What is the most effective music for a particular person on a specific occasion under specific circumstances?" That is, we take into account the music, the person, the occasion, and the circumstance. Most of us assume, understandably so, that music is the key. However, the music is not an isolated phenomenon heard outside the context of listener and situation. By using music as environmental design, the most helpful inquiries are: *What is the goal of the environment, and what is the best music to achieve that goal?*

As we have said throughout this book, the answer to whether or not music is suitable rests in the response of the listener. If a piece is intended to be healing, soothing, or otherwise therapeutic, but instead it irritates, agitates, or annoys the patient, then we shouldn't make the judgment that the patient was wrong for not responding appropriately. So, if any adjustment can be made, it should be in the music—turn it down, turn it off, or change it!

To Like or Not to Like: Is That the Right Question?

In the course of one of our medical workshops, we gave the participating nurses a follow-up assignment. They were each to take a piece of music, play it for three patients, and report back to us. One nurse returned with this story:

Carol had been a patient for the past ten days, in a great deal of pain and discomfort. Her spinal cord injury and the ensuing surgery had left her in a Stryker traction, a metal contraption that straps the patient in, head down and immobilized. This device was a miracle—it countered the detrimental effects of gravity and allowed the spinal cord to heal without weight-bearing pressure. The difficulty, of course, was surviving the discomfort— good for the back, bad for sleep. In fact, sleep deprivation is one of the known and acknowledged side effects of being in a Stryker traction.

On this day, the nurse, Rosie, approached Carol, who had gone without sleep for days. Rosie talked to Carol about listening to The Still Point, *an album we had recently produced for Washoe Medical Center. While the music was very soothing, it was unfamiliar to this young woman who was already dealing with enormous challenges.*

Carol was irritable—understandably so. Her injury was substantial, and the recovery from her surgery would require a lengthy convalescence. However, Rosie was gently persistent. She asked Carol if she would try the music for just ten minutes, and then if she didn't like it, it would be turned off and never be mentioned again. Carol declined, but Rosie asked again. The nurse told her of the workshop and that it was not necessary for Carol to like the music, but it was an assignment. "Could you please help me?" Rosie asked.

Carol reluctantly agreed, so Rosie procured a Walkman portable cassette player and carefully put the headphones on her patient. She adjusted the volume until Carol indicated that it was satisfactory.

"Ten minutes," Carol said.

"Ten minutes," Rosie promised.

Within only a few minutes, Carol fell asleep. She slept for four hours straight, the longest she had rested since she had been admitted. Rosie worried about her promise of ten minutes, but also yielded to the reality that Carol had not been able to sleep for days. The effects of sleep deprivation run the spectrum from irritability to depression. Rosie kept a close eye on Carol, wanting to be there when she awoke since her patient had no way of removing or otherwise managing the Walkman.

When Carol did wake up, she promptly asked that the headphones be removed. As Rosie carefully lifted them off, without prompting or suggestion, Carol said rather defiantly, "I didn't like the music!"

We have often questioned the relevance of the question, "Do you like the music?" It is apparent to us that when considering such an inquiry, it is not clear exactly what information is being sought. For instance, some people might say, "I liked the music, but actually I am a jazz lover," or "I don't care for it . . . I prefer country and western." While it may seem that the answer has been given, from our point of view, the question itself is imprecise and misleading.

In a setting where the purpose of the music is to provide an effect beyond the moment or circumstance, beyond pleasure or entertainment, then any inquiry needs to avoid reducing the assessment down to "like" or "dislike." As musicians, we have had to allow music to serve us, as when the most simple, commercial, and popular music is far more appropriate for the moment than acclaimed masterpieces such as Bartok's *Concerto for Orchestra* or Luciano Pavarotti's most brilliant aria. As such, the effectiveness of any particular piece of music becomes apparent depending on the environment it creates.

Stimulative versus Sedative Music

We have found that the style and sound of a piece determines its utility value. The two main types of ambient music—*stimulative* and *sedative*—differ in rhythm, melody, harmony, and texture.

Stimulative music, as a rule, tends to be active, louder, and more demanding. The goal is to energize and arouse to a higher level. Research has demonstrated that listening to fast music causes our pulse rates to rise accordingly. For example, consider the tradition of East Indian *tabla* drumming, where the solo performer starts at a tempo equal to a relaxed heart rate (approximately 68 to 72 beats per minute), and then gradually increases the tempo and energy level during the course of the solo. The intended result is that the listeners' pulse rates will follow the dynamics of the drumming, resulting in feelings of increasing exhilaration and excitement. Music traditions in many other cultures take advantage of the stimulative effects of fast tempos. Particularly notable in this respect are the various dance forms of Brazilian music and Afro-Cuban salsa. In America, we have upbeat music that is specially designed for aerobics, jogging, and household chores.

Sedative music, by contrast, is less active, characterized by slower tempos and softer volumes. Again, the choice of tempo is designed to relax and slow the pulse. A tempo of 60 beats per minute is commonly chosen to evoke the relaxation response. Sedative music lacks heavy drum beats and demanding melodies. Likewise, sedative music is apt to be characterized by the sounds of sustained strings, for example, as opposed to the harder-edged timbres of electric guitars and drums. Typical applications include massage, meditation, and relaxation.

Regardless of which type of music you may prefer, your choice should be based on your goal, whether the activity in question is running a treadmill, painting a portrait, or healing from a critical illness. These are examples of activities that allow for the *positive distraction* that background music affords. The decision as to whether or not to use environmental music, and if so, which kind, should be based on your own research about what works, monitoring the results in the moment.

The Television Hour

The most easily accessible and available technological tool for music and entertainment is the television. The health-care industry has validated this national pastime by having at least one TV in every room. In recent years, however, some hospitals have instituted pay-television, pay-per-view movies on demand, and other amenities more common to the hospitality industry. The TV is often used to mitigate the boredom factor for patients and families able to watch it, as well as providing cognitive orientation for patients who are in various stages of impaired consciousness. Talk shows are sometimes broadcast in order to bring patients into the present, offering language orientation. It is also used when there is a need for stimulation for comatose patients who have no visitors.

Network television commercials are often several decibels louder than the regular program material, probably to prevent our being able to suc-cessfully ignore them. For patients under medication or otherwise impaired, the result is perceived as erratic noise, often disturbing and totally out of context. Such patients may not be aware that they are hearing commercials; they only hear loud voices, then softer sounds, then loud voices. They may mistake the commercials for people yelling at each other or at them, since they are do not know otherwise.

Talk TV: Is It Healing?

The language of talk TV, like talk radio, is often combative, as are its subjects. The typical gladiator-cheering crowd may be entertaining to some, but for a patient in need of peace and quiet, it is neither soothing nor sup-portive of the healing process. In all fairness to the millions of people who watch Jerry Springer, it must be admitted that such programs may very well serve as a powerful distraction from other worries. However, nurses report that pulse rates and blood pressures are sometimes driven higher in patients who are watching violent or otherwise disturbing programming.

Critical illness—the kind that would call for hospitalization or bed con-finement—is not business as usual. Unless patients are able to choose their own programming, they require an advocate who will act on their behalf. The television dominates any environment in which it is running. If it is not appropriately part of the healing environment, then it is violating it. Many consider talk radio an acceptable alternative to talk TV, but in truth, it may even be worse.

We would be remiss if we ignored the sound quality of the television. The speakers for hospital televisions are often located either in the patient's call control (wired remote) or in the side rails of the gurney. They are not designed to broadcast throughout the room. If turned up too loud, the speakers distort, sounding worse than a bad transistor radio. If visitors decide to watch television and turn up the volume so that "everyone" can hear, it is loudest to the patient. This is true whether the patient is awake or asleep.

Evaluating a Health-Care Setting

We suggest that you use the following guidelines in designing the auditory environment for someone who is ill, including yourself:

1. *Assess the sound environment.* How does the room "feel"? Consider the overall quality of the environment—always part of any assessment. Any health benefit will be derived from the total and collective effect of all the environmental components. The auditory environment includes all audible sound, often extending beyond walls and doors. Therefore, consider whether the noises coming from outside the room are loud enough to disturb the patient or otherwise invade the space. Does the room feel like a place of healing or hurting, of ease or dis-ease?

2. *Is the music appropriate?* Nightingale distinguished between music played on percussive instruments, which have a jarring sound, to the sustained quality of voice or violin music. She wrote:

> The effect of music upon the sick has been scarcely at all noticed. . . .
> I will only remark here, that wind instruments, including the human voice,
> and stringed instruments, capable of continuous sound, have a generally
> beneficent effect . . . Instruments [that] have no continuity of sound damage the sick.

This overall description is accurate: to most people, sounds that are jarring, erratic, and percussive are not music to sleep, rest, or recover by. In designing an environment, focus on the therapeutic needs of the patient. Music should be responsive to the patient's needs—it should not cause alarm or irritation, but rather should be soothing, inspiring, and comforting.

3. *Does the music fit the time of day?* A healing environment is in sync with the temporal pacing of the day-night cycle. This means that it may be quite appropriate to have more upbeat music in the middle of the day, depending on the condition of the patient. However, it need not be either overly passive or unduly stimulating.

The day-night cycle—known as the *circadian rhythm*—significantly affects how our bodies function. Sunlight is critical to our well-being, as is respite from intense sensory stimulation. Thus, nighttime provides balance and time for our bodies to regenerate. Often, during a critical illness, this day-night cycle is interrupted. If we are at home and do not sleep well at night, we might find ourselves trying to sleep during the day. This turn-around results in our day-night cycle being out of sync. Usually, when we recover and return to our normal activities, the cycle corrects itself.

In the hospital setting, it is still more difficult. The pacing of hospital care is based on 24-hour observation, a practice established at the time of Florence Nightingale. Most patients report that their sleep is interrupted by a nurse taking their vital signs, giving medication, or medically intervening in some other way. In intensive-care units, however, medical observation is increased because of the severity of the patient's condition. Often these units are without windows. Therefore, not only is the sleep cycle disrupted, but the deprivation of natural sunlight and the inability of the patient to discern day from night has resulted in *ICU psychosis,* a severe clinical disorientation that is relieved by being moved into a room with windows.

Design the patient's environment to support the natural pacing of the day-night cycle by programming restful music in the evening and more active music during the day. If, however, daytime sleep is needed for any reason, then of course the auditory environment can easily respond to the immediate needs of the patient.

4. *How loud is the room?* Every space has a volume. If you have ever watched *Star Trek,* you may have noticed that there is a low rumble of what

we all assume to be the engine noise of the starship *Enterprise.* We experienced a similar sound while working on cruise ships—the rumble was loud enough that when the ship was in port and all the engines were off, the quiet was unnerving and the magic of the ship seemed diminished.

The sounds of illness become part of the "sick room." They may include normal to labored breathing, expressions of pain and suffering, the beeps and pings of monitors, or the hums of ventilators and other devices. If doors and windows are open or vulnerable to being penetrated by outside activities, then add into this chorus the sounds of conversations, phones, televisions, and traffic.

Music may serve several functions in shifting what may seem an intrusive environment into one that is therapeutic. First of all, music can create a therapeutic presence by being appropriate in its content and affect. In addition, it can mask outside sounds; if loud enough, it can cover the most continuous ambient noises. To use music for relaxation, the volume need only be adjusted. If it is used as an accompaniment to something else, such as guided imagery or prayer, then volume is again the key. For the music to have an even more pronounced effect, to be the sole focused event or the driving force of our concentration, the volume and the choice of music may need to change. Be aware of these different options and the changes in the ambient noise levels so that the music is appropriately prioritized according to its purpose. The questions to ask include:

- What is the primary sound event in this space?
- How does music position itself within this space?
- How loud must it be to support the intention of the environment?

5. *How high is the restfulness quotient?* The *restfulness quotient* can be defined as the amount of quality sleep or rest the patient gets, as compared to the number of hours spent in bed. Pain, anxiety, noise, overstimulation in the environment, and the like can all cause disturbed or agitated sleep. However, the obvious goal is to put the patient at rest so that the body can devote itself to restoring health. Is sleep improved by the addition of any particular kind of music? Are the number of hours increased, or the quality of rest improved?

Restfulness and pain management go together—pain is a great factor in preventing sleep, although sleep offers a respite from pain. If the environment lowers the restfulness quotient, then the patient becomes more exhausted by the process of having to cope with pain, and may even require more medication in order to cope. If the restfulness quotient is higher, by virtue of environmental design, then obviously the patient will experience an increased ability to cope with pain and less hours spent in pain. In her treatises, Nightingale specifically addressed the need to avoid disturbing the patient. It remains the best way for the body to repair itself.

St. Charles Medical Center in Bend, Oregon, recently conducted a survey of methods used for pain management, including everything from medication to meditation, guided imagery to healing touch to The C.A.R.E. Channel. The results indicated that The C.A.R.E. Channel was used as much as medication—almost 80 percent of the time. In three critical-care units, Henry Ford Hospital in Detroit combined C.A.R.E. With Music, a custom sound-delivery system, with staff education on how to design a healing environment. Their results showed a significant reduction in the use of patient restraints, indicating less agitation among ventilated acute patients. St. Luke's Episcopal Hospital in Houston, as part of a hospital-wide initiative, redesigned one of their intensive-care units to be a healing environment. In addition to utilizing both music and The C.A.R.E. Channel, they mounted nature pictures on the walls, painted the overhead fluorescent lights to look like clouds, and redesigned other visual elements. They found that music lowered the noise levels and provided a positive distraction from the stress common to critical-care units.

Early in their efforts to use the environment as a therapeutic protocol, South Nassau Communities Hospital in Oceanside, New York, reported the case of a 37-year-old woman who was dying of an acute heart condition. In her final days in the intensive-care unit, she was agitated and frightened. Neither medication nor any other treatment had been successful in alleviating her combined physical and emotional distress. When the staff provided music, nature imagery, and massage therapy, she responded with a substantial lowering of her measurable stress levels. Although she died within 36 hours, the staff and her family knew that she had died in peace, rather than in fear.

At Craig Hospital in Englewood, Colorado, which exclusively serves patients who have incurred catastrophic spinal-cord and brain injuries, the results were immediate. Patients who had experienced their most difficult hours at night while attempting to rest were finally able to sleep with the presence of the "Midnight Starfield," a computer-generated image provided by The C.A.R.E. Channel for that purpose.

Much of the input we receive from our client hospitals is anecdotal; however, Dr. Jayne Standley, a music therapist and researcher at Florida State University, extensively analyzed 30 studies on the use of music in medical and dental procedures, and documented that analgesics—pain medications—can be more effective with the use of music as an adjunct therapy than they are alone. This result is only one component of the larger impact that music has in creating a space and time where healing is possible.

Exercising Your Personal Choice

We live in a world that vehemently supports our right to exercise personal choice. However, in the event of illness, our desires may change; when the situation is critical, the obligation to make a choice can become burdensome. There are times when we want to be taken care of and not have to make any decisions.

Many of the issues of personal choice regarding sound and music are age-driven. Those of us in the baby-boomer generation are not universally "addicted" to music. In fact, we may have lived some parts of our lives without any musical counterpart.

Younger people use and experience music differently. Instead of growing *into* the technology, they grew up with all of it: remote controls, CD players, boomboxes, and more. They are more comfortable with audio technology because they have never known life without these musical conveniences. However, in all fairness, this age group is also healthier and less likely to undergo a hospital admittance or be bedridden at home. Most young people will not be shy about requesting what they want, unless they are too ill to do so, in which case we must make decisions on their behalf that honor who they are and what may best serve them.

While music may be important to the elder generation, it may still be regarded as a luxury. In a crisis, dealing with doctors, hospitals, Medicare forms, and their own diminished capacity to manage it all may make the challenge of technology—VCRs, tape players, CD players, and having to choose the music—so complicated as to seem insurmountable. Therefore, we will need to assist these elders in taking advantage of the ability of music to decrease stress and anxiety and to facilitate pain management. That may mean providing the player, choosing the music, and basically making it very accessible. Both of us have had to strongly encourage our parents to use music, have purchased CD players for them, and have then had to remind them of this option.

The Great Equalizer

Illness can be a great equalizer, making us aware of the true values of time, health, and relationship. It can also make us aware of how vulnerable and fragile we are. If the situation is serious, we may have the real option of changing the way we live to remedy the future. If our condition is grave, we may be forced to alter our hopes and expectations of ourselves and others. We may also find that circumstances and settings that have long been part of our daily lives do not serve us well when illness or health crises occur—which is why environmental design is so critical.

Music changes our spatial and temporal orientation. It can make an otherwise ordinary space into one that is sacred. If that is to happen, however, it may not be the same music we choose at other times, under other circumstances. It may not be the music by which we get married, make love, dance, or drive to work. In fact, our absolute favorites for those contexts may be inappropriate or even upsetting. A therapeutic environment, one where the hope of healing is palpable, varies from those common to other circumstances.

Susan: When my mother died, nothing seemed normal. For the first time in my life, I could not bear hearing music that I otherwise loved. It wasn't more than a few days after her death that my father and I had to secure airline tickets, deal with Social Security, and buy some groceries. Perhaps the feigning of life-as-usual as represented by the music I heard every day felt disrespectful, an affront to the seriousness of the situation. While the world goes on as if nothing were different, most of us will detach from day-to-day life until we are ready to rejoin. Until then, new rituals appropriate to the meaning of the situation must be designed.

How to Take Care of Yourself

In the hospital, the opportunity to create your own environment has never been easier than in the present. Since hospitals have recognized the value of patients having more control over their own circumstances, policies at some institutions have included allowing patients to wear their own bedclothes, installing kitchens for families to prepare meals, and encouraging patients to surround themselves with personal effects such as pillows and family photos. Taking responsibility for your process includes bringing the tools that will create an environment where you feel nurtured. Bringing in music that you are comfortable with, which might feel like an old friend to you, will immediately change the stark and perhaps sterile clinical environment into your personal space. This is true whether you (or someone in your family) are going to be admitted for a procedure, are going through outpatient surgery, or are going through a diagnostic process.

If you are being admitted for an elective procedure, then certainly take advantage of your opportunity to prepare by choosing music to bring with you. If there is an emergency for which there is no time to prepare, hopefully you will have made your musical preferences known well enough that those who act on your behalf will know what would be helpful to you.

Music therapy research has shown that preference positively impacts the effectiveness of therapeutic music. However, in a crisis that brings our lives to a halt, music whose sound or association does not support our personal needs or respect the seriousness of the situation should be replaced by other kinds of music. Make determinations based on your own sensitivities and evaluation of the situation.

As a starting point for you, consult our appendix of artists and composers whose music is broadcast, along with nature imagery, on The C.A.R.E. Channel, the environmental programming we produce for hospitals. This list is not intended as a comprehensive catalog of "healing" music. Rather, it is music that has been found to be helpful and enjoyable to patients and staff in hospitals around the country. Certainly assemble your own personal collection of music that makes you feel good and creates a supportive sound environment that you can access on an as-needed basis.

*"It is not important to know whether the music itself is doing
the relaxing or if it simply assists the body in relaxing itself. . . .
It may be that music is basically amplifying the body's
own healing and relaxing abilities."*
— Steven Halpern, in *Sound Health*

About Headphones

Isolation during an illness is quite different from personal quiet time. When we are ill, our diagnosis immediately separates us from others and from the rest of our lives. On the other hand, personal solitude may still be desirable at times. Therefore, headphones, providing music at any time, in any place, at a desired volume, should be used with due caution. They are designed to separate, both to keep in and to shut out. While this may be completely satisfactory on an ordinary day, being sick changes the rules.

Headphones also have their own side effects: They impede normal auditory responses. Wearers talk loudly because they cannot hear themselves, and others have to shout in order to be heard. In a clinical setting, patients and families raise their voices to communicate, violating others' space and making privacy all but impossible.

Nonetheless, under specific circumstances, we have found headphones to be advantageous, if not necessary. Because of the known benefits of music for patients undergoing medical procedures and in order to remedy the potential disadvantages of headphones, we developed The Sondrex System®. It is designed to insulate patients undergoing medical procedures from extraneous noises without isolating them from their primary caregiver. The cushioned, closed-ear headphones are not soundproof, but they do block out most extraneous sounds without having to use volume alone as the masking agent. The physician or nurse can speak directly and unobtrusively with the patient using a microphone that comes with the system. Since its development, we have found that those hospitals using it have become more cognizant of the environment and the value of intentional communication, and more conscious about the benefits and liabilities of headphones.

An environment is a space that holds events, relationships, hopes, and fears. Headphones create an environment for *one*. However, the health-care event involves families, caregivers, professionals, friends, and others whose relationship to the patient is important. Our advice is to use headphones with caution.

Therefore, the decision of whether to use headphones, or an external music system such as a boombox, should be based on the patient's comfort, who else is in the room, and most important, whether a solitary listening environment is appropriate.

When Our Parents Are Ill

Lest we think it is all imagined, research has shown that our adaptive capacities are only as strong as our physical and mental condition. If we consider the issues of the elderly, many of the solutions regarding diminished capacity lie in the physical design of various environments. Improvements can include lighted walkways, bathrooms with higher commodes, rails in the tubs, and seating options that make it easier to sit down and stand up. Clearly, when we are healthy, we easily adapt to unfriendly environments, whereas in poor health, we are less able to do so.

Without a doubt, most of us will at some time be taking care of our parents or other older family members. Our dear friend Rose, in her later years, was good-natured and skilled at covering up her inability to hear. Some people presumed that she could not hear, and talked privately around her. Others mistakenly assumed that she understood what was being said to her when she had given up even attempting to participate minutes or hours before. It left her isolated and somewhat exhausted by the process. We learned to speak directly to her and make no assumptions.

However, a telling instance occurred while Rose was spending a night with us. I had been raising my voice most of the day to make sure that she could hear me. She, of course, never told me not to yell. However, I began to question the need to continually speak so loudly. While Rose was sitting on the sofa reading, I walked over to Dallas, who was on the other side of the room. I bent down and whispered something rather erotic in his ear.

Rose laughed.

I never again presumed that she would not hear, or yelled at her. I did,
however, take precautions when I did not want her to hear!

In spite of concerns that many older patients may be acutely hard of
hearing, anecdotal stories from our client hospitals regarding elderly
patients and The C.A.R.E. Channel report improved restfulness, deeper
sleep levels, reduced need for nursing assistance, and less overall anxiety.
The specific concerns in caring for the elderly are, however, more complex.
As we discussed, the hearing capacity of older persons varies greatly and
affects their ability to communicate. Also, they may have difficulty separating sounds in order to fully understand what is being said to and around
them. Moreover, if they are not wearing their glasses, they cannot use their
eyes to help them hear.

Irritability, increased frustration, and depression are not uncommon on
the part of an older person who is totally aware of the disconnect between
what they hear and what is being said. Add to this the effects of medication
and confinement—whether at home or in the hospital—and the situation
becomes even more critical. In 1997, *The Journal of Gerontological
Nursing* published a study indicating that mealtime agitation and other
behavioral symptoms exhibited by dementia and Alzheimer's patients (ages
64 to 84) diminished significantly when quiet background music was
played. Music was used to affect the environment in order to mask noises
and prevent startling or stimulating anxiety.

Although studies have documented the positive impact of using soft
background music for the elderly, hearing impairment makes it more difficult to deal with background noises. The ability to separate sounds and the
difficulty in perception sometimes results in older adults resigning themselves to not being able to hear, or becoming agitated. Music played at a
volume low enough to not compete with conversation can still mask erratic
noise. Thus, there is a reasonable foundation on which to base the use of
background music to care for an older person.

Life Transitions

In recent years, the mystique surrounding death and dying has evolved
into an open and candid discourse about the varied and complex processes

that may be involved. Respect for the sacredness of human life and the challenges of terminal illness have forced improvements in palliative care. When "aggressive and heroic measures" are no longer desired or appropriate, the objective shifts from "treatment" to the relief of suffering. For someone who is going through the final stages of a terminal illness, however, we can offer more than relief from physical pain. We can create the space for healing to occur.

Music thanatology, pioneered by harpist Therese Schroeder-Scheker, focuses on the power of music to assist the transition through the dying process. The Chalice of Repose project, based at the St. Patrick Hospital in Missoula, Montana, trains practitioners to play prescriptive harp music from 11th-century Cluny, France, which is believed to help patients deal with the inevitability of their own death, and ease the process of "conscious dying." This is the first music therapy protocol identified for the compassionate and purposeful facilitation of death.

Healing health care holds healing and curing to be independent of each other: The integrity of the spirit, the heart, and the mind may heal regardless of the processes affecting the physical body. In the face of an incurable illness, when life represents only the elongation of suffering, healing may still occur, for one can heal into life or heal into death. A healing environment eases either process. Therefore, the protocols described below are applicable regardless of the prognosis.

The use of music is contextual but may function on both an environmental and a prescriptive level. Our capacity to be sensitive to the moment is perhaps more poignant when the outcome is without ambiguity, as in a life-or-death situation. However, the best choices will be found by focusing on the intention—the outcome desired. Make every instant stunning and loving, sacred and caring. Let the music and the spirit of the moment bear the burden of teaching us how to be together in such profound times at the end of life.

Programming for Healing

> *"Within the boundaries of the 'sick room,' the sounds of*
> *illness become the only song that is heard unless the*
> *environment is programmed for healing."*
> — Susan Mazer, from the article "Sing a Song for the Sick and Tense"

Programming the environment for someone who may not have a preference, or be unable to express it, is a challenge and a responsibility. Caregivers become the ultimate auditory designers and the custodians of the space.

Because neither commercial background music nor radio and TV had been found helpful during acute illness, we were asked by our client hospitals to provide programming specific to the acute-care setting. The following criteria were used in developing The C.A.R.E. Channel and C.A.R.E. With Music:

1. *Instrumental music:* Instrumental music requires the least effort on the part of the listener, while reducing stress and anxiety. Words use a specific part of the brain and require a relatively intact cognitive function in order to be understood. Furthermore, in a condition of semi-consciousness, the words may be misunderstood.

For instance, if we are fully cognizant and hear music with vocals in a language foreign to us, we generally let go of striving to understand meaning. However, under the influence of medication or an illness that impairs our capacity, we may not be able to grasp the fact that the language is foreign, and our minds will struggle to define meaning, or assume a meaning in error. As Nightingale said, it is best not to tax the mind of the patient, but to provide music that is soothing and restful.

Regarding vocal music: Although we do not use vocal music for hospital-wide broadcast, we do not want to totally eliminate this option. There are many opera lovers who would prefer to wake up to Pavarotti, or county and western lovers who would crave Dolly Parton, or jazz lovers who would be in ecstasy to recover to Natalie Cole. We suggest that the conditions under which the music will be *heard*—the patient and the circumstance—be the determining factors.

2. *Music that is easy to listen to:* melodic, accessible, and not too dissonant or rhythmic. The act of listening should not be work. I (Susan) have often said, in a moment of exhaustion, that I do not want to learn anything, meaning I do not want to further tax my brain. Certain kinds of music, especially the jazz and classical genres, are intellectually challenging. Their forms are complex and intended to stimulate thought and feeling; they often evoke a powerful emotional response. This music is not intended to be rest-

ful or sedative. Rather, it is meant to engage, incite, arouse, or provoke. For someone involuntarily impaired, it may even be irritating and counterproductive. Remember, music's purpose as environmental design is to serve the ill, act as a physical and emotional cradle, and be nurturing and safe for the patient *and* the caregiver.

3. *New music, or music free from association:* We suggest that, unless specifically requested, you avoid music that represents major life events or celebrations, such as wedding songs, anniversary favorites, songs that were heard during courtship (or divorce), songs played at someone else's funeral, or any music that is unduly maudlin or inappropriately exciting.

4. *Music appropriate to the situation:* music that will guide the actions of visitors and other family members accordingly.

If the patient needs rest, quiet talk, and a quiet ambiance, then create that kind of space. When others are invited in, they are more likely to automatically respond appropriately to the environment.

5. *Other sound options:* There are other sound elements that offer many of the benefits of music, while being perhaps more neutral in character. Try the following:

- **Wind chimes:** Wind chimes offer both pleasant sounds and variety of tone (since the wind does the playing). There are many styles and qualities available. Larger chimes that have a richer, deeper tone are most soothing. For an older person, high-pitched chimes may be irritating. It is best to listen, try them out, and make the appropriate choice.

- **Water elements:** We are a two-fountain family. However, their use is determined by who else is in the house. The sound of water can be soothing but can also stimulate the bladder. For someone with a hearing aid, it could also be distracting if the water is very loud. Again, experiment.

- **Nature recordings:** There are many commercial recordings available of a wide variety of nature sounds, such as summer rains, ocean surf, rivers and brooks, or bird sanctuaries. For many, they offer a restful ambiance. Try it.

Note: Patients who are asleep or otherwise not fully conscious often listen to sounds out of context. That means that if they hear water, it may sound like distortion common to the radio; if they hear birds, they will not know where the high-pitched chirp is coming from, and that could be irritating. The body responds the same to actual running water or the recorded sound of running water.

6. *Music that creates Sacred Space:* This is *it,* the real work—to design the "sick room" to be a place where life is sacred. Each action and effort must be directed toward this goal. If only one component is incompatible or accidental, it violates the natural inclination of the body and soul to heal.

The Healing Health-Care Environment

"Any environment is a mirror of the individual and of the culture. The environment reflects what individuals think about and feel and therefore echoes the values of the culture. An effective environment needs to be filled with cultural symbols that are meaningful especially an environment aimed at healing."
— Nancy Moore and Henrietta Komras, in *Patient-Focused Healing*

The healing health-care environment fortifies and honors the human process when it is in peril. It has a definitive feeling, rather than a specific sound or look. For most of us, entrance into a hospital, whether in the role of patient, friend, or family, is something that calls out for personal caring. Unfortunately, in the wake of technological growth, the part of health care that speaks to both *health* and *care* has often been put aside. Our sole objective is to create health-care spaces that inherently offer support to the healing process beyond providing clinical protocols. While issues of life and death are not ours to dictate, the processes that occur along the path can be held and honored so that those who are most affected, including both patients and caregivers, are positively served by the environment. Music, in this context, is not used as a medicinal agent, but rather as an environmental context that holds the processes of healing.

It has been our observation, in developing this work, that the human spirit is often fed by the invisible. Indeed, the sounds of illness, the impersonal nature of institutional settings, and our struggle to discriminate between the controllable and uncontrollable all speak to the need for a redesign of how we hear our own pain and the pain of others. Indeed, the pain of a patient and loved one is often felt deepest in the darkness of the midnight hours, listening to the silence, waiting, and not knowing how to gain respite from the ongoing fear. It remains a privilege to serve the unspoken needs of this process and to empower you to be the designer of sacred healing space.

Chapter Twelve

Designing Learning Environments

"If, when a child learns to speak, he is also taught to sing,
he will never know life without music."

— Ali Akbar Khan, Indian master musician

What We Do Not Remember Learning

If we were to take a guess, we might reasonably assume that when you read nursery rhymes such as *Twinkle, Twinkle, Little Star*, you also sang them. We would also imagine that you do not remember the day you learned that song or who taught it to you. In his book *Everything I Always Wanted to Know I Learned in Kindergarten,* Robert Fulghum reminded all of us that the fabric of our relationship to the world is woven early in our lives. We might also add that the music in our lives becomes who we are at that time. With age and experience comes increased variety and repertoire. However, a profound relationship to music has already developed.

A healing setting is an environment that inspires, encourages, and builds self-esteem. Whether we are referring to a child learning the hand movements for *The Eensy Weensy Spider,* or to an adult being informed about the procedures required to increase the chance of recovering from cancer, the environment acts as either an advocate or an adversary to the learning process. Considering the *when, who,* and *how* of healing makes it obvious that answers are difficult to quantify. Patients heal and students learn—but how each process happens remains a mystery. Perhaps the body naturally restores itself, facilitated by treatment and prescription. Likewise, perhaps teachers impart information and skills to students whose minds and sensitivities are naturally engaged. However, our means of internalizing information remain elusive.

Current efforts to hold teachers accountable for the education of their students has proven controversial, if not confusing. As with a hospital patient, there is no standard, generic student. Rather, each student is a unique individual, with a wide variety of capacities. The role of a teacher in relation to the performance of a student is not merely a linear stream of knowledge, passed from one to the other. Rather, teaching is a complex venture that involves individual responsibility, capability, potential, and objective achievement.

Furthermore, *where* does all this happen? Using the traditional educational equation, if you build a room, fill in would-be students, and add a teacher certified to have mastered specific knowledge and appropriate skills, then *it* happens: The teacher teaches, and the students learn. But is that really what occurs? More important, is that *how* it happens?

In the same way that healing involves more than direct human intervention, so learning occurs with or without instruction, a classroom, or formal educational paraphernalia. The role of the teacher may not be fixed, but may be passed from person to person, voluntarily and otherwise. Furthermore, the chronology of learning may not be the linear and authoritative delivery of information from one person (or medium) to another that it is often assumed to be.

Educational psychologist Jeanne Gibbs suggests that ". . . there is no such thing as 'teaching'—only the inner (intrinsic) learning out of reflection on sequential experiences." Nonetheless, learning theories have long hypothesized about exactly how the brain and mind acquire knowledge, hoping to arrive at a way of predicting, thereby being able to cause, the successful transmission of usable knowledge. Textbooks are written from beginning to end with careful attention to the ordered unveiling of information. The hope is that the sequence in which information is imparted will support the transformation of the textbooks' content into knowledge.

However, our experience in working as teachers, both one-on-one with students and in the classroom, has shown that learning is dependent on a complex relationship between the subject matter and its meaning to the student. Holistic in nature, authentic learning requires engagement on the most intimate level, combining both cognition and creativity, the heart and the mind. Indeed, even in our years as students, the quality of the educational process was directly related to the personal relevance of the subject matter. The role of the teacher, perhaps, is to make the information meaningful to the student, to merge the student with the information. If learning is to occur, there must be no separation between teacher and student. Neither should information that may seem foreign to students remain elusive. The transformative nature of learning is like that of healing: The knowledge becomes the student becomes the knowledge—for a lifetime.

In our early years, from birth until school age, we are discoverers. We are born intent on living, and then intent on learning. Our curiosity leads us fearlessly into the world, into the unknown, which, when we are infants, includes literally everything.

Our niece and nephew, Rachel and Ari, constantly remind us that learning is a hunger, not a task, and is seldom without some kind of musical component. We gave Rachel a music program for the computer when she was four. The various exercises began with a wonderful room full of musical instruments strewn in a way that made them very accessible. When Rachel "clicked" on an instrument, it would come to life and play a short musical riff, just long enough for her to hear its sound. Then there was a follow-up game in which small animals race to the finish line lest they be captured. Their salvation relied on Rachel's ability to identify the sounds of the instruments she heard.

We watched Rachel pop the CD into the computer, turn it on, and click on the appropriate icon. She easily recognized the sounds. But, to our concern, she waited until the last minute to save the animals. Seeing our dismay, she said, "Don't worry, I just want to see what happens!" Then she nonchalantly clicked, winning the game over and over. Rachel's learning process continues to be clearly driven from inside, not through motivation or a set of directions given by anyone.

Our nephew Ari, two years older, is an avid reader in his leisure time. He easily reports in great detail the facts from the books he reads. When he recently started playing clarinet, he came to Uncle Dallas, who immediately encouraged him to give up "reading" the notes and to start playing by ear. Ari easily read the notes or numbers from the page, but like many students, he had not been trained to listen—a most critical habit. Although frustrated and claiming "impossibility," it took a only a couple days for Ari to be able to play "this cool jazz lick" in the lower range of the clarinet, something he took back to school with great pride.

Yet another, unrelated example of how mysterious the learning process is occurred when Ari was nine. He asked to hear "Waters of the Earth," the theme from an album he'd first heard when he was five. He said it was his favorite piece.

We were not there when Rachel learned to identify the sounds of orchestral instruments, when she learned how to use the computer's mouse, or when she learned to manipulate the computer as if it were an extension of her own mind. Ari was alone on the day he went from a reluctant reader to one fully engrossed in his own extensive library of favorite books. The children's capacity for learning is clearly evidenced by their performance and demonstration. The role of teacher, however, is not so clear—not fixed in any single person, place, time, or methodology. The learning process remains a mystery.

One day, Ari could not read. The next day, he could.

One day, Rachel spoke but a few direct words. On another, she knew words that no one had taught her.

One day she was hearing the jingles of a rattle. What seemed like only a few days later, she sat down at a small harp and composed a piece of music—which she remembered a week later.

How? When?

Innocence

At the age of four, life is simple and learning is play. Everything is new. Awkwardness is forgotten, if not forgiven, and embarrassment does not exist. As we mature, however, information becomes more complex and expectations are heightened. Pride and fear begin to pollute our pure thirst for knowledge. How do we retain and transform the "natural" innate learning process into one that is by design? How do we learn to learn?

Today, the lifestyles of the young and innocent are not easy. They include social, economic, and circumstantial pressures over which children and parents have no control. The hours spent in school comprise a larger portion of the lives of the young than the time spent anywhere else. The impact of experiences and relationships that occur there is lifelong and can override other challenges. It can bring hope and new light into a child's life, as well as inspiration and possibility.

The environment, then, is the advocate, if not the partner, in the educational process. It is the place where objective information becomes relevant, and where inspiration develops individual potential.

Learning Processes

In the learning environment, music can affect three important areas of learning: *cognition,* or clarity of knowledge; *motivation,* or inspiration; and *retention,* or personal keeping of the knowledge. It brings knowledge from the holistic field into the academic, acknowledging the soul of the child as well as the mind.

Just as in the health-care setting, the relationship between those involved—here, the teacher and the student—depends on communication, the physical capacity to accomplish the tasks at hand, continued inspiration, and the capacity of the space to mirror and enrich the self-respect of both student and teacher.

William Strickland is the founder and director of the Manchester Craftsman's Guild, a city-wide arts institute for inner-city students in Pittsburgh. His facility is designed with art, fountains, and other aesthetic accoutrements because he believes that students should be "surrounded by excellence." The sounds within the academy, while reflecting varied levels of activities, are tempered and respectful in accordance with the visual and spatial milieu. For every visual cue, there is an auditory counterpart. This institute is free from graffiti, litter, and inappropriate auditory chaos. Quite simply, that is not part of the culture or environment.

The quality of the learning environment predicts it own outcome. For a teacher, it is difficult to teach or model discipline while amidst aural chaos or surrounded by chaotic graffiti. For the student, it is ever more difficult to acquire knowledge in an environment that is itself without obvious intent.

The complexity of the learning process dramatically impacts relationships, perceptions, interpretations, and expectations. The ability to learn is a function of the intellect and the soul. The qualities of desire and of inspiration to learn reside in the deeper, inner places of the heart and mind. Music reaches into all those places. It can create quiet in the midst of confusion. By providing an environment in which students can be protected from distraction, purposefully selected music provides both freedom and discipline.

The challenge of the learning environment is to balance mental activity with calm pursuit—to create a place where healthy curiosity and incentive can thrive amidst the pressures of academic performance. *Any environment in which information is exchanged is, if it has immediate or long-term relevance, a learning environment.* So, ambiance, which predetermines what we hear and how we are heard, is critical to the processes involved.

Can You Hear Yourself Think?

Thinking is auditory. We talk to ourselves, silently saying in the privacy of our own minds all that we might speak. The auditory environment sets the baseline for how we hear and speak words, and as a result, it influences our capacity to think. Perhaps the first questions that must be answered are whether a space is capable of supporting the learning process, and what is required to make it so.

Other evidence of the relationship between hearing and language is the speech affect of the hearing impaired, which approximates what speech of the hearing sounds like. Sign language imitates the dynamics of spoken language; the physical hand and arm gestures add meaning to words in the same way that inflection and dynamics of the voice can when speaking. Thus, in the inner recesses of our own minds, we think as we speak—in full sentences, with dynamics, pauses, and expressive nuances.

The exclamation "I can't hear myself think!" describes the kind of frustration most of us feel when we have to function mentally and intellectually in the midst of chaos. Subtleties of inflection, volume, and expression can be vital in the transmission of information—we need to hear ourselves think!

Similarly, how many times have we said, "It's so noisy, I can't think straight!" In this context, "straight thinking" means being able to concentrate, focus attention, think in complete thoughts, and retain what we hear.

Therefore, when considering the design of learning environments, the direct relationship between thought and language, between hearing the dialogue in our heads versus sounds and words around us, increases in importance.

Recent research has focused on the ability of specific music and sound environments to help students concentrate and retain information. Children's television programs, computer games, and talking toys are extremely stimulating; this stimulation directly competes with the sensitivity and sophisticated listening skills that are most beneficial to children.

Given that any environment may be used as a place of learning, it becomes important to optimize the capacity to study and to maximize the learning potential.

Music and Learning

"Music is more than just another learning technique. It is part of our lives and our history. Great music connects to studying and learning by way of its meaning, its power, its quality, and its ability to affect thinking and creating. We use this music, great music—music that has stood the test of time and examination—because of its unmatched capacity to elevate us emotionally and intellectually."
— Arthur Harvey, *Learning with the Classics*

Much has been written about music, the brain, learning, and childhood development. Building on research begun in Bulgaria, Sheila Ostrander of the University of Iowa talks about "super-learning," increased retention generated by listening to music at 60 beats per minute in 4/4 time. Subsequent studies have claimed that it opens up more pathways in the brain, enhancing long-term and short-term memory.

In *Learning with the Classics* by Andersen, Marsh, and Harvey, *whole brain learning* is described as the most comprehensive means for increased retention. It is theorized that the right brain—the side that deals with creativity and emotions—and the left brain, which holds facts and objective information, are each optimized when concurrently engaged. The suggested protocol balances didactic learning and creative inspiration. This theory rec-ommends Baroque music at a tempo of 50 to 70 beats per minute, played at a relatively low volume. While studying, the creative part of us is not dis-tracted but engaged by the music, allowing us to access the "whole brain."

Based on its unique balance of melody, harmony, and accessibility, the music of Mozart has been proposed to be the best for this purpose. Mozart is not as mechanical as Bach, as dramatic as Beethoven, as ethereal as Debussy, or as dissonant as Stravinsky. Music of other composers of the same period, such as Vivaldi and Handel, has also been found to be effec-tive. In his book *The Mozart Effect,* Don Campbell describes numerous studies and practices using classical music to enhance learning.

Enough interest has been spurred by claims of a relationship between increased learning capacity and classical music that the National Academy of Recording Arts and Sciences is distributing one million compact discs of Grammy-winning classical symphonies—"smart symphonies"—to new-borns in order to facilitate a long-term study on the impact of early listen-ing to classical music on intelligence. This mass distribution project follows the lead of the state of Georgia, which, through the efforts of former gover-nor Zell Miller, provided classical recordings to thousands of Georgia schoolchildren.

In spite of compelling claims, however, research has not definitively shown that listening *solely* to classical music—excluding other genres—is effective in enhancing learning. On the contrary, music therapy research places a high value on variety, a diversity of styles, and the need for a var-ied auditory diet. Similar to our sense of smell, we become habituated to continuous, unchanging sounds to the point that we cannot hear them. Current children's TV programs that are designed to be both educational and entertaining—*edutainment*—include new, original songs and dances that successfully teach everything from language to arithmetic to life values to healthy relationships. Our innate need for variety and the increasing tech-nological capability to provide it have yielded a vast array of musical options. Therefore, the more exposure we give our children to different vari-eties of music, the richer their sources of inspiration and delight—and the more skilled they will become at selecting music that is life-enhancing.

More than Music

Just as music is more than simply a combination of tones and rhythms, so is the environment of learning more than the music. The term *life space,* first used by the late Kurt Lewin, is defined as "the individual and all aspects of the environment that influence [that individual's] behavior at any given time." Lewin's learning theory revolved around the life space because he felt that it was impossible to separate the environment from the individual, the learning from the student's response and actions. He further theorized what we find to be obvious: that positive environmental factors were found to be attractive; and negative factors were found to be aversive, "causing anxiety, hesitation, tension, or conflict."

In our discussion about music as environmental design, we have consistently focused on designing the environment to reinforce the positive capacity, spirit, and goals of the individual. This is perhaps the best manifestation of Lewin's life space. Clearly, learning potential is not solely dependent only on innate, genetic gray matter and sequential processes, but is also conditioned by the environment.

Efforts to decipher and explain how we learn and what causes us to process information in specific ways have resulted in more learning theories than we could possibly describe here. However, in the same way that the power to heal is inherent to the human body, so is the capacity to learn. Designing the environment to reflect the highest and most inspired level of knowledge will result in *holistic learning*—the integration of information with the mind and spirit of the student.

Music to Learn Multiplication, Reading, and Science By

As we have noted, many scholars are interested in finding the ideal music that, when listened to, would increase our ability to learn. Given the opportunity, students might request that we come up with specific music that would make difficult subjects easier, make boring subjects entertaining, and further render their teachers more clever and creative than before. As noted, many theories and practices have been put forth to assist efforts like this. However, none of them have been widely accepted enough to become part of our culture.

Nonetheless, what has been accepted by scholars and experienced by most of us is that the environment and our learning about the world can be enhanced by music. For those of us whose personal preferences stray from sounds of Mozart, there is an ever-growing listening repertoire from which to choose. We suggest the following criteria on which to base your choice:

- *Instrumental only:* Remember that thought is auditory. It is difficult, or at least taxing, to have two conversations going on at once—the one in your head and the one on the CD.

- *Moderate rhythm:* Music that has a strong rhythmic background can be distracting. However, music that is too slow or somber can put us to sleep. Research has shown that music at a pace of 53 to 70 beats per minute has been most effective. However, there remains more music to choose from than there are researchers to evaluate it. Experiment.

- *Harmonically pleasing:* Whether we are talking about jazz or classical, music that demands the listener's undivided attention may be ill-suited for environmental use. Music that is too dissonant, complex, or otherwise "intellectual" may simply be unnerving. It can have so subtle an impact that you may not initially know what is wrong. Simplicity and clarity of melody and harmony are good benchmarks.

- *Moderate to low volume:* The primary difference between foreground and background is volume. It will make an even larger difference in your ability to focus on what you are doing. Again, *what you hear outside of you competes with what you hear inside.* Thus, make sure that the music is, as we said, at the back of your mind's queue. If you find yourself distracted, it may be too loud.

- *Familiar or unfamiliar:* It is better to avoid music that you would rather dance to, unless your objective is to dance. Study is a ritual. It requires that you postpone doing or thinking about anything else. If you choose music that draws your attention because it creates an environment intended for some other activity, then you will have to struggle to reach your objectives. This could result in reaching the end of a chapter and not remembering one word that you just read. Other symptoms include confusing the facts of one situation with those of another, or taking three hours to accomplish one hour's work. Choose music that brings familiarity and intention to the subject at hand, rather than to the music. It should become part of the study "ritual."

Intention—Attention—Retention

Curing is to healing what *rote learning* is to understanding. In both cases, the distinctions lie between compartmentalization and holism, between circumstance and authenticity. To learn music by rote is to be spoon-fed—note to note, using short-term recall and repetition as the primary teaching methods. Unfortunately, memory lapses are not uncommon for a music student. Nonetheless, playing music without printed scores can be successfully done either by *memorizing* (learning a sequence of musical notes by heart), or by *knowing* (authentically understanding and remembering the music). Personally, I (Susan) do not forget music that I *know*—it is an indelible part of me.

Authentic learning requires a fully engaged mind. Furthermore, it demands attention to the details and tasks in the moment, which may include facts, skills, or processes. Actualization of the learning process only occurs with retention that allows the learning to become who we are, a part of how we see and act in our lives.

- *Intention* is a requisite, without which there can be no lasting engagement with the process.

- *Attention,* being fully present, optimizes our time and effort, as well as the quality of the process.

- *Retention* is where efforts pay off, where knowledge becomes part of the individual.

The role of the teacher, not unlike that of the physician, is to facilitate and generate inspiration, hope, and enthusiasm in either student or patient. The environment must be designed to support that relationship and facilitate the desired outcome.

Study As Ritual, Learning As Goal

We have spoken consistently of the power of environment as a partner in the human process. Purposeful design readily becomes the silent benefactor of the learning process. The *ritual* of design replaces routine with intention, directly supporting personal growth and potential. While study is the deliberate acquisition of knowledge, the learning environment provides a context that supports, if not assures, success.

The following questions will help to guide your environmental designing process:

1. *Is it* obvious *that the time and place are set up for learning?* Especially with children, the clearer the intention and purpose, the better the chance that they will purposefully comply with the tasks of reading or doing homework. If there is any chance that one could make the room a playroom, then a bright, healthy child will find the opportunity to act accordingly.

Susan: When I was in high school, I had a short attention span and poor reading retention. I was quite driven in my studies and feared not doing well. I also found solace in my books. The problem was that I did not know how to make sure that I would remember everything. In retrospect, I think that I over-studied. I was told that I had poor reading retention, in the 40th percentile—that is, I could not remember everything. I needed a process—something to do—as much as something to read. If the act was too cerebral, too much in my head, my mind wandered. To help, I created a ritual prior to studying.

While I was told many times that I should study in my room, which had a desk, chair, light, and all the necessities for study, I did not like the isolation and the all-too-quiet pressure imposed by the room itself. To this day, I tend to do my work in the middle of things—in the kitchen or family room.

*I had a bottomless pot of tea, which I drank for hours. I had my study note-
books in which I wrote pertinent facts, lest I forget them. In my early morning time—4:00 to 6:00 A.M.—prior to anyone else arising, I had the world
to myself; however, I didn't feel alone. I listened to music to help fill the
hours during which I studied. To this day, I use music as a context of my
mind. It pushes out the distractions and helps me focus, removing the isolation and dissipating the pressure.*

2. *Does the space promote study?* The environmental cues should be
appropriate to study. That could mean making sure that the Sunday comics
are put away, the toys are out of sight, and the television is off. Playrooms
may become learning environments. Spaces normally used for other activities can become learning environments if the "props" are appropriate and
accommodation is made.

3. *Does the space insulate you from outside distractions?* Now that you
have set your *intention,* consider how your *attention* increases or decreases
according to the room. Sometimes we can concentrate enough to ignore the
neighbors next door having an argument, or the kids playing, or the mail-
man delivering. However, our capacity to stay focused determines how
compelling the distraction is. Therefore, insulation protects us from com-
peting interests. Also, the amount of energy it takes to ignore an annoyance
is much greater than that required to focus our attention. Studies at Emory
University documented that "noise even in 'normal' classrooms interferes
with concentration and learning skills." Home is an extension of the classroom for students as young as first-graders. Therefore, optimize the living
room or kitchen, whichever the chosen place is, by minimizing distractions
during the hours of use. This may include turning off the television, setting
times when there are no visitors, and keeping the space clutter-free.

4. *Is there ample and flexible lighting?* Light and sound are partners,
too. Personally, I (Susan) do not like overhead lighting, but rather prefer
incandescent table lamps. The impersonal glare of fluorescent kitchen lights
has never helped me feel focused because they are not focused. Their very
design is about flooding a room with usable light without regard to people
or tasks. Reflected light can also serve to light a wide area with minimal
glare. The nature of a quiet space is both auditory and visual.

Natural daylight is wonderful and can be accessed through either windows or *full-spectrum* lighting, which is increasingly available in the marketplace. Typical fluorescent lights project a green-tinted glow. They reflect a light that looks artificial and dead.

Be aware of the glare and reflections from computer monitors, as they are now commonly used by ever-younger students. A productive and effective learning environment strains neither eyes nor ears, and promotes clarity of thought.

5. *Is there comfortable seating and appropriate table space for reading or writing?* If the table is at the wrong height or the chair is not designed for extended use, your endurance will suffer. In addition, if there are squeaks and other sounds emanating from the tools you use, they will be distracting. Your table, chair, lamp, and you must become *one,* as should the processes of thinking and hearing.

6. *Is the space age-appropriate?* Our capacity to concentrate, comprehend, and retain information changes with age. From birth through early adulthood, our capacity increases. For instance, a high school student may be able to study in a "study hall," where students are seated in small desks, row upon row, with ambient noises and distractions around them. However, as we age, our memories lose their resilience. Our ability to pay attention and concentrate may lessen. Our eyes and ears lose their acuity. While we have the tools and ability to compensate for the changes, we become more susceptible to environmental stressors.

To an older person, it may be difficult to read or concentrate in a noisy setting. A younger child, of perhaps five to seven years, may find it difficult to sit still, concentrate, and not be distracted by everything and everyone. Of course, within what is "normal" there are individual capacities. The good news is that design allows us—gives us both permission and mandate—to accommodate the needs of those present. For instance, whether it is your child, your parent, your spouse, or yourself, knowledge of the specific persons involved should certainly be considered in making decisions.

Susan: Dallas and I have very different learning styles. Dallas can practice the saxophone while listening to the radio and at the same time have CNN on the television in the next room—all at the same time, missing neither a note nor a word. He will then quote detailed news reports word for word, memorize his music in short order, and play flawlessly. He is able to perform multiple tasks while hearing concurrent layers of information.

In contrast, I process information beyond fact, moving quickly from the cognitive process of assimilation to the creative realm of meaning. I move quickly from fact to interpretation, projecting and extending the relationship of one fact to another. I find it difficult to write about one topic while concurrently hearing about something else. My verbal and writing skills, however, have allowed me to write as easily as I speak. I am able to deal with computers, math, and accounting tasks as long as I do so within a contained framework. I like working in relative quiet that is balanced with occasional music.

If I attempt to do what comes so easily to Dallas—multiple tasks, layers of disconnected information—I miss both notes and words, my irritability rises, and I make mistakes. Musically, I might offer that the harp is an instrument far more difficult than Dallas's woodwinds. However, I don't believe that has anything to do with why Dallas and I have such different styles of learning and study. Dallas easily plays by ear and memorizes long nonrepeating phrases. I am an avid reader, sight-reading complicated scores, but I struggle when I have to memorize.

In the many years we have worked together, we have each expected the other to be similar and totally compatible in temperament and taste. In writing this book together, the stylistic chasm and our differences in learning styles have become ever more apparent. We celebrate the differences, accommodate each other, and invent ways for each of us to succeed.

You will find your way if you identify your needs, find what works best for you, and establish your goals. You will further be able to assist your parent, child, or spouse as they set academic goals for themselves. There is no judgment in determining style, nor is there a formula for what is optimal. The goals and outcomes should determine the method, not vice versa.

7. Is the environment specific to the demands of a particular topic?

Q: What is the difference between arithmetic and English literature?
A: English literature renders a calculator useless.

If we think about the ways in which we learn and practice skills, we must also address the various tools used in the process. English literature usually requires a good easy chair, a good reading light, relative quiet, and, yes, no calculator. If we are writing a book review, we might need a table, computer, or word processor, and soft music might help. However, if we are working on complex mathematical formulas and problem-solving, we may need that calculator, as well as a scribble pad and pencil, a computer, good lighting, and a sense of humor.

Thus, the spaces in which we effectively learn must be able to accommodate the tasks at hand and must be able to change if necessary. Even a "music" room, which may hold the piano, a music stand, and chairs for an audience, may also be a living room, study, or a place for quiet reading. Few rooms do only one thing. Few of us have the luxury of compartmentalizing our tasks to our spaces. Most of us use one room to do lots of different things, and, therefore, benefit greatly by being able to alter this special space to our needs.

Q: What do arithmetic and English literature have in common?
A: They are both difficult to study in the shower.

Failing to successfully learn or study because you are in the wrong place is like blaming the bathwater for being wet. While we are all forced to adapt in some ways to surrogate "school" rooms, learning demands every skill we have and takes us to the limits of our sentient capacities. It requires of us that we focus for inordinate lengths of time, file information in the archives of our memories, and be able to access skills to learn yet other skills. Therefore, anything that distracts or otherwise drains our mental capacity may result in our having to re-learn what we thought we had already mastered.

Sensory Overload

Susan: It was noon—lunch was over, and only two and a half hours were left of the school day. The small alcove in the library had ten tables, each surrounded on one side by small chairs. On the left were tall windows, similar to those I remember from my own school years. On the opposite side was a wall of books, only as high as the height of a middle-school child.

When we arrived, the school was prepared for us. They had students available to help us unload our musical instruments from the van. They also had a security guard and assistant principal prepared to spend the next two hours "being present" during the workshop. We requested that teachers attend for several reasons, not the least of which was that we did not want to be forced to discipline students or have to play an authoritarian role.

In the workshop, we talk about process, acknowledging first that all of us, including Dallas and me, have finely tuned skills in judging who we are to each other. Then, we look at how we manage conflict and daily frustrations. The main question is, "What do we do when we don't get what we want?" In a collective group process, we candidly describe our methods of coping, and evaluate whether they are effective and what the results are. Truly an amazing discussion, and the only way to create an open attitude toward healthier options. The workshop objective, as a whole, is to empower choices other than using drugs, alcohol, and violence to manage day-to-day decisions that seem unmanageable.

When the students arrived, I got the chill I usually get. From the inside of my soul, I wanted our music to reach the part of each of them that was still a child. We'd had enough success that it would seem I should have confidence in the process. However, the middle school ages of 11 to 14 are unpredictable years of hormonal torment and confusion. So I did not take anything for granted.

They arrived in groups of four or five at a time, sauntering in with all the enthusiasm of students preparing themselves for a most dreaded and boring two hours. As they came in, the assistant principal immediately exerted her power to direct and control them. She seemed to hope that if there was a preemptive laying-down of the rules, then order would prevail throughout the afternoon. Her efforts were not wholly successful, as the students barely seemed to take notice of her and continued to talk to each other.

As the room filled up, small comments were made to us: questions about the harp, enthusiasm for the saxophone, a tough kind of curiosity that did not betray innocence. When all were seated, I looked at a room filled with students crammed into too-small seats and tables. These were gangly kids— past the awkwardness of 11 into the growth spurts of 13 and 14 that seemed to stretch their bodies almost overnight. Long torsos and legs, small heads and shoulders—just an awkward age between childhood and adulthood.

We always ask that our student audience integrate the whole spectrum: normal, at-risk, high-risk, those who have already gotten into some kind of trouble, and the gifted and talented. This makes our message more accessible about dealing with the issues of conflict resolution and personal decision-making. In our classroom with this subjective subject matter, all would be equal, perhaps for the first time. Also, we did not like to single out kids who had already gotten into trouble. If anything, we wanted to demonstrate authentic respect for them as individuals and create an environment in which they would begin to respect themselves, their experience, and their own power to make decisions.

In the mix we had hoped for, perhaps all these students whose lives and interests were so different could learn something from each other about how life is. However, in this instance, all the girls were stylish—walking, talking, chewing gum, each with the same kind of demeanor, "being cool." The boys—almost men—had a similar gait and posture. All of it spoke to social pressure; none of it represented any sense of anything else. Middle school was tough, and they were tough.

Once the room had filled, the assistant principal again called the group to order, achieving only a slightly lower level of talk. She hastily introduced us, the topic for the day, and the security guard, whom the students all knew as "Coach." Turning the room over to me, she smiled and said she would be in and out during the afternoon, and that Coach would be there throughout. Then she left.

As I began to introduce Dallas and myself, a voice from the back of the room asked, "Why are we all here? What have we done today?" There were more such questions thrown at us, out of order, demanding some explanation as to why all these particular students were here in this room, at this time, on this day.

Finally, after what seemed like an eternal space of confusion, I got it. Each of these lanky, oversized adolescents now facing us had previously gotten into trouble. They all knew each other and each had a certain reputation that followed their actions. All of them were suspicious of us, the upcoming afternoon, and what they had done to deserve this. They were wondering what was up. Their faces asked, "What now?"

"Why us?" "Who are you?" "What is that . . . a harp?" "You gonna play the saxophone?" "I have to go to the bathroom, Teach!" "Ms. Mazer, you buy that yourself?"

And on and on, faster than we could respond.

I had some compassion for their point of view. After all, if you are selected one at a time and find yourself among all those who had previously gotten into some kind of trouble or achieved a certain reputation, then the question to ask would indeed be, "Why us?"

I answered as well as I could. No, you are not in trouble. No, we are not regular teachers. No, we did not "pick" you. No, you are not graded for this afternoon's work. No, this is not a science class. No, you are not taking a test. No . . . well, do you really have to go to the bathroom?

This was after lunch. It seemed as if every student was on a sugar high, and we were faced with more than two hours of wondering if we were going to get anything done at all. I hoped for some kind of idea that would turn the chaos into order, establish engagement instead of defiance, and transform distrust into mutual respect.

"Let's do an experiment!" I heard my voice say aloud, over the din.

It got very quiet.

"Let's find out how long time is. How long is one minute?"

No one answered.

"How long is one minute?" I asked again. "This is not a trick question."

"60 seconds," one student answered.

"Right. How long is two minutes?"

"120 seconds."

"Right." It was now quiet for the first time. What was I up to?, they seemed to wonder.

"Is it long?" I asked.

Silence. They had to think about it.

"Is it long?" I repeated, pushing a little.

Finally, someone said, "Sometimes." Then, another said, "It's short." Then still another student answered, "No, man . . . it's looooonng!"

"Let's find out. This is what we are going to do. We are going to sit in silence for 120 seconds. Then, Dallas and I are going to play music for 120 seconds. Then, we are going to sit in silence for another 60 seconds. Then, we'll talk about it."

For some blessed reason, the students—all of them—went for it. Dallas counted off. "Ready. Begin." Some students put their heads down, others just looked out the window. A few tested the waters and made some noise, but their troublemaking didn't spread; no one else joined in. Finally, they sat quietly.

The room was astonishingly quiet. Truly quiet. It was a long two minutes—like a cease-fire. For every second that passed, there was a chance the next second would hold.

On cue, Dallas and I began to play very quietly, trying not to shock the silence. We improvised, with the low bass note of the harp laying a carpet of sound. The fluid notes of the wind synthesizer slid in on top of the harmonic richness of the harp, like a silk ribbon being stretched across a body of water. No matter how many times we had performed together, I think that this moment was one of the most inspired.

This was our own two minutes during which we might have a chance to introduce these young hearts and ears to the magic of a musical moment unlike any other they may have experienced. It was live music, not on record or radio, being played for them. New, in the moment, reaching out of the silence to their own souls.

The two minutes of music seemed rich and long enough—and ended appropriately, as if we had written the piece before.

Then, the next minute without music returned the room to its own quiet; however, it was different. It had been transformed into a different kind of room.

When Dallas indicated to me that the time was up, almost in a whisper, I quietly asked, "How long is 120 seconds?"

One student, who had clearly been uncomfortable earlier—loud and defiant—softly asked, "Why can't we do this instead of being sent to the office?"

The "this" to which the student referred was putting a halt to chaos, spending two minutes insulated from inner and outer noise. Current school designs, as well as home-study settings, are often cluttered on both auditory and visual levels. While both young children and adolescents crave and benefit from varied and intensive stimulation, it is possible for them to experience sensory overload. They become unable to clearly process everything going on around them, and they respond appropriately. As a result, retention and productivity, as well as performance, are affected. In the course of our work, we investigated with them what would most improve their capacity to manage emotional stress.

Teachers and other adults often make assumptions regarding students' capacity to appreciate any music other than "their own" music.

Unfortunately, children's and teenagers' exposure to diverse music has been relegated by default to the music industry, to radio program directors, to industries and interests that have agendas far from the hearts and souls of these kids.

The wisdom of the young is at risk of being lost due to the judgment of those of us who don't ask or listen. Because our focus was using music to design healthy environments, we looked at the kinds of music kids listen to, how it impacts them, what they like, and what their parents like. We consistently found that, given the opportunity and a place where their opinions were respected, where candidness on both sides of the question was offered, and where they had concrete alternatives, the students knew what would work best.

What seemed to be missing was balance between quiet times and noisy times—a space where thinking became as valuable as talking, and listening as critical as speaking. The students taught us who they were and what affected them. As evidence of the insight and clarity with which these students knew themselves, here are some of the statements that summarize what they concluded:

- Don't listen to rap when you are angry.
- It's better to mellow out if you are really upset.
- Quiet and soft music can help you mellow out.
- Quiet time is better than being sent to the principal's office.
- We already know how to protect ourselves from harm.
- Being candid comes from trust, respect, and being listened to.

All Environments Can Be Learning Environments

Whether in the kitchen, classroom, study, family room, physician's office, or automobile, our craving for personal accomplishment and for a continual exchange of information demands that any place or space in which we find ourselves should have the capacity to be a learning environment. Learning does not require a computer or a pen and paper. It requires a willing student for whom the information has meaning.

When the environment acts against the learning process, we risk self-doubt, impaired performance, and mistaken judgment of our own capacities. The studies that showed that the development of young children may be hampered by noisy environments were conducted in neighborhoods that were economically challenged. It is too easy to mistakenly link social class and intelligence when the real issues may lie elsewhere. Likewise, our elderly are often judged by others and themselves to have reduced capacity, when the real problem is the room and circumstances under which they receive and must respond to information.

Determining our own needs and styles of learning becomes part of designing the space. Like many others, my (Susan's) parents judiciously purchased a desk and chair for me to study at without evaluating whether or not that kind of setting would be optimal for who I was. You have many choices, and there are no formulas. Even in the classroom, there are choices and options, some of which are better than others. The optimal learning environment respects, acknowledges, and accommodates the capacities of the individual student.

Lifelong Learning

Regardless of how any of us felt about school in our youth, we are students for a lifetime. Furthermore, some of us elect to return to the academic setting of formal education during our adult years. The question, then, is what kind of environment can support our continued learning process. Sentient capacities of sight and sound change with age, as does the ability to perform multiple tasks at once. Retention, once based on academic recall, is now challenged by a preoccupation with the adult responsibilities of living that prioritize and tax our memories.

Nonetheless, the drive for knowledge is enduring, and we continue to seek more. Thus, all truths applicable to a child apply to each of us as adults for a lifetime. We learn throughout every day that we arise and venture into the world. We learn about ourselves, those around us, and then from facts and ideas that we come across purely by accident. We find out what we know and what we don't know. Most important, the meaning in our lives is made manifest by the context in which we discover new truths about the world and ourselves.

The role that music plays in this process is most astounding, as our auditory memory survives most stresses of life, including both physical and emotional traumas. Melodies that we knew as children remain forever part of us, as do those we hear later. Indeed, each song, each symphony, and each lyric embraced in the passions of melody becomes indistinguishable from who we are and how we live.

Afterword

Sound, Sight, and Spirit

A Fairytale

*O*nce *upon a time, in a nearby universe, the moons and suns were com-*
peting with each other, as they often did. While they each demanded
their own hours to shine, they had resigned themselves to having to yield to
each other, lest their own light be diminished by glare. Thus, the days and
nights were split with great diligence and monitored with great vigilance.
Although the trust between the entities was guarded, it had become a valued
point of pride for moons and suns to share the task of spreading light.
Neither one wanted to risk a confrontation where they might lose to the other.

However, in the year 2687, the suns and the moons each yielded to their
own greed and tried to dominate the right to light. In spite of a long-held
and negotiated peace that had worked for so many years, there was a Dark
War. In a myriad of subtle and not-so-subtle ways, this planetary political
rift affected those who lived by the light of the various solar entities.

In this world, 11-year-old Chia loved walking. She became easily hyp-
notized by the beauty of the blue sky, vast and deep, as it seemed to meet the
horizon. Much like the softest of silk drapes, the heavens were ever-forgiving
to the ragged mountains and peaks that met their edge. She would often run
and jump amidst the carpet of wildflowers that seemed so free and bound-
less. Grateful for the world she saw, she walked lightly as only a child can.

On one of the most astounding days that Chia had ever seen, the sun
went down too early and a moon stubbornly refused to rise. Unbeknownst to
her, one of the suns of Gartoneo had been embattled with its nearest moon.

It had become convinced that its own radiance was dimmed by the hours of early moonlight that illuminated Earth on many a night. Such galactic conflicts were rumored, but no one had suspected such a drastic measure would be taken. Chia had gotten used to playing outside until sunset; now she was instantly constrained to playing in the dark. It was a new experience.

At first Chia was frightened, for her eyes could not adjust to such profound darkness. Where were the flowers? Where were the majestic trees that seemed to tower graciously so far above her? The night had come before the moon had risen. There was not even one shadow or glimmer to lead her from the forest to her home.

She took a single step, not even remembering the terrain of the land around her. It was rocky and she feared falling, so she stood where she was, moving not even an inch. She closed her eyes, trying to visualize the vastness in which she had walked for so many hours.

Suddenly, she began to hear the music of the night. She heard the rustle of the leaves as the wind shuffled them like a small deck of cards. Turning to face the wind, she became aware of the night owl, whose singular and pure voice told her that the trees were close at hand. Then she was serenaded by the melodic rhythms of the river, whose waters danced continuously on the rocky banks. The sounds of night creatures chorused in song from land, air, and water, woven into a symphony of a thousand instruments.

As the wind and the water played a rhythmic duet, Chia realized that what her eyes could not see would become visible by the crisp and clear sounds of the night. The many nocturnal voices called to her and helped her negotiate the path. The sounds came from far away from where she stood, offering a larger universe than she had ever experienced. The tap of her own foot on the ground became her handshake with the earth, whose rich and diverse terrain sounded to her like a symphony of sights and sounds.

Can it be, *Chia thought,* that my eyes have falsely thought that they alone defined my world? Is it true that my ears see more than my eyes, and the darkness reveals what I was too blind to see?

And so it was, by the time the sun and the moon both rose to reflect each other's glorious and rich light, that Chia had learned to sing from those whose very powerful presence in her life began only when she started to listen.

Joseph Campbell spoke of a "sacred place where temporal walls may dissolve . . . where [we] can simply experience and bring forth wonder." Music can create that sacred time and place, even within the bustle of activities that draw us away from ourselves. The sound environment is within and without, a marriage between who we are and the world around us. It is holistic in nature, impacting both reality and perception, painting and sculpting the many dimensions of the physical and emotional world.

The philosophy of environmental design, then, reiterates to us the truth that we are our environment. The philosophy of sacred space ventures further, as Joseph Campbell did, to say that there is a place where all separation ceases—between ourselves and the world around us, between who we are and where we are.

You, with your unique sensitivities, experiences, and perceptions, are the singular thread that connects all your environments, whether home or work, learning or healing. Therefore, if we are to be successful designers of our lives, we must be able to design the spaces in which we live.

Kahlil Gibran wrote that the "soul of music is of the spirit, and her mind is of the heart." Perhaps we could say that the soul of a place is in *our* intention, and its mind is in *our* design. Music becomes the color, light, and form that makes both meaning and authenticity palpable. To design our living spaces to reflect who we are, we must call on our sensitivity to relationships, circumstance, and ourselves.

The music in our lives intentionally combines sounds that resonate the sacred within all of us—our passions, innermost thoughts, feelings, histories, and cultures. What we actually hear is a duet between the music and our thoughts, enhanced by the surrounding sounds of life and their meaning. The auditory environment, as a rich orchestration of our hopes, enthusiasm, inspiration, thoughts, and actions, is life expressing itself in all its dynamics, rhythms, and melodies.

Appendix

Choosing a Sound System

A sound system is to music what lighting is to a great painting. The technology of sound reproduction is just as important as the music itself. In the last century, we have progressed from the scratchy sounds of the Victrola's 78-RPM records, to long-playing records, to 8-track tapes, to cassette tapes, to compact discs. We've gone from monaural to hi-fidelity, to stereo, to quadrophonic sound, to surround sound. Whew!

With every new generation of sound technology, our ability to hear the difference has improved. Most of us have scarcely mastered the use of our current sound system when the next enhancement becomes standard. Thus, given the importance of technology to the sound environment, we felt that the following basic information might be of value to those of you who are still trying to keep pace:

1. *Hardware quality* determines how accurately sound is reproduced—are you hearing the music the way it was recorded? Each component (speaker, amplifier, tuner, CD/cassette player, and so on) will affect the total sound. Ideally, sound reproduction is *full frequency,* reproducing music to match the full range of human hearing. This is measured as *frequency response,* which should be about 20–20,000hz (20hz–20khz). This is common to most CD players. *Durability* and *reliability* are also functions of hardware quality—you don't want it to break too soon. Brand names such as Aiwa, Sony, Panasonic, JBL, JVC, Marantz, and Bose offer a range of cost-effective models that differ in power capacity and features.

2. *Function* refers to the purpose of the sound system. For instance, it may be designed for background music, foreground entertainment, voice paging, or another function. Know how and where you are going to use the system.

3. *Size* refers to the volume of sound produced by the system. Requirements should be based on the size of the space and how it is going to be used. The power of a system is measured in watts, so if a system has 80 watts of power, then each channel or side of the unit has 40 watts.

4. *Price* is an important consideration for most of us. The good news is that advancing technology allows quality to keep increasing as costs decrease each year. For example, right now a portable system of moderate quality can be purchased for as little as $100! The best (and most expensive) systems usually consist of separate components. This raises the price considerably compared to bargain-priced combination units. The highest-priced audiophile systems can cost many thousands of dollars.

♪   ♪   ♪

When choosing a sound system, most of us go into a stereo store, where a salesperson takes us into a room filled with all the various systems. The salesperson proceeds to play, at loud volume, music that we may or may not like. After choosing one system, taking it home, and setting it up, we might find that our choice does not suit our specific needs.

In order to assist you in acquiring the right sound system, we suggest the following steps as guidelines:

1. *Take a CD with you that you know and love.* This will allow you to compare different systems playing music with which you are already familiar.

2. *Listen at the volume level you are most used to hearing.* Many systems sound great when they are played loudly, but they lose their clarity and pizzazz at lower volumes. Most of us listen at much lower levels than the blasting common to audio emporiums.

3. *Don't overbuy.* Any salesperson would love to increase their commission by selling you an expensive system. Sound systems can range from $100 to $50,000. Yes, there is a difference between these extremes; however, the difference between a $250 and $400 system may only have to do with features you don't need and wouldn't use.

4. *Make sure you choose your system according to your needs.* If you expect to use your system to provide dance music for occasional parties, you will need to purchase a larger system capable of being broadcast at loud volumes without distortion. But if you plan to use your system primarily to provide soothing music prior to retiring at night, a system of less power will suffice. If you want to hear the same music in different rooms, you might want to invest in additional satellite speakers that can be powered from one central system. More expensive systems allow remote control of the central system from any room. Make sure that the system provides you with power sufficient to provide music with full-frequency sound.

♪♪   ♪♪   ♪♪

Here are some answers to frequently asked questions regarding different features:

1. *What is the "loudness" button or "loudness contour?"* The loudness button on most stereo systems, including the one in your car, is a low-frequency boost for use when you are listening at softer volumes. This feature was developed when manufacturers realized that most people listen at lower volumes that, because of the physics of sound, would result in audibility at only the higher frequencies. Because our listening has been conditioned to expect a rich, full bass sound, they added this boost to compensate.

2. *What is the difference between tone controls and equalization?* They are the same. Equalization (EQ) is the technical term for tone controls. Sophisticated EQ devices can control up to 30 different bands of the frequency spectrum—not unlike how the color balance on your television is controlled by modifying the primary colors. However, home stereo systems generally do not have such complex equalizers. The objective is to compensate (equalize) for the acoustic qualities of the room—for instance, if the room is too bright, or if it overemphasizes or deadens the bass or treble.

3. *Some systems have built-in, ready-to-use EQ for particular styles of music. What are these for?* Different styles of music, such as classical, jazz, pop, or rock, have very different frequency contours. For instance, rock

music emphasizes a booming bass and is generally written and performed with relatively little variation in volume. Pop also has a strong bass, although not as pronounced as rock. Classical music, however, is more acoustic and has a much wider dynamic range. Manufacturers decided that it would be a marketable feature for a user to only have to press a single button to accentuate the preferred sound based on the kind of music. Some systems, for instance, have EQ presets that say "Classical," "Jazz," "Pop," and "Off." Experiment to hear the difference.

4. *Is it necessary to buy a CD player that plays five or more CDs in random order?* This allows for continuous, nonrepetitive play for hours, with the pieces being selected by a computer program, jumping from one CD to the next in no particular or predictable sequence. Personally, we do not listen to CDs that way. We tend to listen to one CD at a time, in the order in which it was recorded. Musicians and producers carefully sequence the pieces on a CD to create the most effective listening experience. However, for those who want their home to sound like a radio, multi-CD players provide more variety—different pieces played in random order. However, do not overbuy. If you prefer to listen to one CD at a time, don't pay for a feature that you won't utilize.

5. *Satellite speakers—what are they?* These are speakers placed at a distance from the main amplifier. The result is a wider sound space. They may be mounted in different areas or rooms and may have their own volume controls. If spread out to multiple rooms, you can freely move around the house or office with continuous access to the music. Lower-cost systems come with prewired speakers and allow only a limited distance from the main amplifier to the speakers. Satellite speakers allow you to create a *stereo field,* which is larger than is possible if the speakers and amplifier are all located close together.

6. *What is the benefit of an AUX output, or an AUX/Video input?* An AUX (auxiliary) output allows you to take the sound from your smaller system and plug it into a larger system, if you choose. A video input allows you to connect outputs from your VCR or TV (or other source) to this stereo system, which will most likely sound better than your TV by itself.

7. *What is "surround sound?"* This feature makes your living room into a theater by providing three-dimensional sound. It requires up to six speakers (front stereo, rear stereo, center dialogue, and subwoofer), physically placed to create the illusion that you are in the middle of the action. This is obviously not necessary for straight CD listening, but is very effective for watching movies. You will notice that there is specific design as to how the sound is distributed. The spoken words come from the middle-front speakers, the bass seems to be everywhere, and the sound effects come from the rear speakers.

Consult your salesperson if other issues arise. Remember to buy for your own use, not for a sound that may not be applicable to your situation.

Sound Choices
Artist Resources

The following record labels, musicians, and composers are featured on The C.A.R.E. Channel and C.A.R.E. With Music programming. We encourage you to visit their websites and purchase their albums. In doing so, you will be supporting the creation of new music to enhance and promote the design of healing environments.

Record Labels:

1. **Sugo Music** • 650-726-0696 • **www.sugomusic.com**
   790 Main Street, Half Moon Bay, CA 94019

   Selected titles: *Sugo Collections, Volumes 1–4*
   Tranquillity; Harmony; Vitality (various artists)
   Seasons; Guitar Masterpieces (Stevan Pasero)
   Voyage; Isle of Dreams (Brad White/Pierre Grill)
   Secret Harbor (Michelle Sell)
   Piano Portraits (various artists)

2. **Consensus Management** • 503-228-5113
   3479 NW Yeon Ave., Portland, OR 97210

   Selected titles: *Four Corners Suite; Tropical Dreams;*
   Light on the Mountain (Scott Moulton)
   Winds Across the Water (White-Eisenstein)
   The Grace Note Series: Selected Classics Volumes 1–3

3. **Access Music** • 800-306-3008 • www.choiceradio.com
   1705 Peggy Court, Suite 1, Petaluma, CA 94954

   Selected titles: *Songs for a Dreamer* (Lee Eisenstein)
   It's About Time; A Perfect Match (Tadamitsu Saito)
   Torches on the Lake (Spencer Brewer/Paul McCandless)

4. **Global Pacific Records** • 800-545-2001
   www.ninegates.com/global.html
   PO Box 2001, Sonoma, CA 95476

   Selected titles: *Paradise Lost; Across a Rainbow Sea* (Steven Kindler)
   Dolphin Smiles (Steven Kindler/Teja Bell)
   Nocturnal Afternoon (Rojo)
   The Fruits of Our Labors (Anthology)
   Valentine Eleven (Jordan de la Sierra)

Individual Artists:

1. **Steven Halpern's** Inner Peace Music
   800-909-0707 • **www.stevenhalpern.com**
   P.O. Box 2644, San Anselmo, CA 94979

   Selected titles: *Spectrum Suite, Natural Light, Inner Peace,
   Connections, Higher Ground, Among Friends*

2. **Michael Allen Harrison** • 503-255-0747 • **www.mahrecords.com**
   c/o MAH Records, PO Box 30448, Portland, OR 97294

   Selected titles: *Emotional Connection, Passion and Grace,
   3rd Avenue, Circle of Influence*

3. **Susan Mazer and Dallas Smith** • 800-348-0799
   www.soundchoices.com
   Original compositions for electric harp and woodwinds.
   Box 8010, Reno, NV 89503

Selected titles: *HeartSong, The Dance of Life, Look to the Mountain, The Nature of Hope, Waters of the Earth, The Fire in the Rose,* Ballet music from *Maxfield Parrish: A Love Story, Inner Rhythms, Carol for the Planet, The Still Point, Magic Garden, Stellar Voyage.*

4. **Kate and Richard Mucci • CROSSWYND**
   Gothic harp and 12-string guitar
   www.CROSSWYND.com

5. **John Nilsen • 503-657-4018 • www.magicwing.com**
   c/o Magic Wing, Box 222, West Linn, OR 97068

   Selected titles: *Twelve Shades of Light, Night Garden, Above Me, Where Rivers Run, From the Sky*

6. **Mike Strickland • 800-825-6453 • www.mikestrickland.com**
   Mike Strickland Productions, PO Box 19443, Seattle, WA 98109

   Selected titles: *Time Remembered, Traveling On, Floating, On the Wind*

Other Contributing Artists:

Jon and Susan Allasia	Gary Lamb
Craig Evans	*BareTraks* (Christine Pyle and Michael Pyle)
Gert Matthias Wegner	Sky Canyon
Jonathan Marmalzat	Marcus Allen
Steve Hallmark	Christian Paulin

Bibliography and Suggested Reading

Adams, Hunter "Patch." *Gesundheit!* Healing Arts Press, 1993.

Andersen, O., M. Marsh, and A. Harvey. *Learning with the Classics.* The Lind Institute, 1999.

Baker, C. F. "Sensory overload and noise in the ICU: Sources of environmental stress." *Critical Care Quarterly* 1984; 6; 66–80.

Berleant, Arnold. *The Aesthetics of Environment.* Temple University Press, 1992.

Blood, D. J., and S. J. Ferriss. "Effects of background music on anxiety, satisfaction with communications, and productivity." *Psychol-Rep.* 1993 Feb; 72(1) 171–7.

Campbell, Don. *The Mozart Effect.* Avon Books, 1997.

Chuang, Jeffrey. "Experts say noisy classrooms may hinder learning." *The Toronto Star.* July 24, 1997, *LIFE,* pg. 5.

Goddaer, J., and I. Abraham. "Effects of relaxing music on agitation during meals among nursing home residents with severe cognitive impairment," *Arch Psychiatr Nurs.* 1994 June, Vol. 8, pp. 150–158.

Grumet, G. W. "Pandemonium in the hospital: Noise abuse in acute care facilities." *New England Journal of Medicine.* 1993,328:433-437.

Hamel, Peter Michael. *Through Music to the Self.* Shambhala, 1979.

Halpern, Steven, with Louis Savary. *Sound Health: The Music and Sounds That Make Us Whole.* Harper & Row, Inc., 1985.

Hansell, H. N. "The behavioral effects of noise on man: the patient with intensive care unit psychosis." *Heart Lung.* 1984;13:59–65.

Harris, David A. *Noise Control Manual for Residential Buildings.* McGraw-Hill, 1997.

Hodges, Donald, ed. *The Handbook of Music Psychology.* Second edition. San Antonio: IMR Press, 1999.

Jourdain, Robert. *Music, the Brain, and Ecstasy.* Avon Books, 1997.

Lanza, Joseph. *Elevator Music.* New York: St. Martin's Press, 1994.

Longhurst, Brian. *Popular Music and Society.* Blackwell Publishers, 1995.

Magill, Levreault L. "Music therapy in pain and symptom management." *Journal of Palliative Care.* Winter 1993; 9(4): 42–8.

Marcus, Clare Cooper. *House as a Mirror of Self.* Conari Press, 1995.

Marley, L. S. "The use of music with hospitalized infants and toddlers: a descriptive study." *Journal of Music Therapy.* 21, 126–132. 1984.

McKinney, Cathy H. "Music therapy in obstetrics: a review." *Music Therapy Perspectives.* Vol. 8, 57–60. 1990.

Meyer, Leonard B. *Emotion and Meaning in Music.* University of Chicago Press, 1956.

Miller, J. D. "Effects of noise on people." *J. Acoustic Society of America.* 1974: 56:729-64.

Nadel, L. "The touch that heals." *American Baby*, pp. 28, 31–34. April 1987.

Nakamura, H. "Neurobiology of physical environmental stress," *Nippon-Eiseigaku-Zasshi.* 1992 Oct; 47(4): 785-97.

Nivison, M. E., and I. M. Endresen. "An analysis of relationships among environmental noise, annoyance and sensitivity to noise, and the consequences for health and sleep." *J Behav Med.* 1993, Jun 16, pp. 257-276.

Oehler, J. M. "Developmental care of low birth weight infants." *Nurs. Clin. North America.* 1993 Jun:28(2): 289-301.

Ostrander, S., and L. Schroeder. *Superlearning 2000.* New York: Delacorte Press, 1994.

Poldinger, W., and R. Kocher. "Pain in society and in medicine." *Schwiez-Rundsch-Med.-Prax.* 1993 Mar 2; 82(9):255–

Pope, Diana Spies. "Music, noise, and the human voice in the nurse-patient environment." *J. Nursing Scholarship.* 1995; 27(4), 291–296.

Regova, V., and E. Kellerove. "Effects of urban noise pollution on blood pressure and heart rate in preschool children." *Journal of Hypertension.* Vol. 13, pp. 405–412, 1995.

Santo Pietro, Nancy. *Feng Shui: Harmony by Design.* The Berkley Publishing Group, 1996.

Schorr, J. A. "Music and pattern change in chronic pain." *ANS-Adv. Nurs. Sci.* 1993 Jun: 15 (4): 27.

Secretan, Lance H. K. *Reclaiming Higher Ground.* Macmillan Canada, 1996.

Smith, B. J., R. J. Peters, and Stephanie Owen. *Acoustics and Noise Control.* Addison Wesley Longman, Inc., 1992.

Standley, Jayne M. "Music research in medical/dental treatment; meta-analysis and clinical applications." *Journal of Music Therapy.* XXII (2), 1986, 56–122.

———. *Music Techniques in Therapy, Counseling, and Special Education.* St. Louis, MO: MMB Music, 1991.

Storr, Anthony. *Music and the Mind.* New York: Ballantine Books, 1992.

Stratton, V. N. "Influence of music and socializing on perceived stress while waiting." *Percept Mot Skills.* 1992 Aug, 75 p. 334.

Swan, James A. *The Power of Place.* Quest Books, 1991.

Tolson, D., and J. McIntosh. "Listening in the care environment—chaos or clarity for the hearing-impaired elderly person." *International Journal of Nursing Studies.* Vol. 34, Number 3, June 1997, pp.173–187.

Venolia, C. *Healing Environments.* Berkeley, CA: Celestial Arts, 1988.

Zappa, Frank. *The Real Frank Zappa Book* (unpublished). 1989.

Websites

The Association of Healing HealthCare Projects • **www.ahhcp.com**

Florida State University, Center for Music Research • **www.fsu.cmr.edu**

Healing HealthCare Systems • **www.healinghealth.com**

League for the Hard of Hearing • **www.lhh.com**

The Mozart Effect® Resource Center • **www.mozarteffect.com**

Music and Science Computer Archives • **www.MuSICA.com**

The National Academy of Recording Arts and Sciences • **www.naras.com**

The National Campaign for Hearing Health • **www.hearinghealth.net**

Weinberger, Norman. Music and Science Computer Archives, University of California at Irvine • **www.MuSICA.com**

Index

—T—

tabla, 156
Tchaikovsky, Peter Illyich, 32, 66
technology
    advances in, 31-32
    see audiophile listeners, 40
    hernobyl, 93
    in hospitals, 151
    risks of, 116
    role of, 43
    sound masking, 130
    sound reproduction, 204-5
    younger generation's relationship
        with, 162
television, impact of during illness,
    157
thanatology, music, 168
time
    nature of, 152-3
    sense of, 35
    waiting, 72

—V—

vibration therapy, 12

—W—

Washoe Medical Center, 14, 71, 154
Watts, Alan, 2
white noise, 130
whole brain learning, 179

—Z—

Zappa, Frank, 41, 101

About the Authors

Susan Mazer and **Dallas Smith** are acknowledged pioneers in the use of music as environmental design for health care facilities. They co-founded Healing HealthCare Systems, Inc., which produces The C.A.R.E. Channel®, Continuous Ambient Relaxation Environment®, a 24-hour closed-circuit television format for hospitals; and also C.A.R.E. With Music, music programming for hospital-wide broadcast designed specifically to create and support healing environments. Their work has been featured in major health care conferences including The National Symposium on Healthcare Design, The Association for the Care of Children's Health, and The Healthcare Forum. Their innovatios in health care include developing The Sondrex System®, a proprietary personal music delivery system for patients undergoing medical procedures. The Sondrex allows the physician or nurse to speak directly to the patient through closed-ear headphones. Susan and Dallas are on the founding board of The Association Of Healing Health Care Projects.

As musicians and composers, they have recorded more than 20 albums and have been featured on The Discovery Channel, *NOVA,* and National Public Radio. They are the 1997 recipients of the Leland R. Kaiser Founder's Award for their work in healing health care. Susan and Dallas are married and live in Reno, Nevada.

They can be contacted at the following address:

Susan Mazer and Dallas Smith
c/o Healing HealthCare Systems, Inc.
100 W. Grove St., Suite 175
Reno, NV 89509
www.soundchoices.com

Notes

Notes

We hope you enjoyed this Hay House book.
If you would like to receive a free catalog featuring additional
Hay House books and products, or if you would like information about
the Hay Foundation, please contact:

Hay House, Inc.
P.O. Box 5100
Carlsbad, CA 92018-5100

(760) 431-7695 or **(800) 654-5126**
(760) 431-6948 (fax) or **(800) 650-5115 (fax)**

Please visit the Hay House Website at: **www.hayhouse.com**

About the CD

The enclosed CD contains selections from the five-album series available through Hay House. The music is especially chosen to support the listener and the intention of the spaces being designed. This original music is instrumental, composed and performed by harpist Susan Mazer and woodwind performer Dallas Smith. The tempo, mood, and overall feeling of each CD varies; we encourage you to use the sample selections as you deem appropriate to create life-enhancing environments. The repertoire is flexible—feel free to be creative. The following sample tracks are included:

From *Sound Choices for Children*	Time
1. Children of the Fields	4:40
2. Kalimbo	5:09

From *Sound Choices for the Home*	
1. Living Easy	5:45
2. Kids on Camelback	4:20

From *Sound Choices for Healing*	
1. Heart Song	4:25
2. Queen Emma's Theme	5:45

From *Sound Choices for Work*	
1. Sierra Winds	3:44
2. Soaring	3:21

From *Sound Choices for Relaxation*	
1. Song of the Hills	5:31
2. The Spirit of the Lotus	6:52

Susan Mazer, *electroacoustic harp*
Dallas Smith, *electric wind instrument, silver flute,*
    bansuri (bamboo flute), soprano saxophone, clarinet
Andy Heglund, *percussion*; Luigi La Marca, *percussion;* Eric Middleton, *percussion*
Kim Atkinson, *percussion;* Tony Savage, *drums*
All compositions ©℗1987, 1990, 1996, 1997, 1998,
    Avicenna Publishing (BMI)/Oscar Dallas Music (BMI)